M. R. G. Davies abandoned a successful career as a newspaper editor to write fiction. As an author, he completed Desmond Bagley's thriller *Domino Island* for posthumous publication and has written two sequels, *Outback* and *Thin Ice*, both published by HarperCollins. His debut play *Rasputin's Mother* won the Bristol Old Vic playwriting competition and subsequent work for the stage includes *The Seagull Has Landed* (Power Plays festival winner), *MacHamLear* (UK tour), *Reality* (Royal & Derngate) and the book and lyrics for *Tess – The Musical* (workshopped at the RSC). He has written narrative non-fiction for worldwide television, had short stories and poetry commissioned and published, and contributes regular essays for theatre programmes.

www.mrgdavies.com

instagram.com/michaeldaviesauthor
facebook.com/michael-davies-author

Also by M. R. G. Davies

Novels

THE BILL KEMP TRILOGY:

Desmond Bagley's *Domino Island* (as curator)

Outback

Thin Ice

A COSY CRIME CLUB MYSTERY SERIES:

Murder by the Book

A Game of Murder

From Murder with Love

Stage

The Seagull Has Landed

MacHamLear

Tess – The Musical (with composer Michael Blore)

South Sea Bubble

Reality

Rasputin's Mother

Television

Meet, Marry, Murder

A Killer's Mistake

Made for Murder

A GAME OF MURDER

A Cosy Crime Club Mystery

M. R. G. DAVIES

One More Chapter
a division of HarperCollins*Publishers*
1 London Bridge Street
London SE1 9GF
www.harpercollins.co.uk
HarperCollins*Publishers*
Macken House, 39/40 Mayor Street Upper,
Dublin 1, D01 C9W8, Ireland

This paperback edition 2026
1
First published in Great Britain in ebook format
by HarperCollins*Publishers* 2026
Copyright © M. R. G. Davies 2026
M. R. G. Davies asserts the moral right to be identified
as the author of this work

A catalogue record of this book is available from the British Library

ISBN: 978-0-00-875506-5

This novel is entirely a work of fiction. The names, characters and incidents portrayed in it are the work of the author's imagination. Any resemblance to actual persons, living or dead, events or localities is entirely coincidental.

Printed and bound in the UK using 100% Renewable Electricity
by CPI Group (UK) Ltd

All rights reserved. No part of this publication may be reproduced, stored in a retrieval system, or transmitted, in any form or by any means, electronic, mechanical, photocopying, recording or otherwise, without the prior permission of the publishers.
Without limiting the exclusive rights of any author, contributor or the publisher of this publication, any unauthorised use of this publication to train generative artificial intelligence (AI) technologies is expressly prohibited. HarperCollins also exercise their rights under Article 4(3) of the Digital Single Market Directive 2019/790 and expressly reserve this publication from the text and data mining exception.

To old friends

Richard and Mel
David
Alex
and Keith

You have to learn the rules of the game. And then you have to play better than anyone else.

> US Senator Dianne Feinstein

Disce aut discede.

> The Latin Society

Lord Quaint had never liked the cold. Even in his cramped rooms at Cambridge, where his grizzled old bedder had frequently indulged him with an extra lump of coal for no more recompense than a gruff nod when he handed over his bedpan, he had found the winter months gruelling and almost personally offensive. As each Christmas and New Year passed, he would dread the onset of the Hilary term, with its interminably frosty January, relentlessly miserable February and a March only fleetingly brightened by the annual circumnavigation of his birthday.

Here, in the remote wilderness of the Arctic tundra, stranded somewhere between Søsterbekk and Bjørnfjell, he hated it perhaps as much as he'd ever hated anything in his life.

'This place is colder than Hell,' he muttered into his fur-lined sealskin neckerchief.

The man standing at his left shoulder, wrapped almost completely from head to toe in a polar bear overcoat, shook his head. Quaint *would have missed the movement entirely inside the man's flamboyant outerwear were it not for the fact that he also sported a chain of reindeer bells around his neck and thus jangled irritatingly with every motion.*

He spoke with a light Norwegian accent.

'Not so, my lord.'

'I beg your pardon?'

The man leaned forward inside his capacious hood, the better for Quaint to hear him above the bitter wind, and shouted.

'I am sorry to be correcting your Lordship but this place is not, in fact, colder than Hell. Although the village of Hell lies some four hundred miles to the south, just outside the pretty boundaries of Trondheim, it suffers an unusually cold winter climate, with temperatures falling to twenty-five degrees below zero, which is broadly comparable to those of this region. Consequently, it cannot truthfully be said that this place—'

'Yes, thank you, Thor,' interrupted Quaint, his patience running thinner than the air in this part of the coastal crinkly bit that hadn't so much crossed the Arctic circle as made an enemy of it for life by destroying its livelihood, seducing its wife and eating its pet chihuahua.

Sometimes he regretted having to turn to local law enforcement agencies to do the technically legal aspects of the job: it would make life far simpler if he could just arrest the culprits himself, mete out some succinct but apposite physical sanction (nominally for the purposes of temporary restraint), then hand them over to the authorities at some later date of mutual convenience. As it was, he was too often reliant on a jumped-up functionary beyond his capabilities for the official duties of apprehension and incarceration. He could understand the theoretical logic of the position – that allowing a strict amateur to deliver the coup de grâce might open a Pandora's Box of vigilante-style hoodlums to wreak havoc in their communities – but Lord Quaint was not of their ilk. He had proved time and again, to police forces across the globe, that his particular skills were unique. Surely that should afford him some latitude in the immediate administration of justice?

Thor Bjørnson was an especially egregious example of the type. Educated at boarding school in deepest Sussex before the war, he had acquired a knowledge and execution of the English language that outshone most of Quaint's contemporaries at Cambridge, but in the mouth of a foreigner merely served to aggravate his intolerability in the eyes of any native speakers he might encounter. He had, Quaint knew, enjoyed a near meteoric rise through the ranks of the Tromsø police force largely by dint of being its sole employee following the tragic death of his father in a bizarre whaling accident some years earlier, and now enjoyed seniority over the handful of officers who patrolled the northern reaches of the Norwegian Arctic. In Quaint's book, that put him roughly on a par with a detective sergeant in the Met, but the gentleman sleuth was currently in no position to argue. He had been assigned this paragon of Scandinavian justice and, in the grim vastnesses of the barren landscape, he would have to make do.

From their slightly elevated position on the hillside, Lord Quaint looked down on the abandoned train and the frozen lake beyond, wondering for the umpteenth time how he had allowed himself to be commissioned for this nightmarish investigation. The reason stood on the other side of Thor Bjørnson, handcuffed to the policeman and shivering in the freezing air: Quaint's oldest chum, Penworthy Glitch. Quaint recalled once more how Glitch – drawing heavily on a friendship that dated back to dark schoolboy doings in the dorms at

Eton – had strongarmed him into taking a cabin on the wretched *Arctic Voyager*, and he had come to realise that the purpose of the strongarming was the exact purpose in which he was now engaged. It was Quaint, and Quaint alone, who could identify the real killer of Glitch's young and beautiful new wife Lavinia, of whose murder on board Glitch now stood accused and for whose demise he was sure to face the hangman's noose.

Billed by the overenthusiastic marketeers of the Norwegian Polar Express Company as 'the train journey to end all train journeys', it did indeed bear the hallmarks of being the final resting place of the recently wedded Mrs Glitch.

But Quaint was all too aware that the dozen or so unfortunates huddled together in desperation on the hillside below him knew different.

'Ladies and gentlemen,' Quaint called out in his sternest Army voice, refined on the playing fields of Sandhurst and ripened in the heat of the Transvaal. 'If I may have your attention, please?'

Two dozen eyes turned on the aristocrat, every one of them shifty and nervous behind the frozen lids. He surveyed the assembled group with considerable distaste and wondered how his friend had managed to acquire such a motley collection of acquaintances. Their individual connections with the disgraced banker had been largely unknown between them prior to departure, but Quaint had established beyond all doubt that each person ankle-deep in the snow before him had played their part in his downfall.

Now, Penworthy Glitch's life rested in the hands of Lord Quaint.

'You have all, by now, learned the truth about this unusual train journey,' he began, watching the glances flit from one to another as suspicion fell where it might among the group. 'What has almost certainly escaped each and every one of you is the reason why you were all brought together.'

Quaint made out some mutterings among the group and was about to quell the mild insurrection when another sound caught his ear. In the distance, from behind him over the crest of the slope, came the unmistakable sound of a light aircraft.

He hurried to complete his oration.

'However, it has long been clear to me, if not to the spinning wheels of Norwegian justice'—here he glanced sideways at Thor Bjørnson—'that Penworthy Glitch is an innocent man.'

This time he let the murmurings go unchallenged until they reached a natural end.

'Thanks to the evidence you have each provided over the course of the past few days on board the Arctic Voyager, I can now conclusively confirm that Mr Glitch stands wrongly accused of a heinous crime.'

He pointed suddenly at an expensively dressed young man near the centre of the group, his arm around a prettily vapid girl of eighteen.

'You, Count Oblimov, claimed to have witnessed the murder itself in the corridor outside Mr Glitch's cabin. Your fiancée there, Miss Snetterton, has corroborated your story from the beginning. But you are both lying.'

A cry went up from the left-hand end of the line-up as the elderly American heiress Mrs Vance Cooper gasped melodramatically and reached for her smelling salts.

'And you can save your histrionics for the courtroom, Mrs Cooper: you have been less than consistent with the truth yourself.'

The old lady whipped off her spectacles and was about to launch into a speech when Lord Quaint raised a commanding hand in her direction and cut her off before she'd even begun.

'I have more to say, Mrs Cooper. You will await your turn.'

The aircraft was getting closer. Quaint couldn't tell if the group below him were aware of the sound yet, but if they were they gave no sign of it.

'Every one of you here assembled had a motive to do Penworthy Glitch down, and when the opportunity arose, you snatched at it. From the depravities of Sir Elbert's private life – a secret that threatened to ruin him if Glitch were to reveal it – to the financial irregularities of Colonel Trask's business dealings, which Glitch was on the point of exposing, each of you wanted him out of the way. When his new young bride Lavinia came to you in turn, offering you the perfect solution to your respective problems in return for a hefty sum of money, you were each tempted beyond endurance, regardless of the inevitable consequences for the poor, innocent victim of her wicked deception.'

He began to raise his voice over the sound of the engine that was now unquestionably approaching from behind him.

'But you reckoned without the formidable brain of Lord Rivereaux Quaint and the plain inability of the Norwegian rail network to offer a reliable service under such barbaric temperatures at this lofty latitude. Finding ourselves marooned here, I have no compunction about revealing the crux of this case to you all.'

Before he could finish, a seaplane crested the hill above his head at a height of no more than thirty feet and swooped down over the crowd.

To a man (and woman) they ducked.

Consequently, only Quaint saw the seaplane heading for the frozen lake. Only he knew that it had arrived, by prior arrangement with the Norway Postal Service, to retrieve none other than his Lordship himself. He would embark on the small aircraft for its return journey to Narvik, leaving the dozen unwitting co-conspirators in the custody of Thor Bjørnson to await the arrival – who knew when? – of a team of train mechanics to repair their stranded transport and remove them to a subarctic gaol.

He returned his attention to the group, who were now staring at him, open-mouthed.

'The simple fact of the matter is that Lavinia Glitch, the pleasant young wife of the aforementioned accused man, was not, as you all affirmed so confidently to the local police, the victim of his hideous bludgeoning in the corridor outside their cabin. Nor, as some of your more lurid narratives proposed, was her body done away with in a bath of acid in their cabin or tossed from the window of the moving express into the snowy wastes beyond. No, the truth is not only that Penworthy Glitch is not a murderer, but that his deceptive new wife was…'

He paused and surveyed the company as they teetered on the brink of his final pronouncement. They made a sorry picture, but he felt no sympathy for them. They would have seen his friend hang and barely turned a hair.

'… not even dead,' he concluded.

This despicable dozen would face their punishment in an English prison before too long. Until then, he was perfectly prepared to admit that he was delighted at the prospect of their immediate futures, freezing their nether regions in this remote corner of the Arctic.

It was time to wrap things up.

'The notorious Mrs Glitch in fact decamped from the train in secret at our last stop two days ago, when Mr Bjørnson was summoned aboard, and is currently residing with her Italian lover and co-conspirator, Signor Umberto Porcellini, in a rather insalubrious semi-detached villa in the suburbs of Norbiton, where even now the local constabulary are knocking at her door. It will not be long, I suspect, before she is herself behind bars.'

As the wind tore into his sealskin neckerchief and he made his way tentatively across the frozen ice towards the manoeuvring seaplane with his grateful friend in tow, Lord Quaint congratulated himself on solving the sinister case: he had proved beyond all doubt that there had, indeed, been no murder on the polar express.

THE END

The Dining Room

1

Professor Stone did not enjoy being watched as he ate. He could tolerate the other people around the large oak table – he'd endured enough formal meals in academia to be able to survive that, at least – but the portraits were another matter. Generations of stern faces, oddly similar yet distinctly different, stared down at him grimly from the walls. Individually, they looked sombre; collectively they were an ominous army of disapproval. Some were dressed in Tudor ruffs and pantaloons, others in the lacy finery of the Regency or staid sobriety of the Victorians; all were pug ugly.

This was not, however, an observation that Professor Stone felt at liberty to express aloud, given that his host was their direct descendant.

The dining room at Abbots Chantry was hardly the most impressive he had ever seen, but then the house itself did not rank among the top flight of country piles, even within the county boundaries of Norcestershire. Stone knew this because he had done his research. Thanks to the great architectural historian Pevsner, Stone had learned that it was the stately home of the Verity family, whose ancestors were reputed (though not officially recorded anywhere other than via word-of-mouth down the dubious lineage) to have arrived in England with William the Conqueror. The family crest and motto still attested to the ancient roots of the male line: *Vérité et justice*. The property, by contrast, was a later addition to the Old French aristocrats' minor empire, having been acquired in the sixteenth century (verifiable by a musty old document buried somewhere in the vaults of the Norcester Castle Museum) as a ruined ecclesiastical building following the Dissolution of the Monasteries.

Stone remembered learning at school about Henry VIII's aversion to such Catholic fripperies as the Monasteries. It was one of those curiosities that one picked up, safe in the knowledge that its usefulness would be highly questionable in adult life but nonetheless stored away against that rare moment when producing it might engender awe in one's audience. Such a moment had yet to occur in Stone's life regarding this particular historical titbit, but he refused to excise it from his memory just yet. He knew, after all, that many people felt the same about the finer points of his own subject, mathematics, and look how that had turned out for him: a professorship in his late thirties and then two decades of respected practice in the seminar rooms and lecture theatres of Pittingham University.

Never mind that it had all ended badly. Nobody could take away his honorary title now.

'What do you think, Professor?'

Stone was disturbed from his nostalgic reverie by the

familiar voice of his friend and co-member of The Quaint Bookshop reading group, Bella Bourton.

'Mmm? Sorry – what do I think about what?'

Bella laughed diagonally across the table at him. 'Lost in your own world again, Professor?'

She might have been the newest member of the group, and technically the least academically qualified, but over the past few months Stone had developed a decidedly soft spot for her. At least she was – like the rest of the group – untrammelled by knowledge of the personal difficulties that had led to his departure from the great halls of academe a few years earlier. They knew nothing of his brush with the university authorities, or the eccentricities of his wayward colleagues, or the legalities of a contract that should have kept him in comfortable employment well beyond pensionable retirement age but which had, in fact, let him down badly and left him licking his wounds in a mediocre backwater that was the nearest thing to a place he could call home.

There was no need for him to trouble them with any of that.

As for Bella, he relished the fact that she had no degree to encumber her charming innocence: she had no pretensions to high culture but she knew a good book when she read it. In the months since they had first met, Stone had learned much about life from this down-to-earth, newly divorced woman with a fondness for populist authors and a nice line in pomposity-pricking, of which he had first-hand experience.

'Apparently,' he replied, smiling sheepishly at her.

'We were talking about the merits of our latest book,' said Harrison Fforde, a pontificating note in his voice which, Stone imagined, he'd exaggerated from his normal actorly tones for the benefit of the elevated company. Mind you, Fforde could pontificate the telephone directory to an empty phone box when he chose, so maybe this wasn't so very different from his usual delivery.

Did anyone still use a telephone directory? Stone was pretty sure they didn't furnish phone boxes with them any more, even when you could find a phone box that hadn't been converted into a coffee shop or toy exchange or simply used as a public convenience.

His mind was wandering again, even as Lauren Sherwood rested a concerned hand on his left arm. Despite being the youngest in the reading group, she had always been an empathetic creature.

'Professor? Are you all right?'

'Sorry, yes – just miles away.'

A part of the Professor wished he was, in fact, miles away. When the invitation had first arrived, delivered gracelessly to the reading group by the bookshop's rather sullen acting manager Maurice Stapleton, he had initially been inclined to refuse it. The success of the group at solving the murder of the previous manager Felicity Penman – whose body they had discovered slumped between the shelves in the Noir section – had conferred some measure of fame upon the foursome, which Stone had regarded with both suspicion and caution. After the debacle at Pittingham, he had retired to his mother's birthplace of Norcester specifically to avoid scrutiny of any kind, but the group's profile, especially between the pages of the *Norcester Echo*, had risen to such a degree that they now regularly received requests for talks, autographs and even selfies with other bookshop customers desperate for a brush with celebrity. Most of these he had managed to circumvent, pleading shortage of time or simple shyness; the invitation from Lord and Lady Verity to a country-house weekend as guests of honour had proved too much of an inducement to his three colleagues, however, and he had found himself press-ganged into accepting. Now, with the weather turning inclement and dark clouds looming on the distant horizon, across the manicured lawns outside the conservatory, he was regretting the decision once more.

It didn't help that there were three Americans present.

'We want to know,' said the eldest and most leather-faced of the three, who had been introduced as a location manager and spoke with the drawling laziness that Stone always associated with the Wild West, 'what you think of *Murder on the Polar Express*.'

Stone realised he had missed out on a vital part of the conversation. While he was away in his head, musing on the accuracy or otherwise of Lord Verity's family tree, the others had already offered their opinions about the Lord Quaint novel, which the reading group had been studying specially ahead of this weekend after being informed that an advance party from Hollywood would be scouting Abbots Chantry as a possible shooting location for a film of the book. Now, offering his own verdict on the novel would make him look either pathetically unimaginative if he agreed with them, or decidedly curmudgeonly if he took an opposite view. Neither option was appealing but, since he had no idea which he would be exercising, he chose to offer his honest view and hope for the best.

'Not one of his finest,' he said, and stuffed a large head of broccoli into his mouth.

'Oh, Professor!' Bella laughed again and reached for her wine glass. Stone suspected she might be enjoying the lubrication a little too much. 'That's not what you said on Tuesday when we were discussing it. "A neat exposition and an entertaining twist" – that's what you said. I remember it exactly because I had to go and look up "exposition" when I got home. I thought you were talking about the dust jacket.'

She took a large swig from the glass and turned to the American next to her, a well-groomed man in his thirties whom Bella had been flirting with since he'd arrived an hour and a half earlier. Stone could see the superficial attraction – tanned good looks, an easy manner and a practised facility with flattery – but he doubted there was any more substance to the man than that. He'd been described as the director of photography, which Stone presumed put him fairly high up in the film-making hierarchy, and was by far the most inoffensive of the three. The other two – the location manager and the film's director – were comfortably to the wrong end of Stone's scale marked 'uncouth'.

'Yes, well, I've had a chance to reconsider since Tuesday, and I've come to the conclusion that by the end of the book, Lord Quaint is showing distinct signs of being vindictive.'

'Oh, that's all right,' said the third American, a young man in a backwards baseball cap who couldn't have been much more than twenty-five yet held the reins (and presumably the budget) of this Hollywood blockbuster. 'We're changing the ending anyway.'

There was a stirring from Stone's right, where the staff of

Abbots Chantry were seated together. He had noted as they sat down that the reading group had been placed in two pairs, either side of the centre of the table – Lauren next to him, Bella and Fforde opposite – which presented them with the strategic disadvantage of being positioned between the Americans and their Verity hosts at one end, and the assorted staff members at the other. Ranged in the traditionally accepted male-female pattern of alternation, they made for interesting dinner companions.

Beside Fforde sat Bella's sister Ronnie – technically Veronica but, as Bella had stressed, never called by that name, which she found unduly flowery and old-fashioned. Ronnie was one of the numerous volunteers at Abbots Chantry, whose charitable support allowed the place to function as a tourist attraction and without whom Lord and Lady Verity would undoubtedly have to sell up and move to the suburbs. It was Ronnie who had set this whole weekend up, exploiting her sororal connection to the reading group to arrange the invitation that Stone had almost rejected. He hadn't known her long enough to work out the nature of her relationship with her sister, but he sensed a tension between them that intrigued him and could certainly stand further investigation. So far, all he had to go on was Bella's description of her as 'scatty' and his own observations over dinner. As Bella had warned them, she had a tendency – even more so than her sister – towards a loquaciousness which, Stone felt a little churlishly, was rarely merited by the contents of her contributions.

Next to Ronnie was a thin, bespectacled man in a threadbare pale blue pullover, who managed the gift shop at Abbots Chantry.

Stone thought his name was Hemingford Grey but, since that was also a village in Cambridgeshire, he couldn't be sure. On Stone's side of Grey sat Siobhan and Monty Butler, the married couple who lived on the premises and were mainly responsible for the upkeep of the house and control of visitors. Monty was a serious, fiftyish Scotsman in full tartan tweeds, looking every bit the sober estate manager, while Siobhan – younger than her husband by at least ten years, Stone estimated – seemed much more in tune with her role as tour guide, smiling affably at everyone and keen to make sure they all had everything they needed.

To Stone's immediate right sat the source of the stirring: a rather fierce-looking woman of about forty, with greying strands in her otherwise abundant black hair, which fell around her chalk-white skin and velvet-clad shoulders in a way that reminded Stone of Fenella Fielding in *Carry On Screaming*. She was the house's catering manager and her name was Keren Lowe, an unusual forename that Stone had already established was down to her mother's obsession with Bananarama.

'Bloody Americans,' she muttered, loudly enough for Stone to hear clearly and, he assumed, intended to carry at least beyond him to the director of photography on the other side of Lauren, although with enough of a *sotto voce* element to be able to plausibly deny it if she were challenged.

'Don't start,' murmured Siobhan from the side of her mouth, the smile never leaving her lips.

Keren grunted and picked up her wine, knocking back almost half a glass in one draught.

There seemed to be tensions among the household of

Abbots Chantry too, and Stone wondered if bringing them all together socially like this was the brightest idea Lord Verity had ever had. If his intention had been to woo the Americans with the charms of an English country house and its denizens, the chances of that backfiring spectacularly looked reasonably high from where he sat.

Bella had evidently caught Keren's drift, if not the actual words, from the far side of the table. She hurried to change the subject.

'It's looking rather grim outside, isn't it?' she asked nobody in particular. 'Looks like there could be snow.'

Stone realised she was right. That sense of foreboding that comes from lowering clouds and a new chill infusing the air was seeping through the walls of Abbots Chantry even as they ate. Maybe that was what was putting the staff on edge. The sunshine of the early afternoon had already given way to oppressive grey cumulonimbus as he'd unpacked his suitcase in the dingy expanses of his bedroom; now the evening was black with heaviness, and snow felt inevitable.

'Hey, that would be fantastic,' said the director, his eyes eager and alert. He jabbed a finger at the director of photography. 'Must get some mood shots for the sample reel. The producers would love that.'

The location manager appeared mildly alarmed at the comment – or at least as alarmed as a laid-back cowboy with a craggy suntan for a face could get.

'Now don't go expecting snowfall in this picture, Colorado,' he said, reaching his hand across the younger man in a symbolic gesture of restraint. 'We'll be shooting in May and there'll be no real snow at that time of year.' He turned to Lord Verity. 'That's right, ain't it?'

His Lordship should have lived a century earlier, Stone concluded. He was one of those people – a bit like Jacob Rees-Mogg – who was born old, and even though in reality he was probably only just entering middle age, he looked like a relic from a different time. His clothes, his house, his demeanour, even his dowdy wife, belonged in an Edwardian melodrama, and he styled himself a good two decades or more beyond his actual years. But no, even that wasn't right: Stone guessed himself to be about a dozen years older than his host, and he didn't go in for the kind of worn, stuffy tweeds and Oxford brogues that Lord Verity had greeted them in earlier that afternoon. Not yet, anyway. Perhaps the time arrived in everyone's life for them to turn into their grandfathers, but Stone was damned if he was going to turn into his, a charmless drunk with a penchant for reckless gambling and jellied eels. No, Stone decided, getting old was a state of mind, one that Lord Verity had clearly adopted from his early days, and he wasn't going to succumb to it.

As Stone dissected his personality, Lord Verity plucked with his fork at a lump of pheasant on the plate in front of him, sending an accompanying plum swooshing across the china and teetering dangerously on the lip.

An awkward silence awaited his response to the American, as did the rest of the table.

It was Hemingford Grey who coughed pointedly and clattered his knife down on a plate. 'One of your guests asked you a question, your Lordship.'

It was an interesting intervention by a member of staff,

Stone reflected, but maybe they were used to their employer's absent-mindedness. Or maybe Grey was niggled by the weather as well. Whatever the reason, it seemed to drag Lord Verity temporarily from his poultry-focused funk.

'Mmm? What? Oh, yes. Shooting in May. But you can't start on the grouse until August.'

The observation was lost on the location manager, who resumed his conversation with his film crew colleagues.

'And before you start thinking about importing any of that fake stuff, you can forget it.' He looked across at the English contingent, apparently about to explain. 'Two most expensive words in a movie script – "It snows."'

Stone wondered how they were planning a film adaptation of *Murder on the Polar Express* without involving snow of any kind. It seemed like a tall order to him, but then he knew nothing of the inner workings of the movie industry, and the Americans' inspection of Abbots Chantry as a potential location for a story set on an Arctic railway had also got him scratching his head. Maybe they were planning to change the title as well as the ending.

Colorado looked again at the director of photography. 'Would be kinda neat, though, wouldn't it, Marin?'

Stone winced. He wasn't sure if it was at the vocal elision or the men's names.

'Marin,' grunted Keren from beside him, disdain leaking out through both syllables.

'I told you,' said Siobhan through her gritted teeth and grin. Patches of scarlet were beginning to bloom on her cheeks and Stone wondered if Keren always wound her up like this. 'These people are our guests.'

'What's that?' asked Lady Verity, her attention drawn to the *tête-à-tête* below the salt. The Professor had noticed she'd spent much of dinner worrying away at the string of pearls around her neck rather than eating any of the rich food on her plate, and he wondered whether something was troubling her. To his mind, her peacock-blue twinset marked her out as the archetypal aristocratic wife, just as old-beyond-her-years as her husband, and he wondered what sort of troubles might occupy her: which hat to select for Ascot Ladies' Day, perhaps, or how many Vuitton valises to take to Le Touquet?

'Nothing, your Ladyship,' said Monty, shooting a glance that encompassed both his wife and the catering manager. 'We're just discussing the plot.'

'And snow,' joined in Bella, jovially. 'Looks like it's on the way.'

'You'd better hope it isn't,' said Monty darkly.

'What on earth do you mean?' asked Stone, the hairs on the back of his neck nudging involuntarily erect. The Scottish estate manager's accent, coupled with the wary look in his eye, conveyed a sense of doom that would have thrilled his fellow countryman Private Frazer in *Dad's Army*.

'You've seen how inaccessible this place is,' said Monty, his gaze flitting round the table. Stone got the feeling he wanted to make sure everyone was listening to him. 'One B-road running past the gates, a three-quarter-mile single-track driveway with no other entrance to the estate, and sitting in a dell carved out of a loop in the course of the River Nore. Abbots Chantry could hardly be more isolated. If snow blocks the drive overnight, we'll be completely cut off from the outside world.'

The table was silent for at least thirty seconds.

Then Professor Stone laughed.

'Good one, Monty – you really had us going there.'

But with a chill, he noticed nobody else was laughing.

'I'm deadly serious,' said the Scotsman. 'It's happened on numerous occasions since Siobhan and I have been looking after the place. We had two spells last winter, one the year before that, but when it gets really bad it can be weeks before any help gets through.'

'Weeks?' Bella's voice was small and timid.

'Weeks,' Monty confirmed, fixing his eye on her and raising an eyebrow. The accent was pure Sean Connery, the facial expression Roger Moore, but Stone struggled to see Monty as a James Bond figure; if anything, his dark features and solemn look suggested he might be better cast as the villain. Stone wondered vaguely if Abbots Chantry had a white cat.

'He's right, you know,' grumbled Lord Verity, apparently roused from his semi-somnolent state by a subject about which he could expound with expertise: his house. As he spoke, his cummerbund wobbled up and down across his dress shirt and Stone wondered if the family always dressed for dinner or whether this was a sop to the Americans, an attempt to elevate the aristocratic elements of the weekend to press home the property's eligibility as their shooting location. 'Back in eighty-two we were cut off from December to the end of February thanks to the snow. Fortunately my parents had had a rather large shipment delivered from Harrods against exactly such an eventuality and that, together with the estate's own provisions, saw us through. But it was touch and go for a while there.'

Stone was sure he could detect a glint in his Lordship's eye that suggested the hyperbole was for Hollywood's benefit.

He remembered the winter of eighty-two quite clearly: it was his first away from home studying Maths at Forthbury University and was a particularly cold one, with snowfall making pavements hazardous to bicycles and even freezing the river for a brief period. But he suspected there was more than a hint of exaggeration about Lord Verity's recollections. The peer couldn't have been much more than a small child at the time, he reflected, and perhaps that was a factor in his memory: a boy of six or seven would have revelled in the adventures that a snowbound estate could offer, leaving the concerns of simple survival to his worried parents.

'Well, we'll just have to hope it doesn't snow, then, won't we?' Bella was trying to put a tone of resilience into her voice, Stone could tell, but underneath it was a tremble. It might only have been discernible to him and the other reading group members, but it was there nonetheless.

'Agreed,' he said, trying to bolster her spirits. 'And whatever happens, we're not going to let it spoil the weekend. I'm really keen to learn more about the house and gardens. And the main reason we're here, of course – the famous Verity library.'

He picked up his glass and raised it in toast to the company.

'I'm sure there's plenty of excitement for us to look forward to.'

II

B_lithe Spirit_ was one of Harrison Fforde's favourite plays, though he could never be quite sure if it was because it tapped into a deep-seated but utterly unevidenced fear of ghosts, or simply that he'd always wanted to play the role of Madame Arcati. Sadly, his acting career – despite the optimistic Equity name he had devised for himself in an attempt to catch the eye of casting directors on the lookout for something a little different from the usual drama school fare – had never quite reached the heights of being offered female character parts for their comic effect. David Suchet and Stephen Fry might have got away with playing Lady Bracknell in _The Importance of Being Earnest_ and made their respective producers a tidy sum in the process; nobody was going to fork out more than a threepenny bit to see Fforde play Noel Coward's famous medium, and threepenny bits had ceased being legal tender in 1972, around the time he was born. He'd occasionally wondered if the two auspicious incidents – decimalisation of the British currency and the arrival of the infant Harold

Monkton – might somehow be connected, but he couldn't for the life of him think how, and his parents had long since departed to the spirit realm themselves so there was no one left to ask.

What surprised him on the Saturday morning of what he had come to think of as his Hollywood audition weekend, as he opened the heavy curtains in his gothically dramatic bedroom, was that the powers of divination attributed to Madame Arcati appeared to have transferred themselves magically to the reading group's newest member.

For Bella Bourton had been entirely correct at dinner the previous evening.

Abbots Chantry was blanketed with snow.

Fforde had seen snow before. He'd thrown snowballs as a kid, and sometimes as an adult, when the powdery stuff was of the right consistency and there was somebody else around to throw them at who wouldn't beat you up for it. Some years ago, he'd played a rather grumpy Santa in a shopping centre off the Swindon bypass and spent most of January picking bits of synthetic snow out of crevices he didn't know he had. He'd even gone on holiday to Austria with his then wife Selina and watched from afar as she schussed the blue runs while he contented himself with alcohol-laced hot chocolates and a belting fire in the Nachtschnecke und Kopfsalat alpine bar. (He was convinced that holiday was where the rot had set in as far as their marriage was concerned, and it had all been the fault of that bloody instructor Günther, whose insistence on correct pole technique and proper pronunciation of his umlaut had ticked Fforde off to such an extent that he'd refused to ski after the second day, leaving Selina both to the slopes and to

Günther's gruff Germanic charms. He had no proof that anything had happened between them but the chill in the marital chalet bedroom had not entirely been the responsibility of the weather.)

Yes, he'd seen snow before. But not snow like this.

This snow, spread thick and brilliant across Abbots Chantry, was as if a giant Zeppelin filled with cocaine had exploded above the ancient monastery and dumped its load over the estate. In the distance, Fforde could make out a ribbon of black scarring the relentless white where the river wound through the countryside, but otherwise the whole scene was like something out of *Murder on the Polar Express*. He half-expected Lord Quaint to knock at the door with some startling revelations about the other occupants of the house.

'Thick, isn't it?' he said, redundantly but excitedly, as he bounced into the dining room for breakfast.

'The yoghurt?' asked Lauren, looking up from a bowlful of glutinous creamy sludge speckled with blue, straw and other assorted berries.

'The snow,' urged Fforde, wafting both hands at the large windows behind her, where the view down towards the fountain was a uniform tract of white.

'Oh, that. Yes, it's been going non-stop most of the night.'

'You don't sound too cheerful about it,' said Fforde, making his way to a long sideboard at one end of the room, where a vast selection of comestibles was arrayed on silverware that had probably been in the Verity family for generations. Each dish was almost certainly worth more than he could earn in a week on an Equity minimum wage and it was the prospect of enjoying such opulence – alongside the chance to meet a real-life American film crew – that had prompted Fforde to lean so heavily on Professor Stone to accept the invitation of Lord and Lady Verity to a country-house weekend. His fellow reading group members might be used to regular meals and a warm house, but Fforde could not guarantee himself the same luxuries. Not with his precarious freelance existence as an out-of-work actor. He'd hoped he might have been able to leverage the group's fifteen minutes of fame as the amateur sleuths who solved the murder of Felicity Penman into something lucrative – a television appearance or two, perhaps, or a guest spot on someone's podcast – but beyond the annoyance of frequent requests for autographs from members of the public who could do his career no good at all, things had gone very quiet very quickly.

Until this invitation had come along and the doors of possibility had opened up to him again in the form of a weekend in the company of some movie moguls.

'I'm not,' Lauren replied, her mouth full of the glutinous sludge.

'Not a fan of snow, then?'

Fforde wasn't sure which utensils he should use to serve himself from the buffet, settling on a pair of tongs to pick up everything from sausages, bacon and black pudding to a lump of congealed scrambled egg and several baked beans, which he plucked from their dish in ones and twos until he could just about call it a serving.

'Not when it cuts off the power supply,' said Lauren morosely.

'What?'

Lauren jabbed a spoon towards the chandeliers above their

heads, which Fforde now registered hung stubbornly unlit. With the brightness of a wintry sun reflecting off the snow, he hadn't even noticed anything amiss in his room.

'No electricity,' said Lauren, reinforcing her point.

Fforde look back at the sideboard, laden with hotplates and steaming salvers.

'How did they manage to cook breakfast?'

Lauren shrugged. 'A big old wood-fired Aga, I should imagine.'

Now that he thought about it, Fforde realised the whole house had felt a little chillier this morning than it had when they all went to bed. While that might have been attributable to significant quantities of wine, port and brandy over dinner, it now seemed more likely that the lack of electricity had affected the heating this morning. He wondered what back-up plans Monty Butler had in place for when the power went down.

'Is it just us?' he asked Lauren, sitting down opposite her in the same chair he'd occupied over dinner.

Habits formed quickly, he noted.

She looked around the barren table with a spoon in her mouth and stared back at Fforde.

'OK, silly question,' he said, and launched himself into a sausage.

'What are we going to do if the drive is impassable?' asked Lauren after she'd finished her mouthful. 'I've got school on Monday.'

Fforde considered this for a moment. Even allowing for its geographical singularity in the loop of the river, the house could not possibly host such a miniature microclimate that no snow had fallen anywhere else in Norcestershire. If they were really snowed in, he suspected the inmates of Lauren's school, where she'd proudly announced to the reading group that her teaching assistant post had graduated from Reception to Year 2 for the current academic year, would be as unlikely to file into class on Monday morning as she was herself.

'Do you not think there'll be a snow day?' he asked, using his fork to point out of the window behind her.

'You don't know my Head,' said Lauren sullenly. 'It'd have to be drifts taller than the children to make her close the school.'

'Then I think you might be in luck,' boomed a Scottish brogue from beyond the open door, followed quickly by the figure of Monty Butler dressed in a thick herringbone coat over a mustard-coloured knitted waistcoat. A tweed tie and checkered flat cap matched the colour of the waistcoat, giving off a faint Guy Ritchie vibe that Fforde found both mildly distasteful and rather dashing at the same time. 'It's drifting to well over six feet along the drive.'

Lauren seemed to perk up.

'You mean we're stuck here?'

'Stuck, marooned, trapped – whatever word takes your fancy,' said Monty, picking up a fork from the sideboard and stabbing a sausage, which he then proceeded to eat direct from the fork.

For all his enthusiasm about snowballs, Fforde didn't like the sound of trapped. *Von Trapped*, yes, of course – there was always room for another *Sing-along-a-Sound-of-Music* – but locked in by the elements in a creepy, electricity-free manor with a cast of misfitting oddballs was not the weekend he had been hoping for.

'Can't we call someone for help?'

Monty tucked a piece of semi-masticated pork into his cheek before answering.

'Who do you suggest? If we can't get out, nobody can get in. And anyway, the phone signal is down as well.'

'What?' Lauren spluttered the last spoonful of her yoghurt back into its bowl. 'I haven't even looked at my phone this morning.'

'Really?' Fforde was surprised. Personally, he rarely bothered to check his mobile until much later in the day. What was the point? Nobody would be trying to reach him anyway. But he thought every young person – and he considered Lauren a young person even though she must be past thirty – was glued to their phone from the moment they woke up to the moment they went to sleep.

'It's a detox thing. I try not to look at it for the first hour after getting up and the last hour before going to bed.'

'Very commendable,' he said, nodding as he skewered a baked bean. Since first meeting Lauren more than a year earlier, when she'd become the third member of the reading group after him and Professor Stone, he'd always found her to be an unusually sensible example of her generation. She'd been appropriately courteous towards the two older men from the start, without it ever falling into deference, and he valued her different take on life. And books. More than that, her optimism and vitality added a much-needed weekly boost of pep to his otherwise mundane routine, and he'd miss her terribly if she ever left or moved away.

'I don't know about that, but I certainly can't go the whole day without it.'

'Sorry, my dear,' said Monty, turning back towards the door with another sausage between his fingers. 'It'll be more than that. No chance of getting an engineer out before Monday at the earliest – and even that'll depend on the snow clearing, which doesn't look too likely at the moment.'

He didn't wait for a response. He clearly had things to get on with.

Lauren was staring again at Fforde.

'No phone, no electricity, no escape. What the hell are we going to do?'

Fforde shrugged. 'Board games?'

'*Board games*?'

Fforde heard the sound of rising alarm in her voice and attempted to soothe it.

'Don't worry. I'm sure it's just a temporary thing. They'll have a back-up generator or something. It can't be the first time this has happened.'

'First time what's happened?' asked Professor Stone as he entered the room. 'Morning all, by the way.'

The blasé entrance was typical of the Professor. Ever since the launch of the reading group – none of them was ever allowed to call it a book club – the former academic had assumed for himself the default role of leader, despite Fforde's self-evident charisma and authoritative qualities. Maybe it was his age but for reasons Fforde couldn't fathom, Lauren and Bella seemed in thrall to him, and Fforde occasionally found himself resenting the feeling that the three of them were mere acolytes to the

Professor's guiding influence. If Felicity had still been around, he'd have asked her whether such a lopsided balance of power was what she'd intended when she set up the reading group from among the keenest customers of The Quaint Bookshop.

Sadly, the events of six months earlier had deprived him of that opportunity.

'Morning, Professor,' said Fforde, who had long since given up attempting to challenge Stone's hubristic view of himself. 'The power's down and there's no phone signal. We were just assessing the possibility of a back-up plan.'

The Professor looked completely unperturbed.

'Funnily enough, I've just been discussing exactly that with the gardener.'

He went to the sideboard and began loading a plate.

'The gardener? Where did he come from?'

'*She*, actually – Olive. Very nice woman, and pretty skilled with a spanner, if you ask me.'

Fforde felt a twinge of hope. If this Olive had managed to reach the estate that morning, then there must be a chance that the drive wasn't completely impassable. Maybe they would be able to get home after all. He was even prepared to forgo the rest of the country-house weekend if it meant they could safely make it out.

'How did she get here?' he asked.

'She lives here,' Stone replied without turning round from the buffet. 'I went for a walk as far as I could down the drive and met her on the way back. She's trying to rig something up with a generator but I gather the stocks of diesel are low. Probably won't last the weekend.'

He turned round to face them, a mountain of food piled up on his plate.

'Looks like we're in for a bit of an adventure.'

When Fforde finally managed to track down Olive the gardener, she was already being accosted by one of the Americans. Fforde heard the accent before he saw them and thought it was the location manager – the least interesting among the film crew, as far as he was concerned. He suspected Hollywood location managers could do little for the career of an ageing British actor. Directors and DoPs, on the other hand…

'You have to be kidding,' the leathery man was saying as Fforde rounded a corner into the stable yard. The house here had offered some shelter from the snow, which was only ankle-deep, compared to the waist-high banks further out across the lawns, and the blizzard had relented to a gently falling curtain of large, feathery flakes.

The man was standing too close to the woman – whom Fforde assumed to be Olive, leaning on a spade and dressed as she was in wellingtons, grubby green overalls and the ubiquitous flat cap that served everyone from monarchs to minions in these circles – and Fforde immediately felt the discomfort of the reserved Englishman at the brashness of Americans and their inability to recognise social acceptability.

Olive, on the other hand, didn't seem to care. The proximity of her interlocutor and the height difference between them that allowed him to peer down at her apparently had no impact on her and she brushed him off with a nonchalance that Fforde found instantly impressive, mentally noting it for some future character role.

'Not kidding at all, sir,' she replied with equanimity, her West Country vowels giving her deep voice a softening lilt. 'Now if you don't mind, I've got work to do. If you'll allow me to get about my business, I'll be in soon to see if I can get some heat going in the house. I'm sure you and your colleagues aren't used to this kind of weather.'

'Ain't that the truth,' said the American and turned away. Fforde caught a glimpse of his face and saw that the Californian sunshine that had lit him up over dinner last night had darkened with the clouds into a sour grimace.

Fforde waited until the man had rounded a different corner, towards the back of the house, before stepping out into the yard, where Olive had begun shovelling some of the deeper snow to the edges.

'Good morning,' he boomed in his best Brian-Blessed-hailing-from-the-summit-of-Everest voice. 'You must be Olive.'

'Must I?' she replied without looking up.

Instantly, Fforde wondered if he'd got it all wrong. He'd seen the outfit, he'd heard her speak of getting the heat going, and he'd assumed – not unnaturally, he allowed himself – that this must be Olive. She was shovelling like a gardener, her accent fitted the image perfectly and there, poking out of her overall back pocket, was a spanner. In fact, now he came to consider it further, if it wasn't Olive then who the hell was it?

No, it must be Olive.

Mustn't it?

'Sorry,' he muttered, the decibels falling by about three-quarters from his initial greeting. '*Are* you Olive?'

'Depends who's asking.'

She still hadn't looked up.

'Oh, I see.' He didn't but it felt like the right thing to say. 'I'm one of the guests here this weekend. My name is Harrison Fforde.'

Olive – if indeed it was Olive, a question that seemed to be looming ever larger in Fforde's mind with every passing second – finally stopped what she was doing and looked up at him, a broad smile creasing her even broader face.

'Well, well, well,' she said, pushing her thick brown glasses up on to her thick brown head of hair, presumably to appraise him more effectively with whatever version of her eyesight didn't need the optician's prescription.

'And what might you be looking for – the lost ark, the temple of doom or the crystal skull?'

Fforde was grateful, at least, that she hadn't enquired about the dial of destiny. The misguided later addition to the series, in his view, had failed to capture the *Boy's Own* adventure atmosphere in the same way as its predecessors and had, in fact, prompted something of a rethink about his stage name. It had served him well enough at the start of his career, provoking interest and amusement from casting directors and agents, but since settling in Norcester for a life of odd jobs seasoned with sporadic forays into acting-adjacent work such as tour guiding, he had found it increasingly burdensome. Those casting directors and agents had long since ceased to be amused – or interested, come to that – and he had privately been wondering if it had outlived its usefulness. Having the piss taken out of him by Olive was, he suspected, if not the final nail in the pseudonym's coffin, at least one that would hold the lid down while he explored other options.

He gave a little laugh of toleration, one that had been well used over the years, and moved swiftly on.

'I gather you've been chatting with the Professor this morning?'

'Have I?'

She was evidently going to be hard work.

'And who might this Professor be when he's at home?'

'Er, tall chap, early sixties, bit of a goatee – air of authority about him.'

'Oh, Stone,' she said in a way that suggested she'd known him all her life. 'Yes, he's been out to see me.'

'And you told him you might be able to get some power up and running?'

Olive shovelled another spadeful of snow and stopped again to lean on her implement.

'Funny thing, snow.'

'Is it?'

'Never does what you want it to do. Falls thick where it's no help and only slush where you need it. Take this yard, for instance. You might think the lighter fall here would be a good thing.'

'I suppose,' said Fforde, though he was struggling to work out why, or what any of this had to do with restoring the power.

'You might think it wouldn't be so hard getting the genny across from the barn and into the house.'

'Oh, I see,' said Fforde, beginning to understand.

'But thick snow would have compacted easier and made a stronger foundation to drag it on – like huskies pulling a sled. This stuff turns to slush so it has to be cleared away first.'

'Ah, yes,' said Fforde, waggling a finger at the spade in her hands. 'Hence the…'

'It's a bugger of a job, though,' she interrupted, and shovelled again. 'Specially for one person.'

Fforde noticed that she wasn't making eye contact with him but he understood her perfectly now.

If only the beefy Californian had stayed a few minutes more.

'Er … would you like me to help?' he asked tentatively, desperately hoping he'd guessed the anticipated answer wrongly.

'Oh no, Mr Fforde. I couldn't possibly ask a house guest to help me with something like this.'

Fforde had never really known what 'palpable' meant – it turned up in the swordfight at the end of *Hamlet* in relation to 'a hit', although that didn't help him much – but he knew that whatever it meant, his relief was it.

'On the other hand,' Olive went on, 'if a house guest were to *volunteer* their help, then it would be rude, bordering on churlish, of a mere gardener to refuse them, wouldn't it?'

Palpable or not, Fforde's relief vanished like a seven per cent solution of cocaine into Sherlock Holmes's arm.

'Do you … have another spade?' he asked miserably.

'Tons,' she replied, and marched off towards the barn.

They were in the middle of hauling the generator through the freshly shovelled yard when the Wild Westerner reappeared.

'There's talk inside of someone riding out for help,' he announced without preamble. The snow reached substantially lower up his cowboy boots than it had an hour earlier, but they still looked implacably incongruous. His cod-cowpoke language added to the fakery but his suggestion stirred something vaguely intrepid in Fforde.

'Has anyone offered their services?' he asked. 'Because I wouldn't mind having a bash at reaching civilisation.'

'That dog won't hunt,' said the American, which Fforde assumed he meant figuratively. Remarkably for this kind of household, he hadn't noticed a single quadruped of any variety.

'Oh – why's that?'

'Because I already bagged that beaver,' he said, mixing metaphorical critters with nonchalant ease. 'I just came back out to ask Olive here for a pair of those rinky-dink boots y'all wear over here. Wallingtons, or something?'

A little of Olive's resilience seemed to sag.

'Wellingtons,' she corrected him, and turned back towards the barn. She emerged a moment later with three pairs of boots clutched in her arms: a bright yellow ankle-length pair that wouldn't have looked out of place on Paddington Bear, a mid-sized combination in blue and white vertical stripes, and a huge set of green anglers' waders draped over one forearm that almost touched the ground at both ends.

'I'll take them there long johns,' said the location manager, grabbing them from Olive and making his way over to a low wall beside the yard's main gate. He tugged off his leather boots, dropping them into the snow, and began wrestling with the waders as Fforde and Olive stood watching.

'You do know how far it is to the nearest house, don't you?' Olive asked as the man moved on to his second leg.

'Twelve miles, so Mr Butler tells me.'

'Twelve miles *in thick snow*. It'll take hours to reach anyone, and then they won't be able to do anything for days, probably.'

'Lady, twelve miles ain't nothing,' said the location manager, and Fforde thought he meant it. 'I've hiked trails in the Appalachians, climbed mountains in the Rockies and trekked the Painted Desert with the Hopi. You're gonna have to find something more challenging than a bit of snow to stop me getting help.'

When he stood up, he looked at least several inches taller to Fforde, although that could have been a mirage effected by the hubris.

'Aren't you even going to take a coat?' he asked as the man opened the gate and started ambling towards the main drive.

Without looking back, the cowboy waved one valedictory hand and shuffled on in silence.

When he turned the corner of the house, Fforde glanced at Olive, who shrugged.

'Dead man walking,' she said, and heaved at the generator.

The Lounge

I

As Lauren surveyed the dozen or so people gathered in front of her, all eyes in her direction, she concluded it was the perfect audience: captive.

Apart from her brother Simon and her two cats, Romulus and Remus, she rarely had the chance to try out story ideas on actual listeners. Simon, of course, only pretended to listen and usually had hidden earpods blasting the latest grime or house or whatever relentless mechanical churning passed for music these days. The cats, meanwhile, seemed content enough to laze around on comfy chairs or cushions while she explored her latest novel idea in real time, but when it came to offering feedback on her efforts they fell unquestionably into the recalcitrant camp. She often felt she got more helpful notes from the house plants, and they were mostly dead.

Now, though, she had the undivided attention of the lounge, where guests and staff alike had gathered in an attempt to draw heat from the huge fireplace and, perhaps, share some communal warmth from the presence of other people. Given that they weren't huddled shoulder to shoulder in one big mass, but rather spread across various sofas, armchairs and *chaises longues*, it probably wasn't quite as effective as penguins in the Antarctic, Lauren imagined, but the principle was sound enough. There was a hint of polar endless night about the lounge, too, with candles and oil lamps scavenged by the staff providing merely a few pools of light, while the further reaches of the room remained shrouded in gloomy shadow. The grey daylight was, technically, creeping in at the mullioned windows but if it had crept any slower it would have been going backwards, actively dragging light out of the room into the dingy beyond.

Lauren hoped she might be brightening the atmosphere at least a little with the plot of her latest work-in-progress.

'And then the secret agent leaps off the cliff with only his raincoat as a kind of parachute, swims out to the submarine where he overpowers the crew and stops the launch of the nuclear missile by sticking a piece of chewing gum over the red button.'

There was a pause in the room that dragged on marginally longer than Lauren would have liked. It might have been her first attempt at an action thriller, and quite probably what one agent had told her was 'derivative' when she wrote asking for representation, but there was no need to be rude about it.

It was Bella who broke the silence.

'Sounds like you've made a good start on it, love,' she said kindly. 'These works-in-progress are always difficult to share, aren't they?'

Lauren was grateful for her friend's support, even if it was less enthusiastic than she'd hoped. Despite her relative lateness to the reading group party, Bella had quickly become a mother figure to them all, but especially to Lauren. There was little more than a decade between them in age, but Bella had always seemed a woman out of time with her staid clothes and out-of-style hairdo. She felt more like an aged aunt than an older sibling and, when her marriage had fallen apart around the time of her joining the group, she had resisted all offers of support, relying instead on what seemed like limitless inner resourcefulness to see her through the crisis. Now, returned to a spinsterhood that seemed to suit her completely, she had apparently morphed into one of the heroines of the golden-age detective novels that the group went back to over and over again for their timeless qualities of charm and elegance. In fact, now that Lauren came to think about it, Bella could almost be Lord Quaint in female form.

'Anything in it for me?' asked Fforde from the back of the room. He hadn't been there when Lauren started her rundown of the spy thriller and she hadn't noticed him come in, but his question helped relieve the slight tension she felt.

'Almost certainly, I would think,' she replied, smiling at her reading group colleague from her place in front of the fire. 'Know any good producers?'

'I've been out of action so long I don't know any producers – good, bad or indifferent.'

Lauren realised immediately that this remark was intended for the Americans in the room, though they seemed to give no visible reaction. The director, Colorado, was engrossed in something on his iPhone – heaven knew what, since there was no signal – while the cinematographer had been in a world of his own, spending the past fifteen minutes eyeing up the lounge itself, presumably for angles, lighting and any other visual landmarks that would make this a suitable set for scenes from their new adaptation.

Keren Lowe got up from her armchair near the door and made her way over to the fireplace.

'I think we could do with another log or two on the fire,' she said, reaching past Lauren to pick up a comically giant pair of tongs from a set of implements nestling in the enormous grate.

Monty Butler was quickly at her side.

'Let me do that,' he said solicitously. 'No point having a burly Scotsman about if he can't do the heavy labouring.'

'It's not exactly tossing the caber, but if you insist…' Keren gave a little laugh that Lauren, in one of her more florid passages, might have called coquettish.

With the action around the fire taking everyone's attention, Lauren suddenly felt sidelined and she was a little put out about it. Her offer to outline her latest masterpiece had been made in the spirit of generosity, wanting to give them all something to focus on besides the weather and the forlornness of their predicament, but it had gone down considerably less well than she'd hoped. She went to the sofa where Bella was sitting and perched beside her.

Siobhan now assumed command, nudging Keren aside and putting herself next to her husband, who was manhandling logs without the use of any implements and swinging mighty chunks of oak from the stack at one side of the grate into the middle of the conflagration, sending sparks shooting up the chimney into the vaulted darkness above. Lauren found herself wondering how Monty might look bare-chested and kilted, brandishing a claymore like a latter-day Mel Gibson yelling 'They'll never take our broadband!' and charging down the drive in pursuit of a way out.

She filed away the image for her next novel.

'I do apologise for the continued absence of Lord and Lady Verity,' Siobhan was saying. 'In truth, they rarely make an appearance before lunchtime, even when there are guests in the house.'

Lauren thought she sounded personally affronted at the fact.

'But as Abbots Chantry's resident tour guide and occasional librarian'—here she nodded towards Professor Stone away to her left—'I'd like to offer our esteemed visitors a little by way of background to the house and its estate. Because there's more to this place than meets the eye, and some of it is quite grisly.'

Colorado Hughes put down his iPhone and sat up, swivelling his baseball cap from front-facing to backwards and taking ten years off his already minimal age in the process.

'I wanna hear more,' he said, chewing gum noisily.

Lauren tried to work out how much younger than her this supposed *wunderkind* of Hollywood actually was. She knew his name, of course, but couldn't remember whether she'd ever seen either of the movies that had won him worldwide acclaim and the job of director on this new Lord Quaint adaptation. It seemed a strange choice to her: his first film had been a true *auteur*'s semi-autobiographical piece, riddled with drug use and the trappings of privileged wealth, the second a hip-hop version of *King Lear* in which the mad king's three daughters had battled one another in a sing-off and The Fool had been played by a chimpanzee. To go from such niche cultural backwaters to the helm of a vintage classic suggested to Lauren that either he talked a fantastic pitch in the studio executives' office, or he was sleeping with somebody really important. Either was plausible, she supposed, but the latter would make a much more interesting backstory.

'I wanna hear grisly,' the boy went on. 'Lay it on me.'

'That's a kind invitation,' said Siobhan without missing a beat, 'but I think I'll just tell you a bit about the history of the house.'

The bit about being the occasional librarian had piqued Lauren's interest, and she could see that the other three members of the reading group had similarly pricked-up ears. To be fair, everyone's ears had a measure of perkiness about them, which Lauren put down largely to Siobhan's easy personability and a certain facility with words: she seemed to have a way with storytelling that could both intrigue and hold her listeners, and Lauren was more than a little jealous.

Still, that was probably what made a good tour guide.

'The house was founded as a monastery in around 1340, we believe,' Siobhan began.

So far, so conventional.

'Within its first twenty years there had been at least a dozen murders.'

Now that was a way to start a tale.

Lauren sat for the next half-hour agog at Siobhan's crafting and weaving of a narrative that encompassed bubonic plague, warrior monks covering Henry V's back at Agincourt, the disastrous Battle of Norcester (1483) after which the abbot was defrocked in front of a superfluity of alarmed nuns, and the eventual disbanding of the religious cloister in Henry VIII's decisive dissolution of Catholic orders.

And that was just the first two centuries.

Since 1542, when Abbots Chantry was partially destroyed by the Lord Lieutenant of Norcestershire – one of the first to have been appointed by the corpulent monarch in his declining years – the house had been rebuilt and destroyed by civil war, rebuilt and destroyed by fire, rebuilt and destroyed by Nazi bombs aiming for Coventry, and finally rebuilt as the semi-elegant pile it was today. Throughout those near five hundred years, it had been in the ownership of the Verity family, whose ability to side with the winning team in most conflicts had seen them flourish and thrive as well as any of their aristocratic counterparts. The Marlboroughs might have had their palaces, the Howards their castles, but no other English peers had kept the favour of the monarchy so consistently and so hypocritically.

'The Veritys were a triumphant example of sycophancy at its most successful,' concluded Siobhan, adding conspiratorially, 'I can only say that when his Lordship isn't here. Although the family know it to be the truth, they don't like broadcasting it to all and sundry.'

Bella, beside Lauren on the sofa, looked as if she'd added a touch of concern to her thrall.

'What an amazing story,' she said, leaning forward with her eyes wide. 'And I imagine the house itself has a few secrets?'

Siobhan smiled. 'Oh yes. There are the usual priest holes and hidden stairways, but Abbots Chantry has lots more besides – including the obligatory ghosts, of course. We've got corridors that appear to go nowhere, a secret wine cellar that only the family knows the entrance to, and even concealed messages in the plasterwork of the cornices.'

Immediately, everyone craned their necks to study the carvings around the edge of the ceiling in the increasing gloom. To Lauren, it looked like perfectly normal, if rather ornate, cornicing.

'It's called steganography,' Siobhan said. 'From the Greek – literally meaning *hidden writing*.'

The Professor stirred.

'And was very popular with the ancient Greeks themselves,' he said.

Lauren recalled the Professor's passion for Archimedes that had played a part in the mystery of Felicity Penman's murder. When each of them had anonymously been sent a book, offering a clue to the identity of the killer, Professor Stone's had been a dry academic tome penned by the father of mathematics himself. Solving those clues had been instrumental in bringing the murderer to justice, and she was proud of the role the reading group had taken in exercising the kind of investigative skills they'd accumulated in their trawl through golden-age detective novels. Who said reading was a waste of time? Well, actually, that had been her father in one of his more cynical moments, after her brother had been briefly imprisoned for cybercrime, but she and the others had proved him wrong with the Penman case.

And now Professor Stone was revealing that he was clearly a student of wider Greek lore than simply its mathematicians.

Was there no end to the man's secrets?

'Herodotus writes about a couple of examples,' the Professor continued. 'Such as the servant whose head was shaved, then had a message inscribed on his scalp. When his hair grew back, he was sent to deliver the message, which could only be revealed by shaving his head again. And then there was the wax tablet that warned of a military attack thanks to a message written on the tablet *before* it was covered with wax. The recipient melted off the innocuous message on the surface to discover the secret one underneath.'

Lauren was sure she'd seen exactly that technique in one of the *Indiana Jones* films but decided against mentioning it to the Professor.

'This is really interesting to me,' said Marin, the director of photography, peering hard at the ceiling. 'Is there any way we could get a close-up look at some of this stuff? What does it mean?'

'Ah,' said Siobhan. 'Some of that remains a secret – and some we simply don't know. Take the rampant goat over there in the corner by the door.'

Everyone turned.

Which must have made it something of a shock to Hemingford Grey when he came in through the door at that precise moment and found the whole room staring at him.

'Er ... sorry. Have I interrupted something?'

'Don't worry, Hem. I was just pointing out the goat.'

He looked above him. 'Oh, right. Him.'

He seemed to lose interest and Lauren thought he'd probably heard the story many times before.

'I've just come in to grab Keren, actually.' He signalled with a movement of his head for Keren. 'His Lordship has a request.'

As Siobhan resumed her non-explanation of the

representation of a rampant goat in the cornicing of the lounge at Abbots Chantry, Lauren idly watched Keren pick her way between the chairs to reach the door, where Grey handed her a note and whispered a few words before turning and leaving the room. Keren unfolded the slip of paper, read it and frowned. Lauren couldn't tell if it was a frown of disapproval or simply a failure to understand the note's meaning, but whatever its contents, Keren followed Grey out of the room without looking back.

'And we've got a special treat for our guests this morning. Monty here is going to show the film crew some possible locations on the estate – whatever's reachable in the snow – while I've got something much more exciting for our book club visitors.'

Stone coughed loudly, and Lauren was expecting him to correct her terminology to his preferred nomenclature – 'reading group' – but she was diverted by Bella, who turned to her with a look of mild alarm on her face.

It was an expression Lauren had grown accustomed to in the months that she'd known her. Much as she liked Bella, Lauren couldn't help thinking she must live her life in a semi-permanent state of mild alarm. Perhaps she was still getting used to her existence beyond the confines of her recently concluded marriage to the infamous Trevor; perhaps she had always been like that. Lauren resolved to find a quiet moment this weekend to quiz Bella's sister Ronnie on their upbringing. She might be able to shed some light on the innate apprehension that never seemed far below the surface of Bella's countenance.

'What does she mean? I'm not sure I want anything more

exciting than a tour of the library, to be honest. Ronnie's shown me round the place before, of course, but I didn't know about any secret corridors, hidden messages or resident ghosts. It's bad enough that we're trapped here in this haunted mansion without having to know all about its dark corners.'

Lauren rested a hand on Bella's arm.

'Don't worry, Bella. You don't need to be frightened. Nothing's going to happen.'

The Secret Passage

1

Siobhan certainly knew how to ratchet up the tension; Bella could give her that.

The tour guide and sometime librarian waited patiently for the Americans to leave the lounge, led out by Monty in search of potential shooting sites for their film. When the door closed again, there were just the four of them and Siobhan.

'Right. This is where the fun begins,' she said.

Bella hadn't quite been able to figure Siobhan out. Her personality made her a natural in the role of host for the estate, yet she'd seemed to be in a particularly irritable mood over dinner the previous evening. After nineteen years (and a bit) married to Trevor, Bella was all too aware of the need to tiptoe around a volatile temper, but she didn't really think Siobhan fell into the same category as her ex-husband. Now there was a man for whom the word volatile might have been invented. And temper, come to that. Not for the first time, she marvelled at her endurance through such a lengthy relationship when the prime driving force behind their staying together had amounted to little more than her being periodically required to reinforce his very twentieth-century attitudes towards everything from gender politics to football. This was usually best exemplified on Norcester United match days, when she was expected to wear the club scarf, fetch the half-time pies from the food stand and definitely not offer an opinion on the quality of United's back four after yet another opposition forward had succeeded in slipping between their ranks and inserting an easy winner past the stranded keeper. That kind of thing was officially, and perpetually, the exclusive realm of the men, and she should be grateful she was allowed even to listen to their post-match analysis in the bar of the Pickled Gherkin afterwards. She'd only broken that rule on a couple of occasions – once to defend a referee whose eyesight had been called into doubt by Trevor and his mates, and once to challenge a particularly unpleasant remark questioning the manager's maternal lineage – and on both occasions she had regretted saying anything when they got home. Although he was never one for physical violence (she guessed he'd tried it once or twice in his youth and come off much the worse, so had avoided it as an adult, even in domestic settings), Trevor could be psychologically vindictive, with a talent for stretching sullen silences out for days, in some cases.

But where Trevor had been bad-tempered and mean, Siobhan's instinct seemed, at least on short acquaintance, to be to please. Perhaps the pressures of important weekend guests at a dinner with the boss and his wife had imposed a certain strain on the poor woman and the stress had leaked out through her snapping at Keren across the table. She seemed a little calmer this morning without their Lord-and-Ladyships on hand, and she'd been positively effusive when it came to dishing out the secrets of the Veritys' ancestry.

People could be so complicated. Why wasn't everyone just nice to each other all the time? It would make life a lot easier all round.

Siobhan beckoned them all closer to her where she stood beside the fireplace. Once they had crowded round, looking every bit to Bella like a huddle in those football matches Trevor used to watch when the scores were level and they had to decide who was going to take the penalties, she stretched out an arm with a flourish and grabbed a foot-high bust on the end of the mantelpiece. With a wrench, she pulled it backwards.

For a moment, Bella thought she'd broken it. That really would have been volatile.

But then something happened that made Bella believe she might already be in a Hollywood movie, and she almost turned round to look for Marin and Colorado and a big film camera.

The wall behind Siobhan started to move.

Fforde let out a guttural laugh of delight, while Lauren took a pace backwards. Even the Professor had an impressed look on his face – something Bella had learned was rare to the point of competing with sightings of Bigfoot or Nessie. Nothing impressed the Professor.

Except this did.

The entire panel from the fireplace to a distance about six feet to its left slid away with a harsh grating noise and gradually disappeared behind its neighbouring panel. In its place gaped a recess even darker than the room, which seemed to lead Bella's eye into its depths. The blackness was inky, the opening imposing, but it was the stench that emerged from it that had Bella truly reeling. It was as if all the mothballs from her granny's pre-war dressing room had been gathered together, stuffed into a cesspit to ripen, then rinsed with drainwater before being doused in hydrogen sulphide and set alight.

It wasn't a pleasant smell.

'Oh my God,' said Fforde, clutching his hand to his mouth and backing away.

Bella assumed the aroma had reached him.

'Did somebody die in there?'

Siobhan allowed herself a little smile.

'Probably quite a few people, actually. But not in the last couple of hundred years or so, you'll be pleased to learn.'

'Smells like their bodies are still in there,' said Fforde, now gripping the bottom corner of his jacket and holding it over his nose. He may not have appeared on a stage for a few years but he could still muster up a dramatic performance when required.

'You'll get used to it in a minute,' said Siobhan, smiling at their reactions.

'What is it?' asked the Professor, leaning forwards to peer into the darkness. 'A secret closet?'

'Oh no, Professor. It's much more interesting than that. You see over there, in the corner nearest the fireplace?'

Bella overrode her natural distaste at the stench to follow Stone's lead and lean in. As her eyes became accustomed to the blackness, she could make out a rectangular block, six feet high and about three feet wide, that was even blacker than the rest. She realised it was a further opening in the chimney breast behind the grate. And as she looked closer, she could see that the floor fell away where the opening stood.

'Is that ... is that a staircase?'

'Be my guest,' said Siobhan, indicating for Bella to step inside and inspect it more closely.

Bella reached out a hand behind her, where Lauren took hold of it and squeezed encouragingly. When she stepped inside the hidden compartment, where the dim light seemed to vanish completely, she felt a thrill run through her and, mentally exorcising any apparitions that might be lurking, approached the top stair. Visions of the Ghostbusters and their cumbersome apparatus for obliterating, dispensing with or otherwise eliminating spectral beings flitted through her mind but she steeled herself, deciding that was just the movies and she really didn't need anything more elaborate than her own strength of character. A year ago, this scenario would have seemed impossible to her. Now she felt like Sigourney Weaver facing down a killer alien.

Except she wasn't in her pants and vest. That would have been a step too far.

The further she went, the better her eyes could see, and she let go of Lauren's hand to grasp the wall on either side of the opening. Behind her, Siobhan spoke.

'Here – take my torch.'

Grabbing the light, Bella pointed it down into the descending well of blackness, where its beam followed the winding stairs as they turned in a spiral to the right, leading down under the fireplace itself and back towards the lounge. She tried to imagine the layout of the house, wondering where the stairs might go and what was at the bottom of them.

'Go ahead,' said Siobhan encouragingly. 'It's perfectly safe.'

Bella made a decision.

'No. I think, if anything, this is the right territory for Indiana Jones – or at least Harrison Fforde.'

Fforde had allowed Lauren and the Professor to move in front of him as they ventured into the alcove but Bella picked him out with the torchlight.

'What do you say, Harrison?'

'I say you're a mad woman with a death wish,' Fforde retorted crisply, and took a pace backwards. 'Lead on, Macduff.'

In her mind, the voice of Bella's angry GCSE English teacher, Mr Wibberley, echoed down the years as he railed against the common misquotation.

'It doesn't say "Lead on", does it?' he had yelled at her as they read the play aloud in class one hot June afternoon when she'd much rather have been outside making sandcastles in the long-jump pit. 'Look at it again.'

She had.

He was right. It clearly said 'Lay on, Macduff'. Not 'Lead on'. She never forgot that lesson. It was odd, though, that the actor in the group wasn't aware of the error; maybe he'd been in the long-jump pit.

In the light from the torch, Bella could see the faces of the Professor and Lauren watching her expectantly.

'Go on, Bella,' encouraged Lauren with a smile.

She turned back to the stairs and began her slow descent, the others following her closely. It took them several minutes in the confines of the narrow passageway to make any progress at all.

The four of them had tiptoed less than fifteen yards into the tunnel when a sickening scream rang out far above their heads.

The Ballroom

I

For the second time in six months, Professor Stone found himself rounding up his charges from the reading group under his protective care. When he'd first done it, in the immediate aftermath of the attack on the bookshop manager, he'd felt surprisingly paternal about making sure none of them was too traumatised and they were all shielded from the harshest inquisitions of Chief Inspector Miranda Carlton.

He'd never expected to have to perform the same function for them again.

And yet here he was, marshalling the forces of The Quaint Bookshop reading group as they came together in adversity to confront … what?

The truth was, he had no idea what they were dealing with. The scream they'd heard – particularly blood-curdling, he'd thought, even though it had seemed to come from quite a distance away from their subterranean exploration – had stopped them in their tracks. Now he was gathering them together in the spacious ballroom of Abbots Chantry, thankfully with the lights back on, to find out what on earth was happening.

He didn't for a moment imagine the large room – one of the extant parts of the original monastery – had always been used for dancing: that kind of frivolity was hardly the natural terrain of your average medieval monk. Its vaulted ceiling led him to suspect it had perhaps been the refectory in its pre-Henry VIII days, and converted for use as an entertainment space much later. Which of the long line of Veritys had had the bright idea of turning it into a ballroom he could not know for sure, but if he'd been forced to guess, he might have had a stab at the present lord's great-grandfather, who, he'd learned, had been an especially wayward profligate and hosted debauched parties at every opportunity. He and his friends would shoot game (and the occasional unfortunate beater, if the rumours were accurate) during the day and illegal substances at night, carousing to raucous jazz bands and gambling their expensive cars, properties and mistresses between one another until the money ran out and the friends evaporated. The impoverished lord limped on another few years in penury before dying of consumption on a Greek island, but not before impregnating an exotic Cretan dancer whom he'd legitimised by marrying on his deathbed. The rest of the family were horrified to discover that the offspring of this coupling – the present Lord Verity's grandfather – owed his heritage as much to the Hellenic peasantry as he did to one of England's most historic bloodlines, but when he grew up and showed a notable talent for making several fortunes on the stock market, most were willing to overlook his father's peccadilloes.

It was amazing what a little money could do, Stone reflected.

The reverberations of debauchery, if they existed in the crevices of this ballroom, were currently subsumed by a chaotic babbling of people, assembled there for the purposes of enumeration by the Professor. So far, besides the reading group, he'd managed to collect Siobhan from the main stairs, where she'd evidently gone looking for the source of the scream, Monty and the two remaining Americans from the entrance hall, and Olive the gardener from the kitchen, where she was chopping vegetables for lunch, having got the generator working. Her duties apparently extended beyond the grounds and maintenance, and Stone wondered just how varied her skillset was, both inside and out; from the way she was julienning carrots, she seemed just as adept with a Sabatier as she was with her spanner. There was still no sign of Lord and Lady Verity themselves, and also absent were Hemingford Grey, Keren Lowe and Bella's sister Ronnie. All of them knew the house well, so they might have been anywhere.

The mystery they had yet to tackle was the small matter of who had screamed.

Stone found his naturally assumed authority being challenged when Monty Butler climbed onto a dais at one end of the ballroom and called for order.

'Ladies and gentlemen, please,' he shouted, the chatter in the room settling to an anxious murmuring. 'I think everyone heard that scream but does anyone know who it was?'

Everybody looked round at each other, searching for signs that somebody might know what the hell was going on. Every face was as blank as the next.

'Can anyone shed any light on where it came from?'

Again, no offers of light-shedding.

Stone was beginning to wonder why their host and hostess hadn't made it down from their apartments yet: unless they were both particularly heavy sleepers, it seemed odd that at least one of them hadn't heard the scream and woken the other to alert them to something amiss in the house. Even allowing for them to dress for propriety's sake, they would surely have joined the rest of the household by now.

Unless the something that was amiss was in their apartments.

He was about to propose to Monty that someone should check on them when a disturbance at the far side of the room, nearest the doors to the main hall, drew his attention.

Staggering into the ballroom, his face one of the fifty or so reputed shades to match his name, came Hemingford Grey. The blood that would normally reside in the area above the neck seemed to have drained somewhere south of his collar and all that remained to animate his stricken features was a dull, indeterminate hue and a look of haggard horror. It would have been hard to tell if he were alive or dead had it not been for the fact that he was upright and his jaw was opening and closing silently in pale imitation of a ventriloquist's dummy.

Stone could only guess at what utterances the silence was disguising.

'Hem,' said Siobhan, launching herself towards him and grabbing an arm to offer support. 'What on earth is it?'

She helped him to a nearby chair and eased him into it. There was a vacant look in his eye that revealed him to have been traumatised.

'Tell us, Mr Grey – what's happened?' Stone asked, keen to find out exactly what it was that had done the traumatising.

He crossed quickly to the man's side, fearing the worst for their hosts. If pressed, he'd have guessed from its pitch that the scream had been delivered by a woman, but he couldn't be certain, and even if that were true, it didn't mean that Lord Verity was not in just as much peril as his wife. Stone couldn't begin to fathom why anyone would wish them ill – especially among the company invited to join them for this country-house weekend – but matters such as that would have to wait. First they needed to know what was going on.

Hemingford Grey wafted one hand vaguely in the direction of the door, the other pulling a handkerchief from a pocket inside his jacket and clutching it to his mouth. A film of sweat was beaded across his brow and he mopped it with the handkerchief before speaking in a tiny, terrified voice.

'Out there ... in the snow ... under the tower,' he mumbled.

'What's out there?' urged Stone, immediately regretting pushing the poor man so hard. The last thing they needed was for him to clam up in shock.

Grey responded to his urgency by breaking out of his horrified reverie and staring Stone straight in the face.

'Keren,' he said simply. 'She fell.'

It took a moment for his words to sink in. When they did, Siobhan let out a little whimper while Bella said quietly, 'Oh no.'

Stone looked round and caught Monty's eye. It was clear they had had the same thought and both threw themselves towards the ballroom door at the same moment. Stone checked his pace slightly, allowing the Scotsman to go first, then followed him through the entrance hall to the front door. As they flew outside, Monty turned left, Stone on his heels, and followed Hemingford Grey's footsteps in the snow. They came from the north-eastern end of the building, where the old monastery's imposing tower climbed above the slated roof at the highest point of Abbots Chantry, its broad circular structure housing a succession of round chambers, one on top of another, pinnacled by an arch perching on the top, where a solitary bell hung ominously against the thunderous sky. When he'd first arrived the previous evening, Stone was reminded uncannily of the Himalayan convent in Powell and Pressburger's wild psychological chiller *Black Narcissus* – all white robes and dark eyes, mining something weirdly erotic out of the fantasies of a remote sisterhood of nuns.

But Stone was not looking up at the tower now.

He was looking at the crumpled heap at its base.

Monty was already turning away from the body in horror as Stone arrived but neither of them needed to be a medical expert to know that Keren Lowe was dead. The splaying of the limbs and the rapidly pooling red staining the crisp white snow offered a hint; it was the noose around her neck that sealed it.

The rope had snapped some six feet away from where it was tied in an efficient hangman's knot, and the torn end coiled away from Keren's body like an inquisitive snake. When Stone finally looked up to see where she had fallen from, he could make out the other end of the rope, dangling forlornly in the cold wind and disappearing over the guttering towards an open window high up in the tower.

It wasn't just the wind that chilled him. The sight of

another dead body – especially this close up and so broken by the fall – left Stone feeling sick.

The two men stood motionless, staring at the horror before them. As they stared, the others caught up and a little crowd gathered behind them, falling as silent as the snow that had carpeted the grounds.

Alongside the two dumbstruck Americans stood Bella and Lauren, the older woman clutching a hand to her mouth before turning away, the younger more stoically taking in the scene, as if forcing herself her to acknowledge the tragedy out of respect for the dead. Stone noticed her reach out and grasp Bella's hand nonetheless.

The most visceral reaction came from Siobhan, slightly behind the rest of the group, who pushed her way to the front, took one look at the body and screamed. Monty made half a move to follow her as she ran back towards the front door, but Bella held out a hand as if to stop him, and hurried off in his stead.

Siobhan would be in safe hands with Bella, Stone knew.

'What's up there?' he asked Monty eventually, pointing at the stray end of the rope high above them.

'In the tower?' Monty seemed to be suppressing nausea himself.

'Yes.'

'It's only the old billiard room.' Talking seemed to be helping him recover his composure. 'Lord Verity's great-grandfather—'

'The gambler?'

'The gambler, yes. He had it converted into a kind of games den. Billiards, poker, backgammon – you name it.'

As had happened several times during the investigation into the murder of Felicity Penman, Stone found his mind wandering into incongruously inconsequential areas.

'They must have had a hell of a job getting a billiard table up there,' he mused.

Monty nodded. 'Had to set up a rack-and-pulley system and winch it in from outside, apparently.'

'Is it still there?'

'The table? No – long gone. Broken up for firewood, probably.'

'So what's in there now?'

Monty shrugged. 'I think it's empty. Nobody's been up there for years.'

Stone stared once more at the body in the snow.

'That's not quite true, though, is it?'

For reasons Professor Stone couldn't begin to imagine, mere minutes earlier Keren Lowe had been in the billiard room. With the rope.

II

In the long ago days when Harrison Fforde was still getting occasional theatre jobs – before he'd given up hope of ever playing at the National or auditioning to be the next Bond – he'd discovered that his natural resistance to being told what to do could be something of a hindrance when it came to directors. People trying to wrangle a cast into shape for a public performance tended to want other people to work with that they could guide, mould or otherwise instruct to get the outcome they wanted. In Fforde's case, his innate tendency to push back against exactly such moulding on the grounds that he was an individual with autonomy and ideas of his own made him less than popular with a certain type of director: working ones.

As a result, he had unintentionally but assiduously cultivated for himself a reputation within the British acting industry of being somewhat difficult. His name was never mentioned in discussions, but if you scratched the surface of an ensemble working in almost any of the major provincial theatres, you wouldn't have to scratch too hard to find someone who had once been in the same production as a certain middle-aged thespian determined to derail the show because of his own singular approach. Unfortunately, because his name was never mentioned, Fforde had spent the best part of two decades believing the awkward bugger everyone kept talking about behind their hands was someone else entirely – probably that bloke who kept getting all his roles in television dramas just because he'd once played a wrong 'un in a couple of Nineties episodes of *EastEnders* and had managed to forge a career out of it. When it finally dawned on him that maybe the behind-hand conversations weren't about that bloke at all but much closer to home, the damage had become irreparable and no amount of bridge-building could rescue what was left of his working life. The years that followed, playing Santa in department stores or character work (often the victim, strangely) at murder-mystery events, had brought him a certain pleasure and understated pride, but he couldn't help feeling slightly shortchanged by an industry that wasn't robust enough to deal with his idiosyncratic way of working or single-minded dedication to doing things his way.

He also couldn't help repeating the same mistakes.

Again and again.

Which was why, when Professor Stone asked him – quite politely and without any sense of coercion – if he'd mind terribly helping to move Keren Lowe's body, Harrison Fforde's natural instinct was to resist.

Actually, that wasn't the only reason.

Harrison Fforde also, not unnaturally, had an aversion to death.

'Sorry, Harrison,' the Professor said when the actor gave his best grimace of distaste. 'I know it's not a nice job but somebody's got to do it.'

'Have they? Shouldn't we leave it for the emergency services?'

'What emergency services?' Stone pointed at the drive behind him, thick with a heavy snow that had temporarily stopped falling but looked like it might restart at any moment. 'It could be days before anyone reaches us. We can't leave her lying here.'

Despite his misgivings, Fforde had no desire to challenge the Professor on this. He suspected shifting a corpse after a violent death might be regarded by the police as tampering with a crime scene, but he'd let Stone deal with that if the time came. For now, he desperately wanted to find an excuse not to have to move Keren Lowe's body.

Stone had already lined up Monty for the task, and between them they'd rolled Keren onto her back, but Fforde could see that two people hefting her in the time-honoured fashion of grabbing her legs and holding her under the armpits to lumber her unceremoniously out of the snow was not going to be the most decorous or respectful way of moving her. A person at each corner would be much more seemly.

He ran through a mental checklist of other candidates. Hemingford Grey looked an obvious choice, but he seemed traumatised after discovering the body in the first place and moving it now might just push him over the edge. Lord Verity was still nowhere to be seen, and besides, asking a member of the nobility to help shift the deceased remains of one of his staff would, Fforde conceded, have been utterly inappropriate. Ditto getting the Americans involved, even though they were standing not ten yards from the contorted mess that was Keren's body with unreadable expressions on their faces. He wagered that they hadn't bargained for something like this when they signed up for a weekend at Lord Verity's manor.

Olive had already stepped forward to take one of the two outstanding limbs, which really left only him for the other.

He was relieved to see that he was being invited to take Keren's right leg, which meant he could walk forwards with the rest of her behind him. At least he wouldn't have to see her as he carried her, unlike Monty and the Professor, who would have the whole grim spectacle literally laid out in front of them as they shuffled towards the main entrance, holding one arm each and trying not to allow the head to loll too unpleasantly as they went.

'Where are we going to take her?' Fforde asked eventually, moving gingerly towards the vacant limb as the other three leaned down to take their share of the load.

'One of the outbuildings, perhaps?' ventured Stone, bending his knees in the proper fashion for lifting heavy weights. Fforde wondered whether – and if so, why – he'd ever had official training. Stone would surely never have imagined needing to put it to a use as dismal as this.

'There's the barn,' said Olive, facing Fforde and taking hold of the left leg. 'Bit smelly, though.'

'No, no,' said Monty irritably. 'We can't put her in the barn. It wouldn't be right.'

'Where then?' asked Fforde again. He was aware that there were bigger questions to be addressed – such as why Keren

Lowe had thrown herself out of the tower window in the first place – but perhaps now was not the moment.

'Believe it or not, this place actually has a chapel,' said Monty.

Fforde was quite prepared to believe it. It had been a monastery, after all. It didn't seem *that* surprising.

'Perfect,' said Stone. 'Just direct us where to go.'

As they staggered in ungainly fashion across the snow-covered gravel to the entrance, then in through the main hall and off towards the south-west wing of the building, Fforde pondered on the weight of a dead body. He guessed Keren might be around ten stone, converted it into pounds by multiplying by fourteen, as the Americans would doubtless have done, then divided it by two, subtracting a bit more to allow for the imprecision of his calculation. On that basis, in new money, Keren would have been about sixty-five kilos, he estimated. Rounding roughly and ignoring the uneven distribution between the legs, which were the heavier limbs, and the arm end, which would take the majority of the weight of the torso, he came to a conclusion. Between four of them, it came to around sixteen standard bags of sugar each.

The comparison wasn't very dignified, he realised, but he needed something to take his mind off what he was actually doing.

'Just put her down here for a minute,' said Monty as they reached the end of a cold, dark corridor where two huge oak doors barred their way.

They lowered Keren's body to the chilly stone floor and Monty went forward to the doors. Taking hold of one of the large iron rings, he turned it in vain, then shook it hard.

The doors didn't budge.

'I thought that might be the case,' he said, as much to himself as to the others. 'Nobody's used it in years.'

'No bother,' said Olive, reaching deep into the leather satchel that hung from her workman's belt. She drew out a large bunch of keys, strung together on an outsize metal ring, and began sifting through them.

'Try this one,' she said, singling out one chunky key and handing the dangling bunch to Monty.

The Scotsman slid the key into the lock beneath the iron ring in the door and turned it with a satisfying click. When he tried the handle again, the door swung slowly open about six inches before stopping.

'No bother,' Olive said again, and put her full weight against it. The sticking point was wrenched free and the door crashed open, revealing the grey, dim interior of one of the spookiest places Harrison Fforde had ever seen. At first glance it looked like the set of an old Hammer horror film, with three pairs of decaying pews either side of a short nave and tall candelabras flanking a low wooden rail, beyond which an arched stained-glass window towered above what would have been termed the high altar in a cathedral, but here amounted to little more than a trestle table. To Fforde's surprise, it still sported an embroidered altarcloth in deep, velvety crimson, although the fabric – like the rest of the chapel – was shrouded in cobwebs. The overall effect was at marked odds with the reading group's more usual experience of a chapel – the vast old Methodist church that had been converted years before into The Quaint Bookshop, the welcoming, homely space named in honour of the great fictional detective where they had first been brought together by the tragic Felicity Penman.

As he followed the others inside, leaving Keren for the moment in the corridor, Fforde could have sworn he felt the temperature drop by another couple of degrees. He wondered how long it was since this place had been used for its intended purpose: maybe it had stood abandoned like this since the monastery had been dissolved.

'The family stopped using it as a chapel after the last war,' said Monty, conveniently answering Fforde's unasked question. 'One of the younger sons was killed in North Africa and they seemed to lose their faith after that.'

'I imagine the Americans might be interested in taking a look at this,' said the Professor, staring round the small space. 'It's quite atmospheric, isn't it?'

It was the kind of atmosphere Fforde could have done without.

'Can we just get on with it, please?' he said, rubbing one arm with his other hand and backing out of the chapel.

'Yes, of course,' said Monty, a serious tone returning to his voice. 'Let's get her onto the altar.'

It took some manhandling to move Keren into the chapel and up onto the table but it seemed the right thing to do. While any religious connotations of the building had long since evaporated, there was a certain rectitude accorded by the environment that made Fforde feel a little less disturbed about leaving her there. Olive astutely observed that the lack of heating meant the chapel could act as a temporary mortuary, preserving Keren's body until such time as the emergency services could reach the house.

'I don't suppose your skills extend to carpentry, do they?' the Professor asked her as the four of them lined up solemnly before the altar, uncertain what to do next.

'I have been known to knock up the odd cabinet or two. Why do you ask?'

As soon as the question left her lips, the answer evidently occurred to her, and a look of horror passed across her face.

'You want me to make a coffin?'

The Professor shrugged sheepishly. 'It would be a bit more … dignified.'

'Yes,' said Fforde, leaping on the notion of hiding away the gruesome spectacle before them. 'It would.'

Even Monty seemed to like the idea, and the three men eventually persuaded Olive to build a rudimentary casket for Keren.

'Nothing fancy – we're not talking silk lining or anything,' said Fforde.

'I should hope not,' replied Olive. 'I've got better things to be doing with my time, but if you insist.' She addressed this last remark to Monty, which Fforde assumed was in recognition of his senior position on the estate. He wondered how often Monty was able to get away with giving her orders.

'We should get back to the ballroom,' said the Professor. 'There are some serious questions to be answered.'

III

Bella had been worried about her sister's absence from the ballroom when Hemingford Grey had arrived with the shocking news of Keren's death. Aside from the Veritys, whose continued non-appearance was beginning to vex lots of people for different reasons, Ronnie had been the only person missing when the tragedy was announced, and she hadn't materialised during the half-hour or so of discussion and activity that had followed.

Now that Keren's body had been moved to the chapel, Ronnie was starting to worry Bella considerably. Theirs had never been a particularly close relationship, and despite their regular meet-ups Ronnie had never provided what Bella would have regarded as a shoulder to cry on. In fact, she only really used her visits to her sister's little bungalow on the outskirts of Norcester as an excuse to spend an evening away from Trevor. But she couldn't help feeling a natural instinct to protect her, even though it could be argued that, as they were on Ronnie's home turf, it should be she looking out for Bella. Just who was responsible for whom had been a question that had dogged them all their lives, and it hadn't been made any clearer by the frequent misunderstandings they encountered between them. They seemed to speak a different language and their views of the world came from opposite sides of the telescope lens – Bella seeing goodness and beauty in all she surveyed, Ronnie standing by with a cynical eye ready to complain about anything and everything. Sometimes Bella found it hard to believe they came from the same parents, but on the sole occasion she had brought it up, their mother had assured her that they did, and made a point of taking melodramatic offence at the suggestion that she might have strayed from the marital bed.

Come to think of it, Ronnie took more after her mother than Bella did.

When they were all back in the ballroom and the reading group had formed a little enclave of its own near one of the French windows, she broached the matter of Ronnie's disappearance with Professor Stone.

'I haven't seen her since last night,' she confided. 'She wasn't at breakfast and she wasn't in the lounge when Siobhan was telling us all about the house. I didn't really think too much about it until we heard that scream. Since then, I've been worried sick.'

The Professor patted her arm gently and offered an avuncular smile.

'I'm sure she's fine,' he said, though Bella didn't find him overwhelmingly convincing. 'I'm more concerned about the Veritys, if I'm honest.'

'Why?'

'Well, I know Siobhan said they rarely appeared before lunchtime, but I do think someone should notify them that there's been a death on the premises.'

Bella tried to think back to conversations she'd had in the past about Ronnie's role at Abbots Chantry. Had she ever talked about her ultimate bosses, Lord and Lady Verity, and if so, what had she said about them? Bella struggled to recall any mention of them except for the fact of their existence, and certainly didn't recollect anything about their morning habits. It was a strange omission, now she thought about it: Ronnie was verbose to the point of irritating on many subjects – not least the ones about which she knew least – but when it came to something potentially interesting, such as the lifestyles of the rich and not-quite-famous, she had been notably reserved. Maybe Ronnie genuinely didn't know much about them, in which case Bella would have to ask Monty or Siobhan instead.

Either way, Bella made a mental note to interrogate her sister when the circumstances were less alarming. It wouldn't take much: with Ronnie, all you had to do was drop a mildly provocative statement into the mix and watch her pick it up and run with it. Bella had heard her express wildly contradictory opinions on subjects as diverse as the faking of the Moon landings, the culpability or otherwise of the fire brigade if their engines caused an accident by jumping a red light, and the respective value for money of trout and salmon. Often it depended on what day you were speaking to her and who her last argument had been with, but over the years Bella had learned either to ignore her sister's more outrageous opinions or to wind up the motor, sit back and enjoy the fun.

Somehow they had managed to reach their forties without ever being particularly sisterly, and now Bella felt a pang of regret about that. Having lost both their parents relatively young, they had continued their lives on parallel tracks – Bella accepting a life of domestic drudgery and football widowhood with the hapless Trevor, Ronnie scouting around for something meaningful to do before settling on a volunteer position at Abbots Chantry. The uncharitable thought flashed through Bella's mind that perhaps her sister was cosying up to the aristocrats with a view to moving in. Perhaps that was why she didn't talk about them: she didn't want to risk Bella queering her pitch if she was on the lookout for a rent-free berth in this stately manor. Bella wondered how such a move might go down with the other staff: what would they make of one of the unpaid volunteers wangling a live-in spot?

As quickly as the thought popped up, Bella squashed it back down into the depths of her subconscious. Ronnie could be irritating, certainly, but cynicism to that extreme was surely beyond her. Wasn't it?

She found herself feeling quite relieved when Ronnie appeared at the doors to the ballroom, tray of mugs in her hands, shouting over the hubbub: 'Anyone for tea?'

'Where have you been all morning?' Bella asked her sister when hot drinks had been distributed and they were able to linger for a moment near the French windows.

'Up in the family apartments for most of it,' said Ronnie,

shuffling the last remaining mugs on the tray to make room for the empties that would soon be appearing. 'Her Ladyship caught me on the stairs as I was coming down to breakfast and asked me if I'd mind helping her find something to wear for the film crew. I think she wanted to look the part – you know, to try and help persuade them to shoot *Murder on the Polar Express* here, rather than at Blenheim or Chatsworth or somewhere gaudy like that.'

'Surely that hasn't taken you all morning?' Bella knew her sister's tendency to chattiness meant that hours could not only slip by unnoticed, they could do the shopping and take in a show before slipping back again under Ronnie's nose without her ever realising. Even so, sorting out her Ladyship's wardrobe could hardly have taken all this time.

'No, of course not. But one thing led to another – you know what it's like – and she began asking me all about my life, and how I'd ended up volunteering at Abbots Chantry, so I was telling her about Mother and Father and growing up in Birmingham, and your ears were probably burning a bit too.'

'What did you tell her about me?' asked Bella, her anxiety rising again. While she didn't feel she had anything to hide, she would just as happily not have her private life shared with all and sundry.

Even if the sundry was an aristocrat.

'Oh, not much. I was telling her how you were alone again after Trevor left you.'

'Trevor didn't leave me,' insisted Bella through gritted teeth. She'd been over this innumerable times with Ronnie, explaining that her membership of the reading group might have been the straw that broke the camel's back as far as her marriage was concerned, but the camel in question had been tolerant beyond endurance for nineteen (and a bit) years before she'd ever picked up a copy of *Murder on the Polar Express* or ventured inside The Quaint Bookshop. Trevor's inability to permit her even such a minor, harmless pursuit without his prior approval had merely been the culmination of almost two decades of suppressing her personality with his enforced domesticity.

Annoyingly, Ronnie didn't seem to be able to grasp the fact that a wife might be just as capable of wanting to leave her husband as vice versa. As far as Ronnie was concerned, the vice could only be one way.

'So you say,' said Ronnie tartly. 'Anyway, we were chatting away like old friends when we heard a scream.'

'Oh, you heard that, did you?'

'Of course. We could hardly have missed it, could we, what with it coming from the tower on that side of the building.'

Bella still didn't understand why Ronnie had remained absent for the last half-hour.

'Well, she didn't want me to leave her on her own, did she?'

'So where was Lord Verity while all this was going on?' Bella was finding it hard to quell her feeling that it should have been his Lordship's job to keep his wife safe, not that of an unpaid staff member who'd happened to be caught on the stairs going down to breakfast. On the other hand, if she knew Ronnie – and she really thought she did know Ronnie, in spite of their differences – her sister would have loved every moment of attention granted to her by the lady of the house. She'd be dining out on the story for years to come.

'Fast asleep in the next room,' Ronnie said, lowering her voice as if she were betraying state secrets. 'Snored through it all. I couldn't abandon her, could I? I only got away just now on the pretence of making her a cup of tea. Speaking of which, I should really be getting back upstairs.'

She was halfway to the door when she turned back. Her face was a mixture of worried frown and wide-eyed curiosity, a combination Bella wouldn't have believed technically possible if she'd read it in a detective novel but which made perfect sense when it came to Ronnie.

'Is it true what Olive tells me? Keren has thrown herself off the tower?'

'It's true, my dear,' said the Professor, breaking off from his conversation with Fforde and Lauren to cut in between the two women. 'Hard though it is to believe.'

Ronnie shook her head sadly and was about to turn away again when Stone addressed another question to her.

'How well did you know Keren Lowe?'

Bella was surprised at the Professor. Although he'd done his best to disguise the tone in his voice, she had seen him at close enough quarters during the Felicity Penman investigation to know that he was probing Ronnie semi-officially. Perhaps in the absence of the powers of law enforcement he felt it his duty – possibly even obligation – to lead his own enquiries, but surely he couldn't think Ronnie had anything worthwhile to add to the mystery of Keren's death?

'Why are you asking Ronnie that, Professor?'

'Oh, nothing ulterior,' he said, but she wasn't sure he was telling her the truth. She knew from little mentions that had been dropped during that earlier case that Professor Stone was a man with his own secrets – though he'd never given anything away at reading group meetings – and from where she stood, poking around among other people's skeletons could open him up to accusations of hypocrisy. They'd visited an old colleague of his at one point in the previous investigation and a combination of loose lips and liberal doses of whisky had meant that the man had hinted unintentionally at events and incidents from the Professor's past which he clearly would prefer remained undisturbed. Occasionally, in the depths of the night when she couldn't sleep and regretted that final cup of tea before bed, Bella would find herself wondering what dark secrets lurked behind the implacable façade, and whether he could possibly be something of a plaster saint. She admired him too much to accuse him herself, of course, and didn't really believe he could have been responsible for anything serious, but she could see how other people might think that way. It also, she feared, made him fair game for anyone who might want to go nosing around in those distant, dimly lit affairs. Harrison Fforde, for instance. She could quite see him wanting to dig deeper into the Professor's hidden past, even if it was just to truffle out a few things with which to taunt the older man. He had a mischievous streak, Fforde, and she suspected he'd latch onto anything that had teasing potential without a second thought. So far Stone had managed to keep a lid on whatever it was, but he'd need to be careful if he wanted to retain the higher moral ground.

'I'm just bewildered by the whole situation,' the Professor was saying. 'Keren was with the rest of us in the lounge while Siobhan was talking about the history of the house. She even got up to stoke the fire, if you recall, before Monty stepped in like a true gentleman. And then Hemingford Grey arrived with a message from Lord Verity to say she was wanted elsewhere, and that was the last we saw of her until...'

He trailed off, not needing to complete the sentence.

'Yes, it does seem a little odd, now that you put it that way,' said Bella, her brain starting to build neural pathways that her mind couldn't keep up with. Not least among the puzzles was the discrepancy that Lord Verity had, according to Ronnie's account of the morning, been fast asleep when Hemingford Grey delivered a note to Keren from him. They couldn't both be correct.

But right now she was more concerned with the state of mind of the deceased.

'To go from that to throwing herself off the tower in a matter of minutes seems – well, strange, to say the least. And if you're going to do yourself in, why choose such a dramatic method?'

Fforde and Lauren had joined them now, and at the mention of drama Fforde leaned in, evidently assuming the mantle of master of this topic. Professor Stone might present himself as the *de facto* leader of the reading group, but Harrison could be just as pompous when he put his mind to it.

'Ah, well, there can be lots of reasons why people choose to behave dramatically. Sometimes it's a plea for attention, sometimes a cry for help. Often it's the quiet ones who make the loudest noise when the straw finally breaks.'

Ronnie was nodding. 'That's really interesting you should say that. Keren has definitely been a bit off at work over the past few weeks. Quiet, like you said. I thought she might be a bit under the weather but maybe there was something else going on.'

By now, most of the other people in the room had gathered round their little circle, presumably sniffing out a more interesting line of conversation than they had been able to muster in their smaller groups.

'That doesn't tally with what she told me the other day,' said Hemingford Grey.

'What did she tell you?' asked Bella, her neurons notching up another discrepancy.

'She said she was feeling particularly chipper at the moment as she'd found a new lease of life.'

The Professor looked bemused. 'What did she mean by that?'

'No idea,' said Grey. 'She didn't elaborate. I was just pleased she was so upbeat.'

'I've got a question,' said Lauren, aiming her thoughts at her three colleagues from the reading group, who had formed a natural ring within the wider circle. 'Who screams when they're hanging themselves from a roof?'

Nobody even attempted to answer that question and it hovered uneasily around them, like the creeping odour of a rotting carcass.

'She seemed to be a bit cross last night,' said Bella at last, recalling the barbs Keren had distributed over the dinner table, drawing the *sotto voce* ire of Siobhan.

'She was,' came a voice from the door, and they all turned to see Siobhan entering, closely followed by her husband Monty. Her previously immaculate make-up looked streaked with tears and Bella realised she'd been hit hard by the tragedy that was still unfolding.

'But not cross enough to kill herself.' There was an edge to Siobhan's voice that suggested to Bella that she had more information to share.

Ronnie moved over to Siobhan, putting an arm round her shoulders to comfort her and leading her to an upholstered banquette at the side of the room. The little crowd followed, making Bella think for some reason of a shoal of fish.

As Ronnie fussed over Siobhan, Monty spoke to the Professor.

'I've been up to the billiard room with Olive, just to see if there were any clues up there as to what happened.'

An irrelevant thought struck Bella. 'Billiard room, ballroom, secret passage – it's like that board game, isn't it?'

'What – Scrabble?' said Fforde.

Bella didn't know if he was trying to be witty or really didn't know what she was talking about, but now was not the moment to chase that frayed thread.

'The point is, there were no clues,' said Monty sombrely. 'No suicide note, no evidence of anything amiss, just the other end of that bloody rope tied to a metal grille in the wall of the tower. It must have snapped as she fell.'

Lauren was still looking thoughtful.

'Unless there was something else going on...'

'What do you mean?' asked the Professor.

'I mean, could there have been somebody else in the tower with her?'

Professor Stone looked as shaken as Bella had seen him

since the fateful afternoon in the lobby of Norcester police station.

'No, Lauren. Surely not. Lightning doesn't strike twice. Felicity's murder was a one-off – wasn't it?'

From behind him on the banquette, Siobhan let out a cry of horror.

'Murder?' she wailed. 'Are you saying my sister was murdered?'

The Hall

I
―――

High up on the wall of the entrance hall, a dozen feet above the mighty door and almost obscured by the impressive shield that hung below it, Lauren could just about make out some words carved into the stone. She could barely discern the letters but they clearly made up a motto. Lauren guessed it predated the ownership of the Veritys, and must therefore have belonged to the monks who once inhabited this place.

She stared harder, until the motto finally revealed itself.

Disce aut discede.

Latin.

She knew the Veritys' motto was *'Vérité et justice'*, derived from their ancient French origins, and she felt she could take a stab at what that might mean without even having to draw on her GCSE language certificate. Latin was a different matter altogether.

Professor Stone might know: in the time that she'd known him, he'd confirmed his role as something of a polyglot, his breadth of knowledge extending far beyond his specialist subject of mathematics. Over the months and across a wide variety of reading material, he'd displayed expertise in everything from the internal combustion engine to the indigenous tribes of South America, while his observational skills and analytical reasoning had put him on a par with the great Sherlock Holmes in Lauren's eyes. In fact, she could argue, he was even more impressive than Sir Arthur Conan Doyle's creation because that giant brain was fictional, whereas Professor Stone was a living, breathing wizard of deduction.

On the subject of Keren Lowe's death, however, he seemed to have become a mass of uncertainty.

When Siobhan had divulged the shocking revelation that Keren had been her sister – which at least went some way to explaining their tetchiness with each other over dinner the previous evening – the Professor had been quick to close down further speculation about the manner of her demise. Siobhan was upset enough as it was.

'Let's not discuss it any further here,' he'd said, but indicated as he drew everyone away from Siobhan's banquette that he might be willing to resume their conversation when it was just the four of them in some private spot later in the day.

After a few minutes of awkwardness with the others in the ballroom, the American guests had excused themselves. Lauren couldn't tell if they were horrified or enthralled by the new turn of events, but they appeared to have no frame of reference for such a development. With no reason to prevent them – Lauren assumed they had been with Monty at the time of the scream – Stone had allowed them to wander off, ostensibly to go back to exploring potential locations for their shoot. There was obviously nothing they were going to be able to say to ease Siobhan's suffering and nothing they could do to change the situation.

After offering a few words of empathy to Siobhan for her loss, Lauren had followed them out into the hall.

'Pretty impressive, huh?' said the director, Colorado.

Lauren turned to see him watching her looking up at the inscription in the wall.

'I suppose.'

'Must have been one hell of a job carving that into the stone that high up on the wall,' he said.

Lauren pictured the artist Michelangelo, craning his neck on scaffolding seventy feet above the floor of the Sistine Chapel for three and a half ridiculous years, and suspected the stonemason responsible for the motto might have had the easier job. By some distance.

'I wonder what it means,' she said non-committally.

'I can help you with that,' said Marin Cypher, the director's colleague. He'd been standing in an alcove further along the hall but now emerged into view and approached Lauren across the deep blue carpet that lined the entrance.

'You speak Latin?' She was genuinely surprised. Although she'd never consciously thought about it, she wouldn't have imagined that the ancient and very dead European language would have been of much interest in schools and colleges in the United States. Their history was much shorter and far more insular than a knowledge of Latin would imply.

Marin barked a laugh. 'No, of course not. I'm not a nerd. But Monty told us all about it when he was showing us round earlier.'

'Oh, I see. So?'

'It means *"Learn or leave"*,' explained Marin. 'According to Monty, the monastery taught all kinds of people wanting to take holy orders, but the brothers were particularly strict about wanting its students to apply themselves. Otherwise they were out.'

'Learn or leave,' repeated Lauren. 'Sounds like a good motto for an educational establishment.'

'Not so good for a family crest, though,' said Marin. 'Apparently, the Veritys didn't fancy adopting it when they acquired the house.'

'I suppose they'd got their own motto anyway.'

'Well...' Marin held out an open hand and wobbled it from side to side, pulling an accompanying face to suggest that this wasn't necessarily the case. 'Seems like Siobhan wasn't giving us the whole picture.'

'Spinning us a ton of garbage, more like,' interrupted Colorado. 'That family story she rolled out? Sugar-coated for the tourists.'

Lauren had had her suspicions. Not just that the Veritys should have tidied up what was probably a rather bloody and gruesome history, but that Siobhan had convincingly persuaded them all that it was the unvarnished truth. Still, if Fforde's tales of his time as a tour guide in Norcester were anything to go by, the whole lot could have been completely made up and they wouldn't have been any the wiser.

'That's why we're out here on the hunt for clues,' said Marin.

'Clues to what happened to Keren?'

'No, not that,' said Colorado, waving a hand dismissively

and starting to inspect the vaulted ceiling. 'That seems pretty obvious. She'd had enough of whatever she was having to put up with and decided to throw herself off the tower.'

Lauren had heard that Americans could be blunt but, never having met one in the flesh, she had nothing to judge the assertion by. Characters in books and films could hardly be relied on as a dependable guide to reality, and these two examples of the genre certainly didn't fit into any easy category of stereotype. Colorado Hughes was far too young to be a film director, far too childish in his dress and manner to be given a role of such responsibility. Most of the film directors she'd ever heard of were middle-aged men taking fiction much too seriously. The brash self-confidence seemed right, though. As for Marin Cypher – could that really be his name? – he came across as the grown-up in the American party, Lauren having long since dismissed the now-departed location manager as a failed stunt man with delusions of machismo, whose self-appointed mission to rescue them single-handedly was probably, even now, ending in a huddle of misguided hypothermia somewhere on the road to the nearest village. That's if he'd even made it off the estate. Marin seemed, at least, to be more mature, more thoughtful than his colleagues, and although he was in all likelihood a decade older than Lauren, she could see herself being attracted to a man as interesting and well-travelled as he clearly was. He had his own hair, as far as she could tell, and if his orthodontist was a regular feature on his domestic calendar, well, who was Lauren to criticise a man for his attention to dental? The sparkly gleam behind his attractive smile looked like money well spent to her.

'No, what I'm interested in is the story behind the story,'

Colorado was saying. 'The events leading up to the tragedy, the storm that cut off the house, the horror of the bloodied corpse in the snow. And the traumatic effect on the rest of the assembled company. *We* know why she did it, but the audience doesn't. At least, not yet. Now look, anyone can shoot a movie based on a book—'

'As long as you've got the right cinematographer,' said Marin, and they both laughed knowingly.

'—but it's not often you get the chance to go behind the scenes, uncover a real-life mystery, then film it as you solve the damn thing.'

Lauren wasn't sure what she was being told. Had they abandoned the idea of using Abbots Chantry as a location for their adaptation of *Murder on the Polar Express*? And if so, what was all this talk of filming a real-life mystery?

'I'm sorry,' she said. 'I'm not quite with you.'

'This,' said Colorado, gesturing around the vast entrance hall.

'Them in there,' he went on, jabbing a finger at the ballroom door.

'You,' he added, staring directly at her.

'Me?'

'Yes, you.'

Lauren was mystified. 'You want to make a film about me?'

'Exactly. Well, not *exactly* exactly. I've always wanted to shoot a documentary about a locked-door country-house mystery, and here we are. One's fallen right into my lap. And you're at the heart of it.'

'But it's nothing to do with me. I'm just a guest at this weekend, like you.'

'Don't you see? That's what makes it so incredible.'

Colorado seemed to be getting excited, and he started to skirt Lauren like a lion stalking its prey. Marin made a rectangle out of his forefingers and thumbs and began sizing her up as if through the viewfinder of his camera lens.

'You're perfect.'

'That's kind of you to say,' she replied, wondering if her story pitch in the lounge earlier on had convinced Colorado that she might be the ideal person to script this new project. That idea had its merits, she could see, and within moments of it occurring to her, she was deciding how to spend her evidently hefty pay cheque. Would she rent a house in the Hollywood hills and host elegant parties for visiting natives wanting to worship at the feet of the accomplished screenwriter? Maybe she'd have a home on the beachfront at Malibu, or a ranch down San Diego way? She'd definitely need a bespoke hand-crafted cabinet to store her Oscars and stables for the horses…

'You've got stuffy Brit written all over you,' said Colorado, and Lauren's thought bubble exploded in a shower of ordure.

'I'm sorry?'

'No need to be.'

'No, I'm not apologising, I'm asking you to elaborate.'

'Then why are you sorry?'

'No, I'm not sorry.'

'I thought you just said you were sorry.'

'I did, but I didn't mean I was sorry.'

Colorado stared at her uncomprehendingly. Then he burst out laughing.

'You Brits and your sense of humour. That's exactly what I'm talking about.'

Lauren still didn't get it.

'You're talking about my sense of humour?'

'It's perfect. For this project.'

'You want my sense of humour for the script of your new project?'

'What? The script? No – I want you to front it. Be the presenter. The talking head.'

Their misaligned exchange was interrupted by a booming voice from the door to the ballroom.

Harrison Fforde had entered the chat.

'You'll be needing a professional for that kind of role,' he said, striding towards Lauren and Colorado with an arm outstretched towards them.

'I will?'

'Of course. Someone with a command of the English language, an authoritative voice and experience of the industry. Someone like an actor.'

Lauren liked Harrison but she couldn't help feeling a little violated at this invasion of her conversation. She might have misunderstood Colorado's original intent when he told her she was 'perfect' but a minor readjustment to her thinking would easily accommodate the possibility of presenting a documentary rather than scripting one. In fact, there was lots to like about the chance to front a film: given her job as a teaching assistant, a path to fame had never been as obvious to her as it would have been when Fforde began his career in theatre, and she had never expected to be recognised on the street in the way he had surely desired his whole life, but that didn't mean she couldn't grab a gift horse like this when it came along. Even if she hadn't yet learned to ride.

And now here he was, muscling in on her opportunity.

'You're an actor?' Colorado was staring disbelievingly at Harrison.

'There's no need to sound so surprised,' he said. Even Lauren felt a little protective towards him.

'No, it's just that I—'

'What – couldn't see me as a performer?'

'I guess,' said Colorado lamely.

'Well, I am. And I'll have you know I've performed with all the greats – Sir Ian, Dame Judi, Ant and Dec.'

'You've performed with Judi Dench?' The director's eyes had widened considerably and Lauren felt she was in grave danger of losing the prize that had dangled before her moments ago.

'Well, when I say *performed*, I've been in the same room when she's been acting.'

'You mean you've watched her on stage?' said Lauren acidly, then instantly regretted it. Harrison was her friend, her colleague, and she had no wish to denigrate him in front of a pair of Americans. It was strange what even the hint of fame could do to a person.

'Look, no offence, buddy, but you're not what I'm looking for right now,' said Colorado, and turned his attention back to Lauren.

Fforde gave what Lauren could only describe as the visual equivalent of a 'harrumph' and marched off towards the stairs. She'd have to patch things up with him later on, but it wasn't really her fault, was it? If the film crew found her more photogenic than him, then there wasn't much she could do about that, was there? Harrison must have been in loads of situations where other people got selected for roles ahead of him, so he must be used to the rejection, surely?

There wasn't time to think about that now, though. Marin Cypher was back to his sizing up, moving from one side of her to the other in an attempt, presumably, to find the best angle and light.

'Erm, what exactly have you got in mind for this project?' she asked uncertainly, starting to feel rather uncomfortable under the gaze of two foreigners who were examining every inch of her with seasoned eyes.

'Not sure yet,' said Colorado. 'But we've definitely found our star. Now all we gotta do is follow you round as you explore'—he panned his hands wide as he tested out an imaginary screen title—'*The Mystery of the Hanging Woman.*'

Lauren shivered as his putative name brought her crashing back to reality.

A tragedy had played out at Abbots Chantry and, as things stood, nobody had any inkling why.

II

Professor Stone was not naturally inclined to be rude, but he knew he had a low tolerance for hangers-on; people who just stuck around beyond their usefulness, or enquired too closely into one's personal business; people who seemed to have no lives of their own but chose to live vicariously through others, either because they were too frightened to pursue their own adventures or too nosey to pass up the opportunity of bandwagoning someone else's.

He was beginning to suspect that Hemingford Grey was one of those people.

'I'm sorry, Mr Grey, but I'm afraid I can't help you.'

'You were there, though, weren't you?' The man's voice, honed from private school and family wealth, Stone guessed, had a slight wheedle to it when he was after something. 'You saw the body in the bookshop.'

In the days and weeks after Felicity Penman's murder had been solved, the Professor had made a vow to himself. It wasn't something he could enforce with the other three members of The Quaint Bookshop's reading group, although he'd suggested it to them and they had seemed to agree. He'd promised himself that he would never talk publicly about the case and their involvement in it. As a result, he had turned down several lucrative offers from what he loosely considered to be newspapers, refused a couple of spotty young producers from daytime television and even declined a generous advance from a publishing company hoping to release a memoir on the topic. He wasn't interested in cashing in on Felicity's memory, so why on earth would he talk freely about it to a casual acquaintance with an apparent nose for gossip?

'I'm sorry,' he repeated. 'It's not something I care to talk about.'

Grey seemed put out by his response. Perhaps he'd imagined Stone would be willing to divulge some of the gorier details of the murder or the reading group's role in working out the killer. If so, he was going to be disappointed.

'All right, then. Please yourself.'

Grey began shuffling away across the ballroom and Stone was about to start up a conversation with Monty Butler when the gift shop manager turned back with a curious look on his face.

'If you won't tell me about the body in the bookshop, maybe you could tell me about the police officer who was running the case?'

His line of questioning took Stone by surprise: why did he want to know about Chief Inspector Miranda Carlton? Or was he just asking about the investigation more generally? It all sounded very strange coming from a man who, less than an hour earlier, had been mopping his brow in distress at discovering Keren Lowe's body at the bottom of the tower. It seemed his powers of recovery from that trauma had been remarkable.

'Why do you ask?' he enquired, trying to make himself sound as innocent as possible.

'Oh, it's just that the whole mystery had me intrigued from the moment I read about the murder in the *Norcester Echo*,' said Grey. 'When I heard that your little group had been invited for the weekend, I couldn't resist wangling myself an invitation too. I'm not supposed to be working today – we're only open Monday to Friday as a rule – but I wasn't going to let an opportunity like this pass me by. I can understand if you feel uncomfortable talking about it, but I really would be most grateful if you could give me the inside scoop, as it were.'

So there it was. Hemingford Grey was merely nosey. Stone wondered how his colleagues felt about him gatecrashing the weekend.

'No, I'm sorry, Mr Grey. That would be like me pressing you on the background details about Keren Lowe and Siobhan.'

'Isn't that what you're doing, trying to find out why Keren killed herself? You've found yourself another nice little mystery to solve and you're off and running.'

Hemingford Grey had hit a sore point. He was, of course, absolutely right: Stone's detective antennae had been twitching away merrily as he'd put on a sombre face and gathered the troops in the ballroom. Was there really that much difference between himself and the rubberneckers who wanted to catch a piece of the action when something awful occurred?

Yes, he decided, there was.

The rubberneckers were, by definition, gawkers with no real business in whatever tragedy it was that they were eavesdropping on. He and his squad of investigative book-lovers were something different entirely: they had put their expertise, gained from years of study in the world of fiction, to decisive use in tracking down and bringing to justice the perpetrator of that most heinous of crimes, the murder of a bookshop manager. They had proved themselves the equal of all the amateur sleuths they had been reading about, only in their case they probably deserved even more plaudits since they had achieved their ambition in real life, not simply between the pages of a novel, where the author's whims and machinations could provide them with brilliantly deduced clues or fiendish red herrings, depending on his or her fancy at any given page number.

No, they hadn't merely outwitted their author; they had outwitted the constabulary too. And that made them the heroes of their own story.

Hemingford Grey might take some persuading, though.

'Well, let me tell you, Professor Stone,' he said, 'we're not all as precious as you about our secrets. There are a few things I could tell you about the goings-on in this house that would curl your eyebrows.'

This time, Grey's departure was much more definitive, turning on his heel and walking purposefully for the door.

Stone had no idea why Grey's divulged secrets might curl his eyebrows, or indeed what his eyebrows might look like curled. In his youth he'd once inadvisedly attempted a perm but the result was so disastrous and so hilarious to his classmates that he had vowed never to go near a cosmetic implement or appliance again, and a little bit of him was proud that he had spent the past forty years sticking to that vow. He had no desire at all to have his eyebrows curled, by artificial means or by hair-raising factual revelations.

And yet he was intrigued by the gift shop manager's teaser.

Following Grey out of the ballroom, Stone saw him striding down the hall towards the back of the house. He nodded a hasty greeting at Lauren, who seemed to be very in with the American film crew, posing for them on the grand staircase and grinning like a mad thing, but he suspected she hadn't noticed. Honestly, here was another unexplained death that the reading group had been dropped right in the middle of, and no one except him seemed to be remotely interested in it. Lauren and Fforde had both left the ballroom, presumably embarrassed by the tears of the suicide victim's grieving sister, while Bella had seemed more concerned about Ronnie's welfare than answering the questions that were piling up around them. Why, for instance, was there such a discrepancy between Keren Lowe's demeanour at dinner last night and her apparent state of mind in the billiard room this morning? What had caused her to climb the unused tower and throw herself out of its highest window with a rope tied round her neck? And why had Hemingford Grey suddenly, and apparently only in the wake of his colleague's tragic death, developed such a thriving interest in the murder of Felicity Penman and the officer in charge of that case?

There might be plausible answers to all these questions, but if so, Stone had no idea what they were.

Hemingford Grey had just intimated that he might be able to help in that department.

As Stone followed the man down the hallway, Grey disappeared through a door to the right, to a part of the house that Stone hadn't seen so far, and when he reached the door he found it open. At the far end of another corridor was a double door with a rope hanging across it. A sign above it announced this to be the gift shop.

It seemed natural, after failing in his bid to plumb Stone for information, that Grey should retreat to his own domain. Stone wondered just how much he'd irritated the man by refusing to talk about Felicity Penman; he'd certainly seemed to be more upset about it than Stone would have expected, and he'd made a quick exit after dropping his bombshell about the house being full of secrets. Perhaps he would feel a little less defensive on his own turf.

There was only one way to find out.

When he unclipped the rope from its mooring on the short metal post and let himself into the gift shop, Stone found himself surrounded by a treasure trove of trinkets and curios that wouldn't have been out of place on an episode of the *Antiques Roadshow*. In glass cabinets, reproduction goblets, necklaces and headscarves were displayed like museum pieces. In the unit nearest to him he noticed a replica medieval candlestick whose original he had observed on the mantelpiece in the lounge. He'd intended to ask Siobhan about its history before events had overtaken the morning, but it looked significant and properly old, unlike its plasticky facsimiles here in the gift shop.

The bases of the items behind the glass were dotted with tiny labels revealing their prices. Stone had little to gauge them by but guessed that they might have been on the exorbitant side of high. Given that its audience was both captive and already under the atmospheric influence of the house by the time they'd reached the shop on their tour, he could quite see why the Veritys might risk inflating their prices to squeeze the most out of their visitors. Even so, the labels on everything from branded tea towels to Abbots Chantry whisky (the monks were reputed to have been master distillers in their day, and why not cash in on that five hundred years later?) seemed at least twenty per cent higher than Stone would have expected in your average high street store, and a good fifty per cent above their online equivalents. Some people were willing to pay a premium for buying *in situ*, he supposed, and it appeared that being able to walk out of the house with your very own slice of carefully curated history must count for something.

Through one of the cabinets he spotted Hemingford Grey, standing behind the shop's till and staring out through a mullioned window at the wintry scene beyond.

'Mr Grey,' he began, attempting a tone of conciliation. 'I fear I might have come across as a little brusque in the ballroom.'

Grey turned and smiled at him, which felt like a good sign.

'Brusque in the ballroom? Sounds like a new kind of dance,' he said genially, and Stone hoped he might have regained any ground he had lost a few minutes before.

'I didn't mean to be quite so defensive about the whole murder thing,' said Stone, reaching the till and looking past Grey at the white wilderness outside.

'Please, don't trouble yourself,' said Grey, sounding as if he meant it. 'I understand that some people are more reserved than others. If you don't want to talk to me, that's fine.'

'No, no – it's not that I don't want to talk to you. In fact, I'd very much like to discuss our current situation, especially given your unique knowledge of the house.'

'I'm not sure what you're getting at.'

Stone weighed up his position. Having just condemned Grey for the crime of rubbernecking, he could hardly go poking about in the secrets of the house without laying himself open to the same criticism. On the other hand, how could you investigate a mystery – such as why Keren Lowe had taken her own life – without asking questions? For a moment, he considered dropping the whole thing and leaving it to the emergency services – whenever they finally arrived – to pick up the pieces. After all, it was nothing to do with him really.

Then the detective in him stepped forward and took the microphone.

'How long have you worked at Abbots Chantry, Mr Grey?'

'About twelve years. Why?'

'And what about Keren Lowe?'

'She started a little bit later than me. Maybe ten years.'

'And her sister?'

'A year or two after that. Look, what are you getting at, Professor?'

Lord Quaint stood at the Professor's shoulder, whispering cues in his ear.

'I'm just trying to establish that the three of you were very familiar with the house and its contents, as well as with each other. You must have known them well – although not as well as they knew each other, of course, given that they were sisters.'

'Ah yes. Sisters.'

'Was that one of the secrets you were referring to earlier?' he asked Grey.

'Not really – they didn't particularly try to keep it hidden, although I must admit it did come as something of a surprise when it emerged by accident at a Christmas party. I don't think anybody knew when they first arrived.'

Hemingford Grey was proving to be something of a goldmine when it came to the backstories of the staff at Abbots Chantry. It amounted to little more than gossip, Stone was quite prepared to admit, but one man's gossip was another man's wellspring of information.

Another thought struck him about the events of the morning. It was a question Grey was in a unique position to answer.

'Mr Grey, do you remember when you brought that note into the lounge for Keren Lowe this morning?'

'Of course.'

'You said it was from Lord Verity.'

'Yes.'

'Did Lord Verity give it to you himself?'

'No.'

'Then how did you come by it?'

'I found it.'

The Professor didn't imagine Grey was the life and soul of many dinner parties. It was like getting blood out of a stone that was not only severely anaemic but also had a strong aversion to needles. Stone's mother used to tell the story of an occasion at kindergarten when the teacher had asked him very gently one Monday if he'd had a nice weekend, only to be met with a monosyllabic 'Yes'. The teacher later confessed to his parents that the thought of any further questioning felt too much like intrusion, and she'd let the conversation lapse. But even that seemed positively loquacious in comparison to Grey's current responses.

'May I ask where?'

'On the side table in the entrance hall.'

There were gaps in Grey's narrative and, like an unusually dogged council roadmender, Stone was determined to fill them in.

'How did you know it was from Lord Verity?'

'I could tell from the handwriting.'

'You're familiar enough with his Lordship's penmanship to know it was written by him?'

'Oh yes. He leaves notes around for the staff when he doesn't want to talk to us. He has a particularly distinctive copperplate style. Everyone in the house would recognise it.'

Though he couldn't quite place why, Stone thought that might be an assumption worth testing at some point.

'When you brought it in, you whispered something to her.'

'Did I?'

Stone didn't know if he was being deliberately obtuse or had simply forgotten the encounter.

'You handed her the note and said something to her before she opened it.'

'I was probably telling her I'd just found it on the side table in the entrance hall.'

Even to a mind attuned to seeking out discrepancies and

clues, this seemed perfectly plausible. He could hardly fault Grey on this piece of his tale.

'Did Keren tell you what the note said?'

Grey shrugged. 'I left before she opened it. That was the last time I saw her. Alive, that is.'

They had got to what Stone couldn't help thinking of as the juicy bit, although his sense of propriety and a concern for the shock that Grey must be feeling meant he would never have put it in those terms out loud.

He was about to frame his next question – something sensitive about Grey's discovery of the twisted, bloody body on the path at the bottom of the tower – when his eye was caught by something outside the window behind the gift shop manager, derailing his train of thought and sending it plunging off the precipice of revelation into the ravine of red herrings.

Outside, carving an inexplicable arc through the snow from the kitchen door towards a high garden wall in the distance, was a solitary set of footprints.

The Billiard Room

I

The Professor had been right about one aspect of this tragic day, Bella thought: it was nothing like Felicity's murder.

Where that had seen the reading group come together as a team – assembling like the Avengers in that film Trevor had made her go to see with him, which she'd actually found rather entertaining although she'd never have admitted it to him – Keren's was a very different death. And so far, there was no sign of any collaboration going on. They'd been invited to Abbots Chantry as guests of honour, she'd been led to believe, although the presence of those Americans had made her think twice. Had the real reason for the Veritys inviting them been to add a bit of local celebrity glamour to the weekend, buffing up the appeal of the house to help convince the Hollywood advance party that it was the place to be seen? And, more importantly, the place to film a blockbuster movie? She was under no illusion about the lowly status of The Quaint Bookshop's reading group in the hierarchy of potential *Hello!*

interviewees, but on the other hand their story had delivered their requisite fifteen minutes of fame, plus a few extra minutes thanks to Harrison's natural ability to hog the limelight, and beggars couldn't be choosers. She was sure the Veritys must have friends in high places, but perhaps their normal entourage lacked the necessary populist allure for a delegation of visiting movie-makers.

She was far from convinced that the reading group did either, but it was the only way to make sense of the Veritys' apparently cavalier attitude to their guests: over dinner last night they'd been little more than aloof, this morning completely absent, so Bella had come to the conclusion that they simply wanted the group there to do the job of beguiling the Americans on their behalf.

Now here she was, at half past eleven on the second day of their visit, being utterly ignored by everyone.

After the Professor had pontificated his verdict on the likelihood of a repeat of what had happened to Felicity, he'd disappeared from the ballroom in the wake of the nice chap who ran the gift shop, while Lauren and Harrison had gone chasing off after the film crew. Bella felt neither qualified nor inclined to make small talk with the remaining household staff, even though they included her sister, so she'd plonked herself on a rather hard chair near a window and had been staring out of it at the snow for the last quarter of an hour.

So much for teamwork.

She began reflecting on the circumstances that had led up to this moment: the power cut that had forced Olive to put her trusty spanner to use on the old generator, the gathering in the lounge with its spooky revelations about the house's history, the underground exploration of the secret passageway, and the dramatic incident that had brought them all together in the ballroom, only to find themselves at a loss to explain what on earth had happened, or why.

As she sat staring into the distance, something called to her.

She looked round to see who was left in the ballroom but realised it was empty. Monty, Siobhan and Ronnie must have taken themselves off somewhere – perhaps to a quiet corner of the house where Siobhan could grieve in privacy – and she was alone in the cavernous space. Decorated in an over-the-top jazz-age art deco, with chubby cherubs plastered into the ceiling and semi-naked women in bronze holding aloft crenellated lampshades, the room was a tribute to its hedonistic creator, the current lord's wastrel great-grandfather. And among all the ornate fixtures and period fittings, one thing stood out to Bella now: hanging from the minstrels' gallery at one end of the room, presumably there to call order for speeches or other special announcements, dangled a large bell.

It was the bell that had called to her.

When they had all rushed outside to witness the horrific sight that Hemingford Grey had alerted them to, Bella had looked up at the tower from which Keren had thrown herself. It hardly needed Siobhan's expert guidance to understand that it had once formed the bell tower of the original monastery.

Now, prompted by the unusual feature in the ballroom, Bella had a sudden urge to examine that bell tower more closely.

If the Professor had been around, she'd have taken her idea to him first. As the longest-standing member of the reading group, he'd always been the senior figure in her eyes, and his natural air of authority inspired admiration and awe in equal measure. While his deductions in the investigation into Felicity's murder had not always been completely reliable, he'd never faltered in his steadfast conviction that they – or, more accurately, he – would be able to solve the case.

And they had. As much by luck as by astute analysis, admittedly, but their collective dedication to golden-age detective fiction had served them well and she had felt proud to be part of the team.

Now there seemed to be no team. As a result, Bella Bourton, housewife, divorcee and newly avid consumer of crime novels, would have to do this on her own.

So what would Professor Stone do first?

There was little doubt in her mind that he would waste no time in finding the stairs that led to the tower. She grabbed her shoulder bag and marched out of the ballroom, trying to assess her position relative to the tower. Ignoring the Americans, who seemed to be fussing round Lauren in the hall, she made her way to the north-eastern reaches of the building. When she came across a roped-off corridor with a hand-drawn 'No entry' sign taped to the wall, she guessed this was a section that was not frequented by paying visitors.

If the dust on the ledges and door frames was anything to go by, it wasn't frequented much by the staff either.

Stepping over the rope, Bella looked back over her shoulder, then wondered why she felt guilty about entering this part of the house. She was a guest at Abbots Chantry and if she wanted to go exploring behind the scenes, then only Lord or Lady Verity could stop her, she decided. And as she hadn't seen them since last night, she put even more resolve into her march and strode down the corridor.

The lack of windows meant that the corridor grew darker the further she went into it, but she could make out a lighter patch in the gloom at the far end and made her way steadily towards it. When she reached it, she realised it was coming from a window high up to her right, at the turning point in a narrow flight of stairs. Convinced she'd found the access route to the tower, Bella began to climb. The steps rose in a series of half-flights, with a window at every second turn. She tried to imagine a team of removal men lumbering a billiard table up these stairs, then remembered Monty saying that they'd used a pulley system to winch it up the outside of the building. Either way, it seemed a crazy undertaking.

At the alternate turns, a door led presumably to a room at each storey of the tower. She didn't bother investigating the first four, but when the stairs ran out at the fifth one, she concluded she must have reached the billiard room. She stared at the door for a moment, wondering if she really wanted to go into the room alone. Monty had said it was empty, apart from the ripped end of Keren's rope, but she still didn't relish the prospect of facing a suicide scene on her own. The top chamber of a medieval tower was hardly a desirable destination at the best of times, and a snowbound, isolated weekend with an unexplained death on their hands was not that.

Steeling herself with the thought that Professor Stone would be proud of her for her resilience, Bella reached out and took hold of the large iron ring that served as a door handle. She turned it slowly, feeling the resistance of decades of rust and disuse, and pushed.

Nothing happened.

She pushed harder.

Still nothing happened.

Bella leaned her shoulder against the door and heaved.

It was clear that nothing was going to happen.

She peered more closely at the iron ring and saw that the metal plate in which it was housed also contained a keyhole.

Escutcheon. That was it. From somewhere deep in Bella's memory, the correct word for the metal plate containing the keyhole popped up in her mind. She'd probably read it in one of the Lord Quaint novels and had to look it up. Or maybe she'd made a note of it, as she often did with words or phrases she didn't recognise, and asked the others about it at their next meeting. The first time she'd done that, with the word *antimacassar*, there had been a rather odd look from Harrison Fforde, as if to say *'This isn't what we're here for'*, but Professor Stone had indulged her and Lauren chimed in helpfully too. After that, even Fforde saw it as a kindness to assist her with unfamiliar words. Antimacassar remained one of her favourite words to this day, although the opportunities to use it in everyday conversation were admittedly few and far between.

And now she remembered *escutcheon*.

It was nice to think she knew such an obscure word, but it wasn't going to help her.

She needed the key.

When she finally found Monty in a bedroom, where he and

Ronnie were consoling Siobhan, Bella was surprised that he didn't have the key to the billiard room.

'I gave it back to Olive,' he told her. 'She looks after the hardware for the house.'

Bella was slightly surprised: she'd have imagined that the estate manager – especially one who wore the trousers like Monty, even if they were tartan trews – would retain control over important things like the keys to the house. Maybe he was more of a delegator than she'd first suspected. Olive certainly seemed capable, so perhaps his grip on the estate wasn't quite as iron as she'd thought.

'Do you know where she is?' she asked him.

He looked somewhat bemused and threw a glance at Ronnie, as if asking her to confirm that her sister's behaviour was nothing out of the ordinary.

Ronnie shrugged. So much for the sisterhood.

'May I ask why you want the keys to the billiard room?'

'No reason in particular. I'd just like to see it for myself, if that's OK?'

Monty gave a little cough. 'I suppose so.'

'So can I tell Olive that you've given your permission for me to have the key?'

Monty rested a hand on his wife's shoulder then stood up. 'Can I leave Siobhan with you?' he asked Ronnie, who nodded and shuffled closer to her on the bed.

He turned back to Bella. 'I'll come with you. It'll be easier.'

Tracking down Olive was considerably more straightforward than finding Monty had been. She was in a boot room off the kitchen sharpening a saw and grunted when she saw Monty and Bella arrive.

'Have you got the key to the billiard room?' Monty asked her without any preamble.

'A please never goes down badly,' she grumbled, making no effort to stop her sharpening.

'Please,' he said with a definite edge to his voice.

Bella was fascinated by the interaction. She'd have expected some deference from the gardener to Monty's authority but found none. If anything, he seemed daunted by her and Bella wondered if her position at the house predated his arrival, giving her seniority in years, if not in job title. Certainly Olive's extreme confidence could be read as brash insubordination by someone who chose to take it that way. Fortunately, Monty seemed even-tempered enough not to be riled by her, even if she did hold the whip hand.

'I'm not sure that's a good idea,' she said, finally stopping what she was doing and turning to face Monty, the file in her hand held out as if brandishing a weapon.

'I'm sorry?'

'I don't think I should give you the key to the billiard room.'

Bella tried to work out if the look on her face was defiance, plain and simple, as it appeared to her, or if there was something else going on.

'What on earth are you talking about? Why shouldn't I have the key to the billiard room?'

Was Olive looking a bit shifty? Was she harbouring a scowl? How could Bella really tell?

'Come on, woman – hand it over.'

It was the first time Bella had heard Monty raise his voice.

Olive turned suddenly meek.

She walked over to a cupboard near the outside door and opened it up, revealing a huge array of keys of different sizes: some looked vast and ancient, like props from a wizards-and-witches fantasy epic, others were shiny and small, as if they fitted a tiny padlock. Some were on bunches that could be slung from a work belt, like the one Bella had noticed Olive wearing earlier that morning, while others hung in solitary isolation, as if too important to be sullied by close contact with their neighbour. Olive selected a large, dull iron key from around the middle of the cupboard and unhooked it before handing it to Monty.

'Thank you.'

Without another word, Monty wheeled round and marched for the door. Bella nodded appreciatively at Olive and followed him out.

What was Olive playing at? Monty's request seemed perfectly reasonable, and his question ditto: why shouldn't he have the key to the billiard room? He'd told them earlier that he and Olive had been up there already, finding nothing but the end of the rope, so what possible justification could Olive have for trying to prevent him returning there now?

Bella couldn't make sense of it, but her focus now was on keeping up with Monty as he made his way back to the tower staircase.

When they reached the top and he slid the key into the lock, Bella found herself holding her breath, even though she knew what to expect when he swung the heavy door open.

The room, Monty had assured them, was completely empty.

Except that it wasn't.

Yes, the snapped rope was attached to a metal grille, as he'd reported it. Yes, the other end of it trailed out through the open window to dangle out of sight some ten feet down the tower wall.

But no, the rest of the room wasn't empty.

In the middle of a bare floor that was dusty with inattention and blackened with age lay a carved wooden candlestick.

11

Professor Stone was familiar with the concept of knot gardens; he'd just never seen one.

'The house has a Tudor knot garden,' Hemingford Grey told him when he asked what was behind the high, sandy-coloured wall a hundred yards or so away in the grounds. 'It was first established by the monks in the fifteenth century. It fell into disuse over time but Lord Verity's father had it restored in line with drawings they found during some renovation work twenty-odd years ago.'

'And why would somebody want to go to the knot garden in this weather?'

He studied Grey as he thought about his answer. The man seemed to be considering his words carefully.

'The film crew, scouting locations?'

'But there's only one set of footprints.'

'The gardener?'

'I can't imagine there's anything for Olive to be doing out

there in these conditions. Besides, she's been rather busy keeping the lights on, hasn't she?'

'Indeed.'

His curiosity suitably piqued, Stone turned and walked out of the gift shop, heading for the kitchen. Grey was close behind him.

When he opened the outside door, a blast of cold air bit through his pullover and nibbled at his ears, but Professor Stone barely noticed. Staring at the ground, he saw that the footprints had been made by a heavy pair of boots and were not fresh: judging by the crisp edges to the indentations, he'd have said they'd been locked into the snow by the previous night's freezing temperatures.

'Looks to me like these were made in the early hours of the morning,' he said over his shoulder to Grey, who was pulling a coat tight around himself and following Stone out into the wintry scene. 'After the worst of the blizzard.'

'It must have been later than the last snowfall, otherwise the prints would have been obliterated.'

'My thoughts exactly,' said the Professor. 'But who would have gone stumbling about in the dark last night to visit the knot garden? I'm sure it's very pretty and historic and all that, but it's hardly a destination for the middle of the night in a snowstorm, is it?'

There was something else that troubled Stone about the footprints, which Grey appeared so far not to have noticed: they only went one way.

The Professor needed to shake off his shadow. Grey seemed far too curious for his liking, and if there were investigations to be done, Stone wanted to do them with his reading group colleagues, not this whiny, enigmatic character who'd admitted he was only there to meet the bookshop detectives in person.

'Mr Grey, I wonder if you'd mind going on a hunt for me? I'd very much like to speak to Monty, if you're able to find him.'

'Oh,' said Grey, apparently reluctant to leave Stone's side. 'All right. I suppose so. I'm not sure where he'll be just now but I can certainly have a look, if that's what you'd like.'

'Very much,' said Stone, giving Grey his broadest smile and hoping it looked at least marginally convincing.

'Right,' stuttered Grey, half-turning back towards the kitchen door before stopping again.

'You're sure you want to speak to him now? Only I might be helpful with more information about the knot garden, if you didn't mind waiting?'

'Now would be perfect,' said Stone, and offered an ushering gesture towards the door. 'If you'd be so kind.'

Left alone after the departure of the gift shop manager on a chase for geese that weren't so much wild as non-existent, Professor Stone began tracing the footsteps in the snow. He couldn't understand why the single set of clear prints ran in only one direction, but a gnawing concern rose in him at the thought that whoever went out to the knot garden in the middle of a blizzard had not come back. Not this way, at least. He mentally ticked off the list of staff and guests who'd shared dinner the previous evening – adding Olive as the only absentee who was also in the house for the weekend – and came to the conclusion that there were only two people he hadn't seen this morning: their hosts, Lord and Lady Verity. Might these footsteps belong to one of them? If so, Lord

Verity was the more likely candidate, given the size of the prints, although he supposed wellingtons could leave a deceptively large mark, regardless of the foot inside them.

When he reached the stone wall, which stood a clear three feet taller than him, he looked to the left, where it disappeared into a thicket of greenery, heavily laden with snow. To the right, the wall ran away blankly for ten yards or more until it turned a corner. There was no sign of a door or any other access to the garden beyond, but Stone had good reason to try this direction: the footprints followed the wall this way.

At the corner, the wall ran off again, but about twenty yards away there appeared to be an arch or arbour of some evergreen bush which, he hoped, might conceal a way into the garden. He trudged towards it, creating prints of his own parallel with those he was pursuing, and discovered that it did indeed hide a small entrance with a wooden door. Stooping to pass through, he found himself in a pristine and sheltered part of the grounds, surprisingly large and open yet walled off from the surrounding area to provide privacy and separation.

Even the sounds of the outside world seemed to be cut off in this secluded patch of emptiness. With the vaulting grey skies overhead putting a dingy lid on the whole garden, Stone felt suddenly claustrophobic and oppressed. His everyday footwear felt hideously inadequate, and he bitterly regretted not borrowing Grey's coat when he sent him back inside the house.

Then again, it might not have been entirely the cold air that made him shiver.

The snow here was immaculate and untouched, save for the prints that led from the doorway to a low circular centrepiece at the heart of the garden. He could tell from the smooth undulations and crafted shapes beneath the blanketing white that the hedges forming the knot garden were carefully tended and maintained in their shape and he assumed that whoever had left the footprints knew its design well, for they went directly and uninterrupted straight to the circle in the middle, following what Stone imagined to be a gravel path under the snow.

The circular section was raised slightly higher than the rest of the hedges in the pattern around it, and at its nearest edge the snow had been disturbed by someone rummaging into the foliage below.

Exactly why was a total mystery to the Professor. Had they been trying to hide something down there? Or perhaps retrieving something previously stashed in a hiding place? Either way, it left him deeply disturbed. A bit like the snow. What possible reason could someone have for slogging out here to bury or salvage something in a snowstorm at night?

The footsteps might provide a clue.

From the spot at the edge of the circle where the snow had been moved, they headed off to the right, presumably along another path. Stone followed them again to the far corner of the wall, where another door appeared almost magically, offering a second, semi-concealed way out.

On the other side of this door, the weight of the knot garden's eerie stillness lifted immediately, and Stone felt himself stand a little taller.

The prints headed back towards the house by a different route, arriving at a single-storey extension that looked like a poorly designed annex to the original building. Its grey brick was completely out of keeping with the sandstone of the main structure, and its twentieth-century uPVC door and windows stood in stark contrast to their mullioned and sash neighbours a little further away to Stone's right.

None of that felt significant to the Professor at that precise moment. His attention was drawn instead to the piece of engraved slate that hung on the wall beside the nasty plastic door. In elegant typeface, the sign announced that this was the estate office.

The footprints led right up to the door.

Stone stood in silence and scratched his head, remembering the words of Lauren Sherwood in the ballroom.

'Unless there was something else going on...'

Was there really something more to Keren's death than the suicide it appeared to be? And if so, what did this set of footprints, leading from the kitchen to the knot garden to the estate office, have to do with any of it? Or was he just letting his imagination run away with him?

As he worked his way back to the kitchen door, completing a circuit with his own footsteps, Professor Stone began to become consumed by a single thought.

Maybe there were some clues to a mystery here after all...

The Kitchen

1

It was clear to Fforde that the Americans were not interested in casting him as the presenter of their new documentary. After hanging around in the hall for half an hour trying to ingratiate himself, only for Lauren to hog their attention, he finally gave up and wandered off to the kitchen in search of something to eat.

All the talk of mysteries had made him hungry. Even if he didn't really understand it. From what he'd heard, Lauren and the Americans seemed obsessed with digging into Keren's past for suicidal motives. He'd seen Professor Stone go beetling off somewhere with Hemingford Grey, as if the shop manager were his best friend and the new Watson to Stone's Holmes. Even Bella had vanished completely, leaving him to be the last remaining liaison between the reading group and the household of Abbots Chantry. While he felt he could hold his own when it came to tall stories for a captive audience, he didn't really think it was fair for the others to have dumped him in favour of their own little quests.

Keren Lowe's death wasn't such a big mystery, was it? Unless they each had other angles they were pursuing without him?

Well, now he had a quest of his own: filling his belly.

As he approached the door to the kitchen, he was surprised to hear animated voices coming from inside, and he was even more surprised when he entered the room to discover Lord and Lady Verity themselves at the heart of a spirited conversation. It was his first sighting of the couple since the previous evening and, as it was now almost lunchtime, Fforde wondered if they'd been deliberately avoiding their weekend guests or if they simply slept in late as a matter of course. Siobhan had suggested the latter, allowing her to divulge some titbits she wouldn't have felt appropriate if they'd been present, but Fforde couldn't help thinking their absence was more than just habit: failing to appear until this sort of time on a Saturday when you have guests in the house was impoliteness bordering on rudeness as far as he was concerned.

As a result, he didn't feel particularly warm towards his hosts as he strolled into the kitchen.

His antagonism towards them deepened when he realised they were having a bit of a go at Siobhan.

The grieving sister of the dead woman was standing at the large table that occupied the centre of the room, buttering a huge pile of bread slices with a ferocity that would have made Gordon Ramsay nervous. Opposite her, with a look of mild disapproval on their faces, stood Lord and Lady Verity, dressed as if for a shooting party and apparently without a hint of empathy for poor Siobhan's situation.

'It's all very tragic, I'm sure,' his Lordship was saying as Fforde entered, 'but we can't let it interfere with the effective running of the house. She was a much-loved and much-respected member of the Abbots Chantry family, and she will be missed by us all'—here he took his wife's hand—'but, as Mr Fforde here might very well say, the show must go on.'

Fforde had never been entirely sure that he agreed with the old showbiz principle. *Why must the show go on?* Noel Coward had once queried in song, and Fforde had asked himself the same question many times during the course of his career. That time he'd had root canal surgery in the morning and the company manager insisted he plough on with a double performance day, matinee and evening, of *The Importance of Being Earnest* had proved a particularly painful example, especially when it came to eating the muffins. But there had been others. His mother's funeral followed by *Abigail's Party*. *Noises Off* after having his elderly cat put down. There were definitely moments when the human being in him felt it should take precedence over the mere actor, and it was only peer pressure or the thought of a stern producer's note threatening legal action or – worse – the sack that had forced him to go along with the ridiculous performers' adage.

'Don't bring me into it,' he said feelingly.

'And anyway,' Lord Verity went on, ignoring Fforde's contribution, 'we all still need sustenance, don't we, and without Keren to fulfil that function, we'll just have to make do.'

By that, Fforde took him to mean that Siobhan would be making lunch.

Fforde studied Lady Verity, clinging to her husband's hand

and declining to make eye contact with the staff. He tried to work out whether she actually agreed with his Lordship or was simply remaining silent out of propriety. She certainly looked more crestfallen than he did about the loss of their catering manager but perhaps Keren had made particularly good sandwiches. Or Siobhan didn't.

'Now, fill me in with what's happening about the power.'

Siobhan stopped mid-spread and dropped the knife she was holding onto the table. She looked utterly worn out.

'Olive's got the back-up generator working, so we're all right for now. We have light and heat but she's not convinced it'll last longer than the day. We never restocked the diesel supply after the last power cut.'

His Lordship tutted and shook his head, reminding Fforde of a walrus toying with a penguin. The moustache was a dead ringer, and the side-to-side movement was exactly as he'd seen it on one of those David Attenborough documentaries about the blue oceans. All it needed was a whispered, cultivated voiceover: *'And here we see the aristocrat in his native habitat, exerting his natural authority over the landscape and sending lower life forms scurrying for protection in their kitchen lairs. With one toss of his huge head, he could crush them completely…'*

'It's really not good enough, Siobhan. How many times does this have to happen for Monty to get some decent planning in place for every eventuality?'

Fforde wondered just how many times this exact scenario had played out. He didn't imagine it could be many. More likely was that odd things would go wrong around the house and grounds, and in Lord Verity's mind they would be agglomerated into repeated issues and mistakes which he could then use to hold against his estate manager at moments like this. It didn't seem very fair, especially since Monty Butler had just witnessed the unpleasant death of his sister-in-law. Never mind his Lordship's cavalier attitude towards the grieving sister.

He contemplated commenting to that effect, then decided against it on the basis that it wasn't his place to intrude on how things were run at Abbots Chantry. Even if he had had the balls to say something, his opportunity was snatched from him by the arrival in the kitchen of Bella and Monty, both looking bemused.

'Ah, there you are,' said Lord Verity, turning on Monty. 'Siobhan's just been telling us that we don't have enough fuel to last the weekend.'

'Probably not,' said Monty, not looking remotely bothered.

'I don't understand how this can be allowed to have happened.'

'Paying the diesel suppliers might help,' said Monty, who clearly was not one to stand for his employer's rank-pulling nonsense. 'I did mention it to you a couple of weeks ago but you said to hold back until we really needed it. Well, now we really need it.'

Lord Verity snorted indignantly, as if to reinforce that this couldn't possibly be his responsibility.

'Well, I need you to come up with a contingency plan before we're plunged into darkness and all freeze to death.'

Lord Verity dragged his wife behind him as he left the kitchen.

'Is everything all right?' asked Fforde, seeing the look on Bella's face.

'What? Oh, yes. Only Mr Butler and I have just been up in the billiard room and we found something rather mysterious in there.'

'Mysterious?'

'Yes. A candlestick.'

'Not just any candlestick,' interjected Monty. 'The antique one from the mantelpiece in the lounge.'

Siobhan had picked up her knife again when the Veritys left the room but now she stopped buttering once more.

'The old monks' candlestick?'

'That's right,' said Monty.

Fforde didn't understand. 'But I thought you said the room was empty when you and Olive checked it earlier?'

'And so it was. Olive locked the room to preserve it in case the police wanted to take a look – whenever they get here.'

'Then how could a candlestick have got there for you and Bella to find just now?'

Even as he asked the question, Fforde felt the stirrings of an old inquisitiveness deep inside him.

He rather liked it.

'That's exactly it,' said Bella, her voice mingling urgency with bewilderment. 'That's the mystery.

'Harrison, I think it's time we got the reading group together.'

11

It didn't take Lauren long to tire of the attentions of the Americans. Like pre-school children or Claudia Winkleman, she could handle them only in small doses, but after half an hour of being told she was 'perfect' and 'sooooo photogenic' while all the while knowing her hair needed washing and her mascara was smudged, she'd had more than her fill of their transatlantic cooing. Harrison was welcome to it.

And there was another aspect of the whole film process that she found distasteful: switching easily from blockbuster to documentary, Colorado Hughes and Marin Cypher had displayed the ultimate in superficial interest in their subjects. Lauren began to doubt whether they were really up for making a movie of the Lord Quaint book at all, so flimsy was their knowledge of the source material and so casual their approach to the whole thing. Now that their eye had been caught by the shiny prospect of a country-house mystery they might be able to flog to Netflix or some other streaming service, they had abandoned their original plans completely and were well into framing a pitch to sell this new idea. They'd already explored the library and conservatory as possible backdrops, and currently had her draped over the banister of the grand staircase.

'That looks sensational,' Colorado told her. 'Now is there any chance you could hitch the skirt a little higher?'

Lauren had never been one for hitching, even in her younger days, and her early supposition that they might be keen to try her out for her analytical mind or her millennial's intelligence had long since evaporated. The request to change into something 'more feminine' should have set off the alarm bells, and the skirt-hitching was a clear red flag, but the final straw had come when Marin had asked her to undo a couple more buttons on her blouse.

'It's just that I need a little more light tone in the image,' he'd argued. 'The hallway is dark, and I'm losing your top against it, so I need something pale to "pop" in the lens.'

'Something pale' presumably meant Lauren's cleavage. Well, she was damned if she was going to put that on display for a pair of lascivious Yanks purporting to be interested in her presenting skills.

'I think I need a break,' she told them, being careful not to burn any Hollywood bridges quite yet but wanting to get away from the pressure.

'Sure, honey,' oozed Colorado. 'Take as much time as you need.'

It wasn't time that Lauren felt she needed so much as a shower. Drenched as she was in oleaginous Americanisms, she had a sudden urge for something trivial and English.

She decided to do the washing up.

Guessing that the breakfast dishes had probably been overlooked in the confusion following Keren's death, Lauren took herself off to the kitchen. It came as a shock to her to discover that not only had breakfast been cleared away, but lunch was in an advanced state of preparation thanks in large part to Siobhan. Among the other occupants of the room, Bella looked like she might have lent a hand with some of it. Monty and Harrison were also present, but from the way they were lounging idly against the dresser, they had evidently made little contribution to the preprandial effort. Lauren was sure Siobhan should have been taking some time to herself to begin to come to terms with the loss of her sister, but Siobhan seemed utterly in control of the domestic chores. The only hint that something might have gone awry in her personal life was a single tear stain in the foundation on her left cheek, and Lauren had to look closely to see that: the casual observer – such as Harrison or Bella – would almost certainly not have noticed it.

She wondered if Siobhan's husband had.

'Let me help with that,' she said, approaching Siobhan at the sink and relieving her of a long brush that she was using to scrub the inside of a champagne flute.

Someone had started early on the Buck's Fizz.

'Oh, thank you,' said Siobhan in a heartfelt voice. 'That's kind.'

'Not at all,' said Lauren. 'You can't be expected to shoulder the whole domestic burden on your own. Not after…'

She plunged a mug into the washing-up bowl to avoid having to end a sentence she wished she'd never started.

'Harrison, why don't you come and dry?'

He stuttered the beginnings of a reply. 'Er ... well, actually, Bella was, um, just suggesting that the reading group...'

'Harrison,' Lauren repeated sternly. 'That wasn't an invitation; it was an order.'

'Righto,' he said jauntily, and trotted over to the sink with an exaggerated spring in his step. 'Happy to help.'

Lauren picked up a nearby tea towel and thrust it into Harrison's hands. He might still be cross with her for stealing his thunder with the Americans, but that wouldn't cut it as an excuse to get out of the chores.

Lauren waited until Monty and Siobhan had left, carrying armfuls of lunchy comestibles through to the dining room, before picking up the conversation with Harrison and Bella.

'What were you going to say about the reading group, Bella?'

Bella came over to the sink and lowered her voice.

'I think we should call a meeting. Here. Today.'

'Really? Why?'

'I just think there's something not right about all this.'

'Of course there's something not right,' said Fforde testily. 'Keren's dead.'

'No, not that. Well, not *just* that.'

Lauren stopped rinsing the trencher in her hand and turned to Bella. 'What are you getting at?'

'I think there's something funny going on here.'

'Funny?'

'Yes, funny. Not ha-ha funny. Weird funny.'

Lauren handed the trencher to Harrison. 'Explain.'

'Don't you think we should wait until we're all together?'

Lauren thought for a moment. She realised she hadn't seen Stone since they all left the ballroom an hour earlier.

'Where is the Professor anyway?' she asked.

Neither Bella nor Fforde could answer that question.

'OK, let's wait until he turns up before we start picking your brains, Bella. But I have to say I'm intrigued.' She tapped a dripping Marigold against Bella's temple. 'What's going on in there, I wonder?'

Bella took the tea towel Fforde offered her and dabbed the side of her head dry.

'You're like Scooby-Doo,' said Lauren. 'You're sniffing something suspicious, aren't you?'

'I don't know,' Bella replied. 'It's probably just the excitement of all this. I've never been a guest at a country-house weekend before, and certainly never been wined and dined by a lord.'

'And lady,' Fforde added.

'And lady. And then for something as dramatic as Keren's suicide to happen right in the middle of it – it's probably just pushed my anxiety levels over their natural limits.'

Lauren took off the gloves and draped them over the side of the sink.

'Don't put yourself down, Bella. We saw from the investigation into Felicity's murder just how handy those twitching antennae of yours are. If you can smell something in the air, I'm perfectly willing to go along with it.'

'Unless it's the drains,' said Fforde. 'Old houses like this – you know.'

'Thanks for that, Harrison,' said Lauren. 'Now finish the drying and let's put some of this stuff away.'

The three of them formed a neat chain from drainer to dresser, Lauren passing the clean items to Fforde by the table before he passed them on to Bella, who seemed to be finding homes for most of them on or in the huge wooden item of furniture. Anything she couldn't place, she put back on the table for Siobhan to sort out later on.

Lauren had reached the penultimate piece of crockery – a rather fancy porcelain dish with a lid that sported an acorn in its centre – when she happened to look out of the kitchen window.

A dark figure was out in the garden, silhouetted against the snow and moving slowly towards the house. She'd almost have missed it among the bushes and trees behind it if it hadn't been for the distinctive motion of its upper body and arms, pulling backwards and forwards in a repeated pattern that could only be one thing: someone was raking the snow.

Lauren peered harder and could now make out the implement itself in the hands of its user. As she stared, she could see that the raker was working backwards, away from a long wall in the distance and towards the house, sweeping over what looked like a trail of disturbed snow from several pairs of feet and leaving a pristine white surface in their wake.

It took a moment longer for Lauren to realise who was doing the raking.

'Why—? What—? Why is Olive sweeping snow in the garden?'

Fforde and Bella stopped what they were doing and joined her by the window.

'Bit pointless, if you ask me,' said Fforde. 'There's loads of the stuff out there, and probably more on the way.'

'Exactly,' said Bella, a thoughtful tone in her voice. 'Which makes it all the more curious that she should be raking it now. What on earth is she up to?'

'Looks a bit fishy, I'll grant you,' said Fforde. 'Almost like she's trying to cover something up.'

'Literally,' said Lauren with conviction. 'How many sets of footprints are there from here to there?'

The others leaned forward for a closer look.

'Can't tell for sure but near the kitchen door it looks like three,' said Fforde.

Lauren considered. 'One for Olive with the rake and two more belonging to persons unknown.'

'Ooh, "persons unknown",' said Bella. 'Very Agatha Christie.'

Lauren took it as a compliment.

And then she spotted something else.

'Have you noticed what's weird about them, though?' she asked, pointing down below the window where the three sets of footsteps followed a clear path out into the grounds.

'What?' said Fforde.

'They're all going the same way. Every one of those three sets of prints goes away from the house. None of them comes back.'

The Conservatory

1

The afternoon was already beginning to darken into dusk when the four members of The Quaint Bookshop reading group finally gathered in the conservatory. In order to preserve as much power from the generator as possible, Monty had requested that only minimal lights be turned on when absolutely necessary, so they had each grabbed a candle from the gift shop and were using these to supplement the grey daylight that was still managing to seep in from the grounds. The resulting effect was like something out of a low-budget horror movie where the cast have been asked to bring their own props and the lighting designer is the leading lady's boyfriend.

It came as something of a shock to Bella to discover that she was in the driving seat, at least for the first part of this impromptu meeting. It came as even more of a shock to realise that she relished the prospect.

If anyone had asked her a year earlier how she'd have felt at the prospect of holding the floor in front of a retired professor, a 'resting' actor and a wannabe author, revealing her nuggets like the amateur but gifted protagonist of some golden-age novel, she'd probably have laughed.

Or run away fast.

Revealing her nuggets was something Bella Bourton had always resisted, not least on that holiday in Spain when Trevor had suggested she go topless on a beach where thousands of others were already as good as naked. It had taken all her willpower to wear a bikini, fifteen years and two stone on from the previous occasion, and when she finally lay face-down on her *Little Mermaid* beach towel and undid the clasp at the back, her fears were proved completely right. Trevor had grabbed her top and yanked it out from under her, causing a nasty friction burn on her bosom and a lifetime's embarrassment chasing after him to get it back.

Now, though, she stood in front of the others, a confidence welling inside her like Norcester United's players must have felt as they ran out onto the pitch for their charity match against Leicester City a few years earlier: they knew they were about to get remorselessly slaughtered but – look! – they were playing at the King Power Stadium. The result didn't matter (although fewer than double figures in the opposition's final account might have smarted less); it was all about the joy of the moment. Similarly, Professor Stone, Harrison Fforde and Lauren Sherwood might be about to shoot down her ideas but she was here, standing proudly before them as an equal. Well, maybe not an equal – Lauren and Harrison were much better at this kind of thing than she was, while the Professor was on a whole different planet of experience – but at least entitled to say her piece.

She just didn't know where to begin.

'Scooby-Doo,' said Lauren encouragingly. 'Remember?'

Bella remembered. Sniffing. Suspicions. Something not right.

She looked at Fforde. 'You remember I said I'd been up to the billiard room?'

'Yes.'

'With Monty.'

'Yes.'

'And it wasn't empty.'

'No.'

Lauren gave her a curious look. Fforde raised an eyebrow. Professor Stone looked impassive, which was disappointing, she had to admit: she'd hoped for a reaction of some kind.

'Bella,' said Lauren, 'what did you find there?'

'Harrison already knows but I wanted us all together before I went any further. Now, do you remember Monty telling us he'd been up there with Olive and found it empty?'

Lauren nodded eagerly. Fforde smiled knowingly. The Professor remained inscrutable.

'Well, it wasn't. Apparently, when they first went in, there was nothing there except the top of the rope Keren had used. But when I went back with him, the room was different. *Even though it had been locked in between.*'

'Because now it had…' Fforde prompted quietly. Bella had never noticed it before but he could speak at a normal volume when he wasn't thinking about projecting his voice in an actorly fashion.

Bella prepared to produce her *pièce de résistance*. She had no idea what *résistance* had to do with it but she'd heard the term all her life and now that the moment came for her to produce a *pièce*, she wasn't going to let it pass by unremarked.

She'd been carrying the medieval candlestick in her shoulder bag ever since they'd discovered it in the billiard room. Having expressed astonishment at finding it there, Monty had quickly decided that the tower should be locked up again in order to preserve what might be viewed by the police as a crime scene, and he'd hurried Bella towards the door. She'd urged him to inspect the torn rope end before they left and, while his attention was drawn by that, she'd felt a sudden impulse to stash the candlestick in her bag. She hadn't been quite sure why, but she didn't concur with Monty's view that it might be central to the mystery of Keren's death; rather, she'd felt strongly that it might be more useful for the reading group to examine it, especially as it resonated so clearly with her earlier notion that the whole weekend was like one big iteration of that board game. (The name would come to her eventually.)

Consequently, she'd felt no compunction about purloining the item from under Monty's nose while he was otherwise occupied.

Now she drew it from her bag in the conservatory with a flourish that Fforde would probably have deemed melodramatic and watched the reactions of her colleagues with pleasure.

'This,' she announced simply.

Harrison reached out immediately to take the candlestick from her. It was no surprise that he should be interested: it was, after all, the physical embodiment of the mysterious narrative she'd unfolded in the kitchen before lunch. It was a shame he'd planted his grubby mitts all over it, especially for a man who'd been so careful to preserve the evidence in the Felicity Penman case, but she was pretty sure it wouldn't have revealed any crucial fingerprints, even if the police had got their hands on it: her own rapid concealment of the curiosity in the billiard room had meant that she'd probably covered it in her own DNA anyway, and any remaining evidence would surely have been wiped off by the lining of her bag.

The damage was already done.

Meanwhile, Lauren's mouth gaped, although whether it was in awe of Bella's audacity or amazement at her stupidity, Bella could not currently tell.

But in the Professor's eyes she saw a flash of recognition and knew she had finally got her reaction.

'That's the medieval candlestick from the lounge,' he said, his eyes widening.

'I don't know where it came from originally, but it was in the billiard room when I found it,' said Bella.

'They've got replicas of it in the gift shop. I saw them earlier, before I went chasing after footprints.'

'Footprints?' queried Lauren, her head whipping to look at Stone. 'Do you mean the ones going out from the kitchen door into the garden?'

'You saw those? I spotted them from the gift shop. They didn't make any sense.'

'Because they only went one way?' asked Lauren.

'Exactly.'

'How many sets of prints were there when you saw them?'

The Professor looked thoughtful. 'Only one – why?'

'Because when I noticed them from the kitchen there were three sets.'

'One will have been mine,' Stone replied thoughtfully, 'but that means someone else followed them out too.'

'Olive,' suggested Fforde. 'We watched her raking them over while we were doing the washing up.'

Bella was worried her moment of triumph might be being lost in all the discussion around footprints.

'Never mind footprints,' she said. 'How on earth did the candlestick from the lounge get into the billiard room in the tower when it was locked the whole time?'

Professor Stone shook his head.

'All right, let's not get all Sherlock Holmes about it, shall we? There's obviously some straightforward explanation to both the candlestick and the footprints. We just don't have all the parts of the jigsaw yet, that's all.'

Bella didn't want to let it go that easily.

'You admit there is a bit of a mystery, though, don't you, Professor?'

'Maybe.'

She counted her thoughts off on her fingers. 'Keren Lowe is dead and nobody knows why; the billiard room is empty but at the same time full of unanswered questions; and we've got footprints in the snow implicating people in this house doing all kinds of unexplained things. Now I agree all that may not quite be in the same category as murder, but it's definitely what I'd call a mystery. And without any police or contact with the outside world, it would make sense for us to do a bit of investigating ourselves, wouldn't it?'

Fforde looked up from the candlestick, which he was

turning over in his hand like Nigel Havers on *The Bidding Room*.

'Almost churlish not to,' he agreed.

'I'm so glad you said that, Bella,' added Lauren, taking the candlestick out of Fforde's hands and wielding it two-handed like a baseball bat.

Bella sighed. Definitely nothing left for the forensics officers now.

Lauren swung vaguely at an imaginary ball inches from Fforde's head and he ducked involuntarily.

'Hey, watch what you're doing with that. It's probably priceless.'

Professor Stone leaned gently across and relieved Lauren of the historic piece. Ah, the full set of prints.

'I don't know about priceless but it could certainly do Harrison quite a bit of damage if you misjudged your swing. Now, as I was saying, let's not start probing something that doesn't need probing.'

'Who says it doesn't need probing, Professor?' Lauren was looking mildly annoyed that he'd taken away her toy. 'I've been wondering what Simon might be doing right now if he were here.'

'Your brother?' The mention of his name caught Bella's attention.

'What do you think, Bella? Would he be sitting around doing nothing or would he be putting his mind to solving the mystery?'

Bella thought back to the crucial role Lauren's brother had played in the investigation into Felicity Penman's murder. His somewhat dubious computer hacking skills had proved invaluable in tracking down the months and years leading up to the horrific attack on the bookshop manager, and she suspected that without him they might never have got to the bottom of the puzzle. Besides that – and notwithstanding the young man's past as a temporary guest in one of His Majesty's more genteel custodial establishments – he'd seemed a very nice boy with a promising future.

What would he be doing in these circumstances? she wondered.

'He'd be asking questions,' she said, her confidence increasing that there really was something more going on than a straightforward family tragedy.

'Such as?' Fforde asked eagerly.

'Well, what was Olive doing, for a start? Why was she raking over the footprints in the garden?'

Lauren joined in. 'Bit suspicious, definitely. And what about the rope? I've been wondering how she could have screamed with that round her neck.'

'Maybe she screamed right up to the point where it went taut,' said Fforde, shivering slightly. 'And then snapped.'

Bella could feel herself getting into her stride. 'Where we were in the secret passage, we had no way of telling if the scream came from inside the tower, before she jumped, or as she fell down the outside. We should probably ask one of the others who heard it from above ground.'

'Or maybe it wasn't Keren who screamed at all,' offered Lauren with wide eyes and a trembling voice.

Bella's own voice came out almost as a whisper. 'You still think someone else might have been up there with her?'

'No, no, no,' said Professor Stone testily. 'This is all getting completely out of hand. There may be questions, I'll give you that much, but let's not get ahead of ourselves. There's nothing to suggest we're dealing with another murder here.'

'Are you sure about that, Professor?' asked Lauren. 'Just think about the events leading up to Keren's death. Ronnie seemed convinced she'd been a bit off, but Hemingford Grey said she was enjoying a new lease of life. We've got two conflicting stories right there – that's suspicious in itself.'

'Hang on a minute—' Bella began, alarmed at the implication that Ronnie might somehow be involved in something suspicious.

'Plus,' Lauren went on, ignoring Bella and holding up a finger as if she had conclusive proof, 'there's still the question of what that note said.'

'Which note?' asked Fforde.

'The one Grey gave her when we were all in the lounge listening to Siobhan. Don't you remember? He came in while we were looking at the goat in the cornice and handed her a note.'

Bella's stomach turned over.

'That was the last time we saw her alive.'

Fforde screwed up his face as if trying to recall the moment. 'Didn't he say Lord Verity had sent her the note – that he wanted to see her?'

'He did,' said Bella slowly. 'But Ronnie told me Lord Verity was snoring away at that time this morning. And why did he want to talk to her anyway? Why send her a note and not just speak to her?'

The Professor intervened. 'Nothing unusual about that. He was always leaving notes for the staff, apparently. Grey told me.'

'So what did Lord Verity want?' Bella repeated. 'Did she even go to see him? He and his wife were in bed all morning, after all.'

Lauren was quick to worm out the ramifications.

'Let's just think about this. Nobody saw the Veritys or Ronnie before Keren's death, right? Ronnie and Lady Verity are each other's alibis, and they can also vouch for the whereabouts of Lord Verity.'

Fforde grunted dismissively. 'It's a presumption that the snoring was Lord Verity. And in any case, we've only got Ronnie's word for any of that.'

Bella was about to express her mounting dismay at the various suggestions that her sister might be trying to conceal something when another possibility crept enticingly into her mind, one that she was aware had little basis in evidence but that snagged at her brain like a kitten teasing a ball of wool.

'Unless the whole note thing was a ruse made up by Hemingford Grey,' she said solemnly.

Three pairs of eyes turned on her. The expressions behind them ranged from confusion to bewilderment, stopping at all stations in between including scepticism, perplexity and even stupefaction.

It was the Professor who voiced their shared befuddlement.

'Why on earth would he do that? What are you suggesting, Bella?'

Even as she spoke, she didn't really know the answer.

'I'm not sure, Professor. I just can't shake the feeling that something's not right about this whole thing. Keren didn't seem to me like someone who was about to kill themselves, and the only clue we've got as to what really happened up in the billiard room is Hemingford Grey turning up with a supposed note from his Lordship asking to see her. Doesn't that seem odd to you?'

'Well, that's easy enough to check out,' said Lauren brightly. 'We'll find Hemingford Grey and ask him if he knew what the note said.'

'I've already done that,' replied the Professor. 'He didn't.'

'Lord Verity, then?'

Bella decided it was time for action. 'I'll go.'

Stone lifted a warning hand to calm the rising anxieties in the conservatory. 'If anyone's going to speak to Lord Verity about all this – and that's a big if – then it'll be me. We need to tread carefully before we go throwing around unsubstantiated ideas about his household. I'll find some quiet moment later on and ask them a sensitive question or two. In the meantime, nobody else is to go blundering about upsetting the staff. Understood?'

Bella's disappointment robbed her of the sense of urgency she'd felt a moment earlier, and she sat down heavily in one of the garden chairs that served for furniture in the conservatory.

'I'm only trying to make sense of it all,' she said forlornly. 'If it looks like a mystery and sounds like a mystery, doesn't that make it a mystery?'

The Professor stood up. It was evidently his turn to take charge of the room.

'It might be a mystery, but it's not the same kind of mystery that we had to deal with before. In the absence of any concrete clues to the contrary, the likeliest narrative is that Keren Lowe tragically took her own life, for reasons we may never understand. Now, in order not to upset our hosts unnecessarily, we need to adopt a cautious approach. If we're going to explore anything, our line of enquiry should be along the lines of *why* she killed herself, rather than whether. Can I get everyone's agreement on that?'

But Bella was only half-listening. Behind Stone, outside in the garden, a scene was unfolding that would obliterate all the notions, theories and cautious approaches they had spent the last half-hour considering.

In the oppressive gloom of impending dusk, Olive, the gardener, was dragging a large wheelbarrow towards them across the snow-covered lawn.

In the wheelbarrow was slumped the lifeless figure of Hemingford Grey.

II

The gaping hole in Grey's chest suggested persuasively to Fforde that he had been murdered.

Lauren and Bella let out a simultaneous cry of horror – pitched almost precisely an octave apart, Fforde registered bizarrely – and both turned away from the conservatory window. The sight of their second bloodied body of the day, its limbs trailing helplessly over the sides of the wheelbarrow, its lifeless eyes gawping unseeingly at the dimming light and a concave pit where its ribs should have been, was clearly too much for them.

By contrast, a grim fascination led Fforde to follow the Professor outside and stare at the ghastliness.

He quickly came to the conclusion that there was little point investigating the possibility that Hemingford Grey might still be alive. Olive had left a trail of red in the snow behind her wheelbarrow, and it seemed reasonable to assume that she would already have ascertained this basic piece of information about her cargo.

Stone investigated it nevertheless, rushing over to take the man's arm and feel for a pulse. At least, Fforde presumed that was what he was doing: the closest he'd ever actually got to a real medic performing that function had been when he'd landed a non-speaking role in *Casualty* as 'Man walking dog' when a pile-up of three ambulances occurred, leaving one of the regular characters in a coma and on the brink between life and death for several episodes while the actor concerned dealt with a particularly virulent case of narcotic attachment. Fforde had stood by, a horrified expression plastered onto his face, while a paramedic held the wrist of another supporting artist before shaking her head meaningfully at her colleague. Everyone understood what that head shake meant: the supporting artist had bitten the dust.

At least Fforde had had something to do, wrangling the horny dachshund they'd given him.

Now Professor Stone gave the same head shake towards Olive, even though the gardener must have known full well that Hemingford Grey had similarly departed this mortal coil in a motion closely akin to shuffling.

With no dachshund to divert him, Fforde felt duty-bound to look at the body in the wheelbarrow.

'He's dead, then?'

Stone grunted. 'I don't think we need Poirot to tell us that.'

'Murdered.'

'Again, not exactly a Marple-level deduction.'

'So—'

'So what?'

The Professor stood from his crouching position by the wheelbarrow and faced Fforde, who felt the same pang of intimidation as the first time he'd met Stone – an older, wiser, more charismatic and generally nicer person than he ever considered himself to be. Fforde had spent most of his life trying to emulate his idols in the world of theatre and had only in recent years come round to accepting that he was never going to be Anthony Hopkins or Ralph Fiennes. In fact, he'd decided, he wouldn't have wanted to be them anyway: all that pressure, attention, fame, money, adulation, glamour…

'So can we agree there's something bloody funny going on?'

Olive spoke for the first time since arriving with her consignment.

'Two murders on the same day? With nobody able to come or go from the estate? I should say there's something funny going on.'

Bella leaned out of the conservatory door, avoiding eye contact with the corpse and addressing herself instead to Olive.

'You think Keren was murdered too, do you?'

Olive put the handles of the barrow down and looked a little sheepish, as if she'd said something she shouldn't.

'Never doubted it. She wasn't the type to kill herself. And besides, there's too many things that don't fit.'

Questions were dancing around Fforde's head like a crazed flamenco dancer, and most of them were aimed at Olive.

'Where did you find him?' was the first one to break free of his cranium and land with the gardener.

She waved vaguely towards the drive. 'Back there, just off the road in a clump of laurel trees.'

'And was he like this when you found him?'

Olive shot him a steely look. 'Are you suggesting he was upright and vocal when I met him, and somehow ended up like this?'

Fforde hadn't been going to suggest that at all, even if he was thinking something approximating it. He did, however, find it interesting that Olive herself had raised the image in everyone's minds.

Olive reached down into the wheelbarrow beside the body and pulled something out. At first, Fforde couldn't work out what it was. It looked like a piece of wood, about six inches long and half an inch in diameter, with one rounded end and the other broken as if it had been snapped off something. The reason for Fforde's initial confusion was that the rounded end was coated with a thick layer of dried blood.

'I found this nearby,' said Olive.

Professor Stone stared at the object in her hand and spoke slowly. 'You think that's what killed him?'

Olive offered the stick up to the hole in Grey's chest. Fforde could see immediately that it had been used repeatedly to create a sizeable crater, but where the individual entry points were distinguishable, they matched the end of the stick pretty closely.

'My God,' said Stone. 'Someone really wanted to do some damage.'

Another question had popped up in Fforde's mind, and he asked it before considering whether it was a wise thing to do at that precise moment.

'Why were you raking the snow earlier on, Olive?'

Before she had a chance to reply, the Professor leaped in to interrupt Fforde's line of questioning.

'Olive, before my friend goes hypothesising about what is or isn't amiss with this whole weekend, do you think we could do something about poor Mr Grey here?'

Olive scowled at Fforde before bending down with a sigh and picking up the handles again. 'I know, I know: another coffin for the chapel.'

When she'd moved out of earshot around the side of the house on her way to the chapel, Fforde asked, 'Why did you shoo her away? I thought things were just about to get interesting.'

'That was the problem,' said the Professor, banging his arms against the cold and heading towards the conservatory door, where Lauren and Bella were both looking shaken and pale. 'I didn't want her throwing in any red herrings until we'd had a chance to talk it through between ourselves. It would seem that there are numerous fingers of suspicion pointing in Olive's direction.'

They were all back inside now, and Fforde closed the door behind him to cut off the chilly blast that was invading the house.

'You don't seriously think Olive could have had anything to do with either of these deaths, do you, Professor?' There was a tremble in Bella's voice that might not have been entirely down to the cold.

Stone's reply reduced the temperature in the room by another degree or two.

'Right now, the only people I trust in this entire house are the three of you.'

Lauren shivered. 'That's a horrible thought, Professor.'

'Horrible, but true. Since we got out of bed this morning,

two people have died. One was murdered, without a shadow of a doubt, and it's looking increasingly likely that there was something suspicious about the other one.'

Fforde couldn't believe that the Professor was still entertaining any doubts about the nefarious end of Keren Lowe. He really could be obstinate sometimes: if the idea hadn't come from him, it was going to take a lot of persuading to convince him of the fact that everyone else in the reading group could plainly see.

'Of course she was murdered as well. It's all too obvious, isn't it? The scream that Lauren so observantly mentioned – why would she cry out if she was trying to do away with herself? And the rope ripping in such an odd way, making it look conveniently like an accident. Then there's the mysterious reappearing candlestick, not to mention Lord Verity's note.'

'Ah yes, the note,' said the Professor. 'There's a new twist on that, now, isn't there?'

'What do you mean?' asked Lauren.

'Well, a few minutes ago, Bella was convinced the whole note thing was a ruse dreamed up by Hemingford Grey to get Keren out of the lounge.'

Bella looked hurt. 'I wouldn't say I was convinced of it, but it did seem a little strange.'

She turned to Lauren as if for moral support.

'It did, you're right,' said the younger woman.

Fforde said, 'The Professor's right, too, though. It doesn't make sense for Grey to have lured Keren away as he's now become the second victim.'

Bella shuddered. 'Oh, don't say that.'

'What, *victim*?'

'Yes.'

'Why not?'

'Because, dear Harrison, it's a stark reminder that two people are dead in the chapel and the person who killed them is chatting away to the rest of the guests in there.'

She pointed towards the main house.

Fforde could feel a familiar sense of trying to wrestle with mist. Among the people mourning the death of Keren Lowe was someone who had recently dispatched Hemingford Grey to join her in the ranks of the unalive. Who they were, and what possible reason they might have to do such a thing, were questions beyond his comprehension.

Fortunately, he had a few sharp-minded fellow sleuths standing around who might just be able to help.

'Why would anyone want to kill the gift shop manager?' he asked, his voice betraying the horror that was starting to sink in at the sight of the second body of the day.

'Why indeed,' intoned Professor Stone gravely. 'He had intimated to me this morning that the house held secrets – and I'm not talking about the priest holes and inscriptions. Maybe he knew too much about something he shouldn't have.'

'What do you mean?' asked Lauren timidly.

'I mean, maybe he had learned of one of those secrets, and the person whose secret it was didn't like him knowing.'

'So they killed him?'

Bella sounded impressed. 'It's a theory.'

Fforde was less complimentary. 'So is the notion that he wandered into the woods, ran into that film location manager, who'd got lost in the snow and gone mad since setting off for help and murdered Hemingford thinking he was a serial killer escaped from a nearby lunatic asylum.'

'Now you're just being silly,' said Bella.

'No sillier than thinking anyone other than Olive killed him. It's perfectly obvious, isn't it? She claims to have found him, she's even brought the murder weapon with her from the scene, like some low-budget Macbeth, and now she's carted off her victim's body so she can hide any evidence and dress him up nicely before the law arrives. Really, Professor, I do think you might have thought it through a bit more before you sent her away.'

Stone's face reddened and Fforde wondered if he'd gone too far. Or maybe he was embarrassed at his blunder.

'I think we might be getting a bit ahead of ourselves,' he said through gritted teeth. 'It might just as easily have been one of the household – or even our host himself.'

'Lord Verity?' spluttered Fforde. 'I don't think so.'

'Why not?' parried Stone. 'Think about it: if he's been having some extramarital rumpy-pumpy with one of the household and Grey found out, wouldn't that be enough motive to silence him?'

Lauren sounded eager. 'Maybe Hemingford was blackmailing him. Maybe he arranged to meet Lord Verity in the grounds, where nobody could hear their conversation, and threatened to reveal the whole thing unless he coughed up lots of money.'

'And how do you explain Keren?' said Fforde, not bothering to disguise the disdain in his voice.

'The extramarital rumpy-pumpy?' suggested Bella, looking between Fforde and Stone like a tennis umpire.

Fforde could feel his patience draining away like the blood from Hemingford Grey's chest wound.

'So Lord Verity killed his mistress, then murdered an employee who tried to extort money from him? And you think that's more likely than the gardener in the grounds with a wooden stake? I know Jack Nicholson went barmy in the snow in *The Shining*, but I didn't think I'd live to see the three of you go the same way. And what makes you so certain it's Lord Verity? It'd be much more interesting if the one who was having the affair was his wife. Maybe *she* was sleeping with Keren and bumped off Grey to keep it secret.'

Fforde was floating ridiculous ideas in an attempt to demonstrate the clear evidence leading to Olive.

He never expected anyone to take him seriously.

'Lesbians, you mean?' asked Bella, looking thrilled. 'Gosh.'

'No, Bella, I wasn't being serious. I was merely pointing out the ludicrousness of any other suspects. You might as well try and argue it was those two American idiots.'

'You might,' said the Professor slowly. 'And isn't that the point? Right now, while we're arguing about motives and marital misdemeanours, somebody in that house is getting away with murder.'

Bella shuddered again. 'What are we going to do, Professor?'

He thought for a moment.

'Well, for a start, we're not going to panic. Let's remember that the vast majority of the people in the house are not double-murderers.'

'Cold comfort,' muttered Fforde. He found the fact that there was a killer on the loose substantially more alarming than the Professor's mathematical logic implied.

'What it means is that we outnumber the perpetrator by a considerable margin. If we all stick together and don't give him—'

'Or her,' interjected Lauren.

'—or her the chance to strike again, we stand a decent chance of making it out of here alive.'

'There's a sentence I wasn't expecting to hear this weekend,' said Fforde.

Stone ignored him. Probably for the best, Fforde thought: he wasn't feeling his most chipper or constructive at this precise moment. He'd been eagerly anticipating a weekend of celebrity status, hobnobbing with Hollywood types who might just offer a glimpse of a revitalised career, and, if all went well, some fine wines from the cellars of one of the minor country houses of England. He'd already had one taste of Lord Verity's collection and it had proved considerably superior to Fforde's own stock of Sainsbury's plonk in a plastic bag under the sink. Now, though, instead of enjoying another slightly sozzled evening in the pleasurable company of a gutsy Shiraz or smooth vintage Bordeaux, all he had to look forward to was a night of mutual mistrust and abject terror. If the weather didn't change soon, it might even be longer than that before the emergency services could be summoned and another killer brought to justice under the noses of the reading group. It wasn't that he hadn't derived some gratification from his part in solving Felicity's murder. On the contrary, the resulting publicity had revived in him something of the thrill of his early days in theatre, when he occasionally found himself mentioned in reviews (it didn't matter whether the crit was favourable or otherwise as long as his name was there in print). But there was a limit to how much excitement one could take from such exploits, particularly when the exploits concerned involved the violent demise of people in one's near vicinity, and that vicinity was severed from the outside world with the culprit on the loose.

'We have to warn the others and then decide as a group what we're going to do,' said Professor Stone.

It wasn't hard to assemble the rest of the household and guests in the ballroom. Fforde felt a sense of *déjà vu* about the whole business but he was glad to see Bella looking so relieved at being reunited with her sister. Ronnie, for her part, seemed somewhat less enthusiastic, but Fforde put that down to her feeling the loss of a co-worker she'd known for some time more heavily than those of the group who were mere visitors this weekend. Lord and Lady Verity were grim-faced and everyone seemed to be allowing them space where they sat to one side on high-backed chairs in plush red velvet. Most were standing in an anxious huddle in the middle of the floor, although the two remaining Americans stood a little apart from the crowd, whispering to one another and fiddling with the handheld video recorder Marin Cypher was carrying. If they'd wanted to place themselves in the suspicious category, Fforde reflected, they could hardly have found a more convincing way of doing it. Except by disappearing in a pair of wellingtons earlier that morning and not being heard of since. Now that really *was* suspicious.

Just what had happened to old leather-face?

Stone was in his element. His only obstacle to complete supremacy was Monty Butler, whose position as estate manager clearly gave him an advantage when it came to jurisdiction. If it had all been down to charisma, Stone would have claimed the crown outright; as it was, it was a matter of a few minutes to establish that he regarded himself as the most senior-ranked among the gathered throng – the Veritys' titles notwithstanding – and he asserted himself accordingly.

'Ladies and gentlemen,' he called from the second step of the low staircase that led to the raised stage at one end of the ballroom. Fforde noted that he didn't ascend the stage itself: that would have appeared crass and uncouth, and the Professor had no need of such gimmicks to demonstrate his authority.

The hubbub fell silent. Fforde glanced around and registered that everyone on the guest list and employed by the house was present, with the sole exception of Olive, who would probably be banging nails into a makeshift coffin even as he thought about it.

'I'm afraid I have bad news to share with you. It would appear that Keren Lowe's death was not the tragic suicide it seemed. In fact, there is good reason to believe that she was murdered.'

Like the good amateur thespian Fforde had discovered the Professor to be, he left a dramatic pause exactly where it was required.

The room erupted.

There was something gratifying to Fforde, even at one remove, in seeing an audience respond like this. The members of the household staff looked at each other in disbelief before breaking out into a hysterical melange of shrieks and wails; Lord and Lady Verity leaped to their feet and began to remonstrate with Professor Stone; the Americans found it hard to control their enthusiasm for the new development, capturing everything and everyone on the camcorder.

The one still figure in the centre of the chaos was Siobhan Butler, a single tear rolling down one cheek.

Stone waved his hands for calm and the noise died down, leaving Lady Verity's high-pitched voice cutting through with the end of a sentence: '… do they think they are?'

If the remark was aimed at him, Stone gave no sign of acknowledging it.

He ploughed on.

'What you will all, no doubt, have immediately realised is that nobody, in this weather, could have arrived at Abbots Chantry, performed the deadly deed and departed again. Which means…'

Another pause.

'… that the killer is still among us.'

The second eruption was even more chaotic than the first, with everyone looking around the room accusingly. Since they all naturally had a clear conscience, Fforde calculated, they could feel entirely justified in placing the blame on someone else nearby. Anyone else.

Except that one of them was pretending.

'Please, please,' shouted Professor Stone. 'There's no point in trying to guess who the killer might be. We don't have any clues and there doesn't seem to be any evidence.'

'Then how do you know she was murdered?' asked Monty, a challenging note in his question.

'Because – and I'm sorry to break more bad news to you all – she isn't the only one.'

'What?' Lord Verity's voice boomed across the ballroom. He was on his feet now and approaching Stone on the steps. 'Are you telling us that someone else is dead?'

'I'm afraid so, your Lordship.'

Fforde watched as all eyes scanned the room for absences. He'd done a mental checklist of the people present before Stone started speaking, but he had the advantage over the others: he, Lauren and Bella already knew that it was only the gardener who was not there, beavering away in the chapel.

Apart from the second victim, of course. But then they knew who he was too.

'Not Olive?' said Siobhan suddenly. 'It's Olive, isn't it?'

For a moment, Fforde thought the Professor was going to lose control of the room. The prospect of Olive having been murdered seemed to send even more of a horrified shiver through the household than Keren's death had a few hours earlier. It was interesting to note that perhaps the least assuming of the employees had the potential to cause the most upset.

'No, ladies and gentlemen – please calm down,' shouted Stone. He had to raise his volume considerably higher than it had been before to be heard above the noise.

'It's not Olive. It's Hemingford Grey.'

Ronnie let out a scream.

In the confusion that followed, two things caught Fforde's attention. The first was the immediate attention that Siobhan gave to Lady Verity: even in her grieving state of mind, she rushed over and began fussing around her employer, fanning her face and plumping a cushion behind her neck to make her more comfortable. This was a woman clearly devoted to her mistress, and in the days of *Downton Abbey* (Fforde's only real reference point for such an era) she might have been what was loosely termed a 'companion'. Fforde had some vague notion that the word might have been a euphemism for other, more sapphic, implications, but either way, Siobhan was obviously a reassuring shoulder for Lady Verity to lean on.

The second thing to catch his attention – and where the first had merely interested him, this properly riled him – was that the Americans had immediately flipped into working mode and were filming the mayhem in the ballroom. In itself, that would not have provoked a strong reaction in him. Two movie men capturing heightened emotions on camera was par for the course as far as he was concerned. The bit that seriously put his nose out of joint – and it didn't take much, having been broken during a soccer game in younger days when the cast of a touring *Charley's Aunt* challenged the stage crew to a match that turned out more *Rollerball* than football – was *who* they were filming.

Posing in front of the video recorder, her best journalistic face to camera, stood Lauren.

'What are you doing?' he shouted, hurrying over to where his erstwhile colleague appeared to have stabbed him in the back with the Americans for the second time that day. 'This isn't an audition – it's a true-crime drama.'

He grabbed Lauren's arm and was on the point of guiding her forcefully away from the film crew when Colorado Hughes stepped forward. Whether he was fired up by the maelstrom of emotions in the ballroom or simply protecting his newest *protégé* Fforde couldn't tell, but he was ready for a confrontation.

'Hey, man, what's your beef?' he asked, the lazy drawl now promoted to something more like agitation.

'My beef?' Fforde looked at the man, trying to work out if he'd be able to take him in a scuffle. He thought he might be about three inches taller but the director had the kind of stocky, bulldog frame that seemed to work advantageously in fights. At least, fights Fforde had seen in films. He'd never seen a fight in real life – never even attended a boxing match – so couldn't really vouch for the veracity of the trope but now he came to consider it he decided he didn't want to put the theory to the test.

'No beef. I just wanted to have a word with Lauren.'

By the time Fforde had eased her away from the camera and back towards the dais, joining Bella at the foot of the steps, Stone had restored order in the ballroom.

'I know this is frightening for everyone,' he announced after filling them in on the manner of Hemingford Grey's death – leaving out the gorier details of his wounds – 'but we need to stay calm and rational.'

He looked at the Americans, still filming proceedings on their camera. 'Gentlemen, I'm sure it would help lower the temperature if you wouldn't mind not filming everyone in the midst of a crisis.'

Marin seemed uncertain and looked to Colorado for

guidance. A small nod from the director and the cinematographer dropped his device from his eye but Fforde noticed its little red indicator was still winking as he held it at waist level, scanning the room for reactions.

'Thank you,' said the Professor. 'Now, we have some decisions to make. Because of the weather, nobody is able to leave Abbots Chantry – at least not for the foreseeable future. We have to hope that our American friend has managed to get off the estate on foot and is, even now, reaching civilisation to send help. But we can't assume we're going to be rescued any time soon, and it certainly seems unlikely that anyone will get here today. Which means we have to work out how we're going to spend the rest of the day and, more importantly, the night.'

The idea that they were all going to have to share the house with a killer had evidently not occurred to some of the occupants. Even Fforde hadn't fully appreciated the gravity of their situation but as the notion sank in, he began to grasp just how serious it was. If they split up, they were laying themselves open to being picked off by whichever murderous guest had already bumped off two of their number. If they all stayed together, they would be sharing a room with the killer in plain sight.

Neither option seemed attractive.

Fortunately for Fforde, the decision was taken out of their hands. While Monty was firmly in favour of everyone staying in the lounge for the night, with Siobhan and Ronnie setting up makeshift beds on the various settees and chairs, Lord and Lady Verity were adamant: no guest of theirs was going to hunker down in an improvised campsite, no matter how comfortable the furnishings. Nobody under their roof was going to be treated with suspicion, as if any of them might be a murderer. And – the clincher as far as their highnesses were concerned – they wouldn't be seen dead in their pyjamas in front of guests.

'Rather unfortunate choice of words,' Fforde whispered.

In spite of the chilling circumstances, Bella giggled.

III

Professor Stone liked to think of himself as a tolerant man but the Americans were severely testing his patience. He'd encountered examples of the nation's boundless exuberance before, not least among the international students who had regularly infiltrated his lectures, and never ceased to be amazed at their confidence in their country's exceptionalism.

America, it seemed, was best at everything.

Despite the lack of evidence to back up such claims, Stone had been able to let them pass him by without being niggled unduly. Even the brash loudness and sartorial misguidedness of many of their number left him unmoved. But when, as now, they simply refused to respond to reason or suggestion, no matter how logical or well-founded the arguments, he rapidly felt his self-restraint ebbing away and his nerves rising to a state of jangling resentment.

To be fair, it wasn't just Americans. It wasn't even all Americans.

But it definitely was Colorado Hughes and Marin Cypher.

He knew he shouldn't let it bother him but even their names got under his skin. He'd never understood people who branded their children with a place name – the Brooklyn Beckhams or Paris Hiltons of this world – and couldn't fathom why anyone thought it might be romantic or evocative. Then again, British place names hardly had the exotic qualities of some of the more *outré* foreign locations. Even the most diehard patriots would surely balk at christening their offspring Battersea or Clacton or Scunthorpe. Maybe Colorado and Marin weren't so outrageous after all.

And he could hardly complain about other people's forenames when he'd spent so much of his life concealing his own. Embarrassed and bullied at school, he'd considered changing it by deed poll when he first went to university, or simply lying about it to make it seem more normal, but a girlfriend in college had introduced him to Colin Dexter's first Morse novel, *Last Bus to Woodstock*, and his view of his name changed instantly. Instead of a millstone round his neck, it could be something intriguing and mysterious with which to lure new friends and lovers, teasing them with a corner of his identity that reeked beguilingly of unknowability. And so he had lived his life, an ineffable enigma to even his closest associates. He recalled how he'd even kept it private when he filled in his customer details for Felicity, and so far he'd managed to persuade the other members of the reading group to call him simply Professor, never divulging the full name behind the initial E. The few people who had ever called him by it were now distant memories.

Professor E. Stone was just fine with him.

'So you're telling us that Olive is alive?' Hughes had said when the main discussion had broken up into smaller groups.

Stone hadn't bothered to grace that with an answer.

Members of the household gravitated towards each other; Bella and Ronnie paired off for a sisterly confab, while Fforde and Lauren picked up where they left off with the exchange of mutual irritation that had preceded the decision-making about where they were all going to spend the night. Stone didn't understand what they were quibbling about but he had bigger things to think about just now and sat down on the dais to work it all out in his head.

For the third time, and in spite of the Veritys' insistence on country-house etiquette, he went over the arguments for and against splitting up overnight. Each bedroom had its own lock and could be fortified from the inside against possible intruders. He would advise everyone to push something heavy against their doors and make sure they'd used the bathroom before shutting themselves away: pity anyone with a nighttime call to micturition.

Maybe the house had chamber pots. He'd check with Siobhan.

Conversely, there was clearly safety in numbers. Anyone with a mind to murder would have their work cut out for them in a lounge containing more than a dozen sleeping people, although he found, worryingly, that he could easily imagine a scenario in which a killer might move silently among them in the early hours, slipping a sharp kitchen knife into the heart of a slumbering victim while placing a hand over their mouth to prevent involuntary noises.

Or maybe the fatal instrument would be something even

more unpremeditated. Hell, even the gift shop had reproduction daggers which, while understandably blunted under health-and-safety requirements, could prove perfectly serviceable as a murder weapon. He ran through a mental checklist of other potential implements – revolver, wrench, lead piping and so on – and discarded them as either too noisy or too cumbersome for easy use in a crowded space.

No, if the killer was going to strike again, it would be with a blade.

To make it feasible to stay together in the lounge, they'd have to take turns keeping watch.

In fact, he realised, they'd have to take turns keeping watch in pairs: no individual (the reading group excepted) could be trusted on their own.

'So where is she?'

The Americans were hassling again.

'Who?'

'Olive. Haven't you been listening?'

Stone looked down at the director and frowned. The man had evidently been jabbering away at the bottom of the steps while the Professor was contemplating what should happen next.

'She's busy. Dealing with … Mr Grey.'

'Oh, right. The stiff.'

Stone winced. He'd left Olive in the chapel with 'the stiff', preparing to build a second coffin to go beside the first one, where Keren Lowe was sleeping the dreamless sleep of the dead. Before gathering everyone together in the ballroom, he'd got the gardener to show him where she'd found Hemingford Grey's body, a hundred yards or so from the house in a clump of laurel trees just off the main drive, exactly as she'd described to Fforde. The ground had been disturbed, as if there'd been a scuffle, but the snow hadn't penetrated into the trees and the killer had evidently fled the scene in that direction, leaving behind no telltale footprints to follow. He and Olive had agreed there were no further clues on offer here and had returned to the house to deal with the fallout.

'Say, do you mind if we take a look at the deceased? I think it might give us some hard-hitting coverage for our movie.'

Stone stared at Colorado Hughes. 'I thought you were making a feature film?'

'We were. But plans change. You gotta stay on your toes in this business. That's what separates the weak from the chaps, as they say.'

Stone would have loved to correct him but the man hadn't taken a breath.

'Yesterday it was *Murder on the Polar Express*. Today? Well, when something as juicy as this drops in your lap, suddenly you become a documentary maker. One body was great, even if it was an easily explained suicide. Two – especially when one of them has had his guts ripped out – is just peachy. Just need to find the right producer when we get out of here and we could be lining up for a Golden Globe. Smart, huh?'

The Professor had his own ideas about what smart might look like in this situation but he didn't suppose the American would pay him any attention even if he were to bestow the benefit of his decades of wisdom from the front lines of social interaction.

In spite of his distaste for the American's insensitivity, he opted for non-committal.

'If you say so.'

'I do say so. Now, about this corpse…'

Stone stood up on the dais, looking down on Hughes and his compatriot from the tallest height he could muster, and spoke slowly and clearly.

'Mr Hughes—'

'It's Colorado,' said the director. 'The only person that calls me Mr Hughes is my mom.'

Stone let the flimsy joke slide by unremarked.

'Mr Hughes,' he repeated. 'I take it that what you're requesting is the chance to view the bodies of two murder victims, currently housed in the most dignified surroundings we could rustle up for them, although that's not saying much, unfortunately. You wish to survey them not for the purposes of conveying your condolences or paying your respects, but merely to gather footage for a documentary you think you might be able to sell about the appalling events that have unfolded here in this house over the past few hours.'

Hughes looked like he was about to speak but the Professor went on without giving him the chance.

'The idea, Mr Hughes, is utterly grotesque and macabre. It smacks of sensationalism and gratuitous voyeurism and any self-respecting filmmaker would be ashamed at even suggesting the possibility of videoing the human remains of such a tragic incident. It is clear to me that you and your team have little to no self-respect, while your treatment of my friends here has revealed you to be opportunistic charlatans at best, morbid ghouls at worst. In your pursuit of a photogenic spokesperson you have chosen to ignore Harrison's obvious talents as a performer in favour of the superficial charms of

Lauren's youth and vitality, which shows a complete disrespect for both of them. Harrison should be an obvious leading man for any documentary; Lauren, meanwhile, is susceptible to being taken advantage of by an unscrupulous bandwagoner. In both instances, you have insulted their intelligence and, as their friend, I take exception to your methods, your intentions and your accents. Kindly remove yourselves from my presence and, if I were you, I'd take steps to stay out of my sight until we're finally rescued. If we ever are.'

Stone felt surprisingly good, even though it occurred to him too late that if either of the Americans had had anything to do with the two deaths, he had just put himself in pole position as the next victim.

Couldn't be helped now.

'Oh, and there's another thing,' he said, turning back to face the gaping pair. 'If either of you goes near the chapel or those bodies, I'll be reporting you for contaminating vital evidence in a double murder investigation.'

When he finished pontificating, Stone realised that the whole room had fallen silent.

He hadn't felt as powerful as this since throwing that student out of the lecture hall for breaking wind into the PA.

Dinner was a sombre affair. Gone were the best platters and glassware from the previous evening, swapped instead for some rudimentary crockery and mugs from the kitchen, where a trio of nervous impromptu chefs were dispatched to knock together something edible. Bella led the contingent, as she told the Professor, in order to relieve the burden on Siobhan, who still seemed to be in a state of shock from discovering that her sister's suicide had, in actual fact, been her murder. Stone had no idea how he'd have reacted in similar circumstances, but Siobhan seemed stoic enough and, indeed, overruled Bella's injunction to take it easy and followed her to the kitchen, accompanied by Monty. The three of them managed to put together a decent enough cold supper of meats, cheeses and bread, but conversation was sparse and everyone spent the hour or so afterwards under a gloom that matched the meteorological conditions.

Fforde drank too much, Stone noted, while he himself declined a second glass of the rather excellent claret that Monty offered him on the grounds that he wanted to keep his wits about him. He was a little irritated that the actor had allowed alcohol to be his chosen means of dealing with the situation: he'd have liked the team around him to be at the top of their game.

After all, it was going to be a long night.

In the end, Monty was overruled and, after a threadbare pretence at weighing up the Professor's pros and cons, Lord Verity had stuck to his guns with the resolution to pack everyone off to their own rooms. Stone had already made the decision to stay awake until next morning if he could, regardless of where they spent the night. Keeping everyone in the same room would have made things much simpler but there was to be no swaying the aristocrat's domestic principles.

Before everyone retired for the evening, Stone took the reading group to one side and whispered conspiratorially.

'I'm sure I don't need to tell you this but I want the three of you to be on extra special guard tonight. Harrison, do you think you'd be able to stay up all night?'

'Why are you picking on me?' he replied, hiccupping slightly.

'Because Bella and Lauren haven't been drinking so they're less likely to fall into a stupor.'

Fforde looked affronted. 'Are you suggesting I can't hold my liquor?'

'I wouldn't dream of suggesting any such thing,' said Stone. 'I just need you to be conscious. I don't want anyone trying any heroics, wandering about the house or anything like that, but it would be a great help if you could all listen out for anything untoward. With a bit of luck, we'll have a quiet night, but we can meet up in the morning to report back on anything suspicious. Does anyone have any questions?'

'Yes.' Lauren sounded anxious. 'What should we do if we hear another attack? We've got no way of communicating with each other and I don't think any of us would feel happy about doing nothing if we thought there was another murder under way.'

It was a tricky one. The Professor had already decided that he would be prepared to leap into action if he got a sniff of something strange happening in the house overnight, but he couldn't bear the thought of putting his friends in danger in the same way.

'I'd like to tell you to stay in your rooms and wait it out, but I think I know you all too well by now to believe that's going to happen. All I can say is that you have no responsibility for what's happened here today, and the fact that we once solved one murder doesn't mean that we're in any position to play detective again. We got lucky last time. I wouldn't want anyone to risk their lives on the off-chance we might get lucky again.'

Bella put her hand to his cheek and rested it there sweetly.

'Bless you, Professor. You can be so naïve sometimes.'

Making the bedtime arrangements was relatively easy, even if Stone retained a measure of apprehension about the decision to split up. With the exception of the Veritys themselves – who could presumably be relied on to look out for each other – all the staff were to be quartered in rooms along one corridor to the rear of the house, overlooking the stable yard and kitchen garden, while the guests and Olive (who had insisted she was not part of the household staff and therefore not subject to their billeting) were housed in more sumptuous lodgings at the front of the house, but again accessed from one shared landing. It was agreed, then, that the staff would go *en masse* to their corridor and the guests together to theirs before simultaneously entering their rooms, keeping one another in sight until the last possible moment. Once inside, they were to follow the Professor's previous instructions and barricade themselves in for the night.

As the staff headed off in one direction and the guests in another – shepherded, at Stone's request, by the other three members of the reading group – the Professor himself fell into step with Lord and Lady Verity, making their way to the private staircase off the main hall.

'Your Lordship,' he began, making the peer jump as he emerged at his right shoulder.

'Oh my goodness! Professor Stone,' said the nobleman. 'I thought you'd gone up with the rest of them?'

They seemed more than a little surprised to find him accompanying them but he made no effort to explain his actions, merely launched into his mission of diplomacy.

'I'll be following them shortly,' said Stone, adopting a tone of gravitas that he hoped would convey the seriousness of his line of questioning. He didn't want to alarm anyone unduly – Lady Verity in particular had had the skittish nerviness of a baby deer throughout dinner – but he needed to pursue the matter that had been raised by the reading group, and this seemed his best opportunity.

'I wanted to ask you a question.'

'As long as it's nothing personal,' said his Lordship.

'I hope not, but I can't make any promises.'

Lady Verity let out a small squeak of dismay.

'Professor Stone, what can you mean?'

'It's about the note you left for Keren Lowe on the hall table this morning – the one that Hemingford Grey delivered to her in the lounge.'

'What note? I didn't leave Keren a note. Not this morning, anyway.'

Professor Stone had not expected this response. During the long, chilly hour or so since dinner, he'd considered what he believed to be every eventuality surrounding the mysterious note, from an innocuous request for a meat preference at Sunday lunch to a dressing down for serving the wrong wine with Friday night's tiramisu. Personally, Stone found sparkling dessert wines a little too boisterous for his taste, and he suspected the same might be true of a conservative couple such as the Veritys, but he wouldn't have classed Moscato as a complete *faux pas*, and certainly not worthy of a written corrective the following morning. Stone had adjudged it unlikely fodder for the note but, sticking to Holmes's adage about the impossible and the improbable and ruling it improbable but not impossible, it remained on Stone's mental menu of possibilities. That menu had also included a wide range of potential spurs to suicide, both within Stone's sphere of knowledge and outside it, even though the Professor now wondered how he could ever have believed that the woman who'd sat at the dining table with them all yesterday, irritating her sister by goading the Americans, could have taken her own life.

Yes, he'd spent much of the day trying to insist that she'd done exactly that, and that they weren't trapped in a nightmarish weekend of horror, but in retrospect he could see how that had merely been a self-defence mechanism, trying to convince himself that history wasn't in the process of repeating.

He had to check. For his own sanity.

'You didn't leave a note on the hall table asking to see Keren?'

'I've told you, Professor, I didn't write her a note today.'

'Or last night for her to find this morning?'

Lord Verity gave a heavy sigh and turned to mount the first step.

'I'm sorry, Professor. I have no idea what happened to Keren, or why she died, but I can assure you that if you're pursuing some phantom note that I'm supposed to have left for her this morning, then you're very much barking up the wrong tree. Good night.'

It wasn't a phantom note. Stone had seen it with his own eyes, in Hemingford Grey's hands before he gave to Keren.

And now she was dead.

He had no idea what to make of it.

'Good night, Professor,' said Lady Verity, pausing before following her husband up the stairs. Her hand on his wrist felt wrong somehow; he should have been consoling her on the loss of two staff members, after all. 'Try and get some sleep.'

Even if he hadn't made a promise to himself to stay awake for the sake of protecting the household, Stone knew there was no way he'd be able to sleep. There were too many ghosts swirling around in his thoughts, too many unanswered questions battering at the door of his brain.

Was Lord Verity lying about not leaving a note for Keren? If so, did his wife know he was lying? Perhaps they were both consummate actors, putting Harrison Fforde to shame with their performances as grieving heads of the house, and the note he had just denied played some vital but as yet indecipherable part in the tragic death of Keren Lowe, and therefore, by extension, that of Hemingford Grey. Stone was a considerable number of miles away from establishing any kind of motive for his Lordship to do away with two of his staff, but that didn't rule it out as a possibility.

Or was he telling the truth, and he had no knowledge of the existence of the note? If so, what was the piece of paper that Grey had given Keren in the lounge? Grey had ruled himself out of suspicion over the murder of Keren by dint of the simple fact that he was now himself supine in a coffin next to hers in the creepy surroundings of the bewebbed chapel. At least, that seemed like a fair assumption to Stone, although it didn't quite fit Holmes's definition of impossible.

Either way, it was too late to ask him now.

Oh, how he would have loved to get the reading group together right now and start throwing ideas around about just what was going on in Abbots Chantry. What he would have given for a healthy dose of Bella's natural wisdom and common sense, or Lauren's youthful energy in pursuing particular lines of enquiry. He'd even have accepted the wild musings of their actor companion, often wide of the mark but frequently useful in nudging a train of thought in one of the others to set them on the right track eventually.

For now, though, under the stringent terms of his own edict, the reading group was out of bounds to him. He could consult them all again in the morning.

First, they had to survive the night.

… The Bedroom

1

The heavy click of the bedroom door behind her made the hair on Bella's neck stand on end. She didn't have much of it, and what there was tended towards the ultra-short, but she sensed the chilling feeling nonetheless.

Unless there was a draught coming from somewhere.

No, it was definitely the chills from closing her door to the outside world – and a double-murderer. In her huge bedroom, one of the many that ran across the front of the house overlooking the drive, lawns and entrance portico, she felt little safer than she had in the ballroom with the others. At least there they had enjoyed safety in numbers, even if one of those numbers was a killer. Here, in the cold and dark of a room that had barely changed for a century, she felt suddenly alone.

She checked her watch: just gone nine o'clock. With the house's limited power, and candles and lanterns providing most of their light, night had effectively fallen several hours earlier, and the anxious activity of the evening – from cobbling together a basic tea to watching the men debate the merits or otherwise of staying together in one room until morning – had made time stretch beyond its natural boundaries. She wouldn't have been surprised if her watch had told her it was past midnight.

Her first job was to lug some furniture about. Quite what Professor Stone expected of her, a woman of hardly monumental stature with a distinct shortage of muscles and a preference for sick notes on school sports days, she wasn't sure, but she would just have to make do.

Making do was something that was stitched deep in Bella Bourton. It was partly the result of several previous generations on her mother's side of women who'd left it very late to breed, forcing early maturity on their siblingless offspring to cater for their ageing progenitors before repeating itself in an unfortunate legacy of resigned stoicism, and partly the almost inevitable consequence of nineteen-and-a-bit years of marriage to Trevor Bourton. In hindsight, Bella could see clearly how the qualities she'd spun as resilience and fortitude were, in objective reality, a worn-down acceptance of drudgery and a dismal reliance on a feckless husband. Despite having freed herself from the yoke of plodding domesticity thanks in no small part to her involvement in the bookshop reading group, Bella found it harder to shake off the shackles of inbred grind that had enslaved the wives and mothers in her ancestry since long before the roots of the family tree dried up. It had always seemed strange to Bella that her sister Ronnie didn't seem to share the innate sense of servitude that had shadowed her entire life, but she supposed that the age difference and carefree privileges of the second-born must have granted Ronnie a certain emancipation she had not herself enjoyed.

She remembered a conversation she'd once had with her on exactly this topic.

'You're so lucky,' she'd told her pre-teen sister. 'You never get asked to do anything to help, you're always given extra pocket money, and any time you want to go somewhere the oldies even pay the bus fare. I never got treated like that.'

Her sister's response had, she now realised, shaped her view of the world for years to come.

'I'm sure you got what you deserved,' she'd said.

Bella hadn't reacted at the time – she was too thrown by her sister's comment to make any response – and it had passed into ancient history before the conversation had come to her mind again, much more recently, as she pondered her future in the wake of leaving Trevor. In the months since, she'd dwelled on it and turned it over in her mind, often in those middle-of-the-night waking hours where reproachful thoughts plague you and slippery ideas present themselves, only to slither away into the subconscious, never to be retrieved, as daylight dawns.

What she deserved. Yes, Ronnie had been right all those years ago. She'd got exactly the things she thought she merited: nothing more, nothing less. She'd expected someone like Trevor as a husband, and Trevor was exactly what she'd got. She'd only ever thought of herself as housewife material, so a housewife she became. She'd adopted the role of resentful big sister, and played it to perfection.

The reading group had changed all that, though.

Professor Stone's natural assurance had taught her what

she could aspire to. Harrison Fforde's good-humoured breeziness through life's adversities had offered her a different perspective. And Lauren Sherwood's bright enthusiasm and childlike energy had reinvigorated her long-latent *joie de vivre*.

She owed them all a huge debt.

She just hoped she'd be around to repay it.

Bella selected a desk that she thought she might be able to manhandle and started shuffling it from the wall where it stood towards the door of the bedroom. The mirror that stood on top of it began wobbling precariously so she stopped halfway across the room and lifted it on to the bed for safety. A few bits and bobs – a hairbrush, a compact, some cotton buds in a pewter jar – had already plummeted to the floor but Bella could retrieve those later, after she'd bolstered the door. She moved from end to end of the desk, picking up two feet and manoeuvring them across the threadbare carpet before doing the same at the other end, and she had nearly achieved her aim when she caught her toe against a bedside rug and stumbled, almost bringing the desk crashing down on top of her. Instead, both its drawers lurched dangerously from their casings and dropped several inches towards her before sticking, wide open, above her head.

Bella gently lowered the arm she'd instinctively thrown up against the impending calamity and realised she had escaped serious injury by a combination of great fortune and a lifetime of unwaxed drawer runners. She mentally thanked the indolent chambermaids whose jobs would have encompassed furniture polishing for their dereliction of duty and extricated herself from the rug.

It was then that she noticed the slim, homemade volume

that had slid out of the left-hand drawer and fallen to the floor alongside the hairbrush.

She'd seen folders like this in plenty of B&Bs and seaside guesthouses over the years. They usually featured on their cover some saccharine and rose-tinted interpretation in pastels of the dwelling in question, while the contents offered anything from local bus timetables to discount vouchers at the zoo. Rarely had Bella found something of real use in one of these visitor guides.

But this one was different.

This one had a pencil sketch that was not only rather artistically rendered, to Bella's limited appreciation, but also unmistakably representative of its subject: Abbots Chantry. Bella knew it must have been a cut above the others she'd seen because the picture was signed. She couldn't make out the artist's name but that was irrelevant: if they'd been a good enough artist to warrant signing it, and the Veritys impressed enough with it to be willing to use it on the front of their guidebook, then Bella was not in a position to quibble with its quality.

Inspired by the cover, and momentarily forgetting the job she was meant to be undertaking, she felt impelled to look inside the folder.

The very first page proved that it lived up to the promise of its artwork.

The Agatha Christie Room, a bold legend announced, underscored for even greater prominence, and below the title lay a black-and-white photograph of the writer herself, in what looked to Bella like late middle age, resting her chin against one hand and lit in the style of movie stars from the heyday of Hollywood.

Turning another page, Bella found herself suddenly deep in a story she recognised from conversations at the reading group. In December 1926, the celebrated Queen of Crime had disappeared for ten or eleven days and a major manhunt was launched to try and track her down. Her first husband had asked for a divorce and, possibly overcome by grief, Christie had vanished from her home in Berkshire. Her car was found near a chalk quarry, prompting speculation that she might have drowned herself, and the press went crazy for the real-life mystery of the mystery writer's whereabouts. Thousands of police and volunteers scoured the countryside and the mighty Sir Arthur Conan Doyle – whose work Bella was now thoroughly familiar with, even if she found his chief protagonist's methods a little laboured – resorted to employing a medium in an effort to trace her. She finally turned up at a spa hotel in Harrogate, almost two hundred miles away, none the worse for her baffling absence.

Officially, no explanation was ever given for the missing ten days. She never talked about it publicly and excised the incident from her autobiography, leaving later chroniclers to speculate that she might have had a nervous breakdown or even that she was trying to frame her wayward husband for murder.

The homemade visitor guide in the Agatha Christie Room supplied another, altogether more prosaic, solution to the mystery.

Agatha Christie had, in fact, abandoned her car and taken the train to Norcestershire, where her good friend Lady

Constance Verity took her in at the family seat for a few days' rest and recuperation following the collapse of her marriage.

She had stayed, for several peaceful days, in this very room before Lady Constance drove her, incognito, to the West Riding of Yorkshire, where she checked into the Old Swan Hotel, Harrogate.

The hair on Bella's neck was at it again.

She stared around the room, contemplating decor that had almost certainly not changed in the century since the greatest crime writer ever was a guest. To Bella's untutored eye, the wallpaper looked as though it could easily predate Christie's visit, and much of the furniture was clearly Victorian or Edwardian, including the desk that had yielded up this gem of personal history. Bella wondered why the Verity family had kept such a significant secret to themselves for all these years: it was a story that would have laid to rest one of the great mysteries of the twentieth century's literary elite, and she imagined any of the leading newspapers would be willing to cough up a small fortune for the rights to break the exclusive. Then again, maybe the family valued their privacy more highly than the financial considerations. In spite of the budgetary hardships she knew from Ronnie hung over Abbots Chantry, revealing the truth to the world would inevitably bring down a hailstorm of press and public intrusion that, if she were in Lord and Lady Verity's shoes, she would definitely want to avoid. They'd happily shared their secret with special guests via the medium of guidebook anecdote, but that was as far as they were willing to go with it. They didn't, it seemed, even want to risk telling this weekend's party, although one look at the Americans with their camcorder would have convinced anyone to keep a secret.

As she flicked through the rest of the volume, she found a note at the back, printed in bold red ink, which confirmed her theory:

> *We ask that you please do not divulge this information to anyone else. It was Agatha's secret and, like the identity of the culprit in her play The Mousetrap, we would like to honour her memory by keeping it on her behalf.*

Bella had to hand it to a century's worth of guests: they had managed to keep the story under wraps all that time.

As she was sliding the folder back into the drawer, she realised she hadn't completed the one task she'd been asked to do: barricade the door. With some more gentle easing of the desk, she managed to place it across the frame so that even if someone tried to push their way in, it would hinder them considerably. It might not stop them entirely, but at least she'd have time to get to the window. There, she'd already ascertained that she could shimmy out onto the narrow roof of the portico and either knock on the window of the room next door or, if push came to shove, risk dropping down to the ground after lowering herself by the fingertips from the portico itself. She sincerely hoped push wouldn't come to shove – she'd never liked the uncouthness of shoving – but the option was there if she needed it.

The thought reminded her that she hadn't checked the window locks. It was all very well planning a means of escape that way, but if she could get out, then it stood to reason that someone really determined could get in by the same route. Once again, any window locks – particularly in a room with fittings of this age – would be unlikely to bar entry completely, but they might afford a few moments in which to flee via the door.

She immediately saw the flaw in that scenario: the door was now barricaded by the desk.

Unlike the Christie disappearance, there didn't seem to be an easy solution to that conundrum, so Bella decided she'd have to revert to that type she was trying to move away from, and make do.

She crossed to the window and reached up to where the sash panes met in the middle. It was slightly too high for her to reach, even on tiptoe, so she gathered up the waste paper bin, lonely now where it had previously stood under the desk, and turned it upside down under the window. She was on the point of stepping up onto it when her eye was caught by a movement in the darkness outside.

On the snow-covered lawn, silhouetted against the moonlit wintry wonderland, a figure in black was making its way across the gardens.

Her neck hair now working overtime, Bella dodged to one side of the windows, where the heavy flock curtains offered her some protection from being seen. She peered round the window frame, ascertaining that the figure was moving away from the house and therefore wouldn't be looking up at her, and took in as much detail as she could manage.

The figure was dressed in black, with the collar of a huge overcoat and a dark hood disguising any facial features. Even with the warm glow of lanterns and candles washing out from the bedrooms further along her corridor, there wouldn't have been enough light to make anyone out in any case, but Bella was disappointed not to be able to identify the figure as positively male or female: its loping gait and slow progress through the snow meant it could have been anybody, and the overcoat was the perfect camouflage for body type. The person wearing it could have been a tiny woman bulked up with layers of additional clothing or a large man in his vest and pants. There was simply no way of telling.

But there was one unanswered question above all the others that were racing through Bella's mind: who was disobeying the Professor's instructions to stay in their room?

When a sudden rap came at her bedroom door, Bella's neck hair finally gave up any semblance of alerting her to danger and simply freaked out. She ran to the desk and threw herself against it, hoping that if someone was trying to gain access, the combined force of the antique wood and her flimsy body weight might do the trick.

Bella had once read an article in *Woman's Own* about the amygdala hijack, in which the part of the brain's limbic system that supervises the fight-or-flight response kicks into action instinctively, before the conscious mind has a chance to rouse itself from its slumbers and stagger into action. In this instance, her instinctive response successfully bypassed her rational brain, exactly as designed by evolution, and she failed to register one salient point: someone wanting to inflict harm on her person was hardly likely to knock on the door first.

Unless it was a double bluff and they wanted to fool her into thinking they were a friend.

But if that were the case, whoever it was wouldn't have

been thinking straight because they should have known that Bella wouldn't answer the door to anyone, as per the Professor's instructions, so it would all have been a waste of their time and they might as well have tried to force themselves in unannounced.

If she'd really stopped to think about it, she'd probably have been grateful that her amygdala had hijacked her.

'Who's there?' she called in the kind of exaggerated whisper that only people in scary films actually use.

'It's me,' came a voice from the corridor.

'Ronnie? What are you doing here?'

'Let me in,' hissed her sister from the wrong side of the door.

'You shouldn't be out of your room,' Bella hissed back.

'Well, we can debate that while I'm out here being hunted by a murderer, or you can let me in. No pressure either way.'

Ronnie really could be maddening sometimes.

Having got the hang of the desktop shuffle on its way to the door, Bella moved it away again much more quickly, avoiding the rug and making a mental note not to share the Agatha Christie secret with her sister: she was surprised Ronnie didn't already know, particularly since the room was named after the writer, but she was absolutely certain that she didn't. If she had, then the whole of Norcester would know by now, and thus the secret would no longer have been a secret. Perhaps Lord and Lady Verity had spotted Ronnie's tendency to verbosity and deliberately kept it from her. If so, Bella judged that a good call.

'What do you want?' she asked eventually, when Ronnie had squeezed past the furniture and into the room.

'I want to stay with you in here tonight.'

'Frightened, are we?'

'Aren't you?'

Ronnie's ability to skewer Bella's pretensions to grownupness hit home again, as it so often did. Ronnie was right, of course. Bella was frightened.

She just didn't want to admit it to her younger sister.

'If there's thunder and lightning too, maybe we can make some dresses out of the curtains,' she said with more than a hint of sarcasm. *The Sound of Music* had been a perennial favourite in their household long after it should have passed its enjoy-by date and Bella knew Ronnie would get the reference.

Bella crossed to a full-length mirror beside the window and began to take off her make-up while Ronnie started a circuit of the room, inspecting the fireplace, portraits and furniture as if she'd never seen them before.

'Can't you sit down for a minute?' Bella asked eventually. 'You're making me nervous.'

'Still getting used to being on your own?' responded Ronnie, with an edge that Bella recognised. It certainly wasn't an innocent question: Ronnie had really rather liked Trevor and Bella's decision to end her marriage, while never openly talked about between them, had created a new undercurrent of tiptoey unease. Of course, Ronnie had never had to deal with the day-to-day minutiae of Trevor, so she didn't have the full picture, but that had never been an obstacle to her expressing an opinion.

Maybe now was the moment.

'I think my nervousness is more about a murderer on the

loose than being on my own,' she said carefully, watching Ronnie in the mirror.

'But you must be finding it difficult?'

'What – being free of Trevor?'

'Free? That's an interesting way of putting it.'

'You have no idea,' said Bella, not really wanting to go into it with a judgemental sister who had never really been on her side since childhood.

'Because from where I stand, it looked more like you abandoning a perfectly good marriage than trying to escape something rotten.'

Bella's buttons were being pushed and she knew it. That didn't make it any easier to resist biting back.

'I said you have no idea, and you really don't,' she barked more forcefully than she'd intended.

'It can't have been easy for him, with you gallivanting about pretending to solve murders.'

'Gallivanting? I wasn't gallivanting anywhere. And we weren't *pretending* to solve murders – we *did* solve them.'

Ronnie grunted. 'You never invited me, though, did you?'

Was that what this was all about? Ronnie was jealous? She'd never mentioned wanting to be involved before: how was Bella supposed to know she'd have liked to be part of the group? Not that she'd ever have invited her – that would have been too much to inflict on the others.

She went for the easy target, spitting out her words.

'You couldn't be part of it. You don't read.'

'All right, all right,' replied Ronnie, making the conventional two-handed, downward-palmed gesture inviting Bella, more than a little patronisingly, to calm down. 'It's just that … you know … maybe you paid a bit more attention to your book club than you did to your husband. If I'd been in his shoes—'

'No,' shouted Bella, turning to face her sister directly. 'You don't get to judge me on whether I paid enough attention to my husband. You don't get to call me out for joining a reading group for my own sanity. And you certainly don't get to empathise with Trevor. Trevor, of all people!'

Ronnie sounded a little less confrontational than she had a moment ago.

'Sorry. I didn't mean to suggest…'

That was exactly what she'd meant. But she backed off to inspect another painting and seemed to have exhausted her line of provocation.

Bella knew she'd get no nearer a proper apology than this from Ronnie. And at least she'd stopped leaning on that button – for now.

Perhaps the best course was to let it go.

She turned back to the mirror and stared at her naked face. She felt more vulnerable than she had in years and realised that an odd paradox of being yoked to Trevor for so long was that it had provided her with an unreal sense of something masquerading as security. She had not, for a moment, regretted her decision to walk away, but there had been unintended consequences that she was still working out.

Ronnie interrupted her study of the strange creature reflected in the glass.

'So can I?'

'Can you what?'

'Can I stay in here with you tonight?'

Years of frustration at her little sister bubbled up inside Bella and mingled with the sickening trepidation this weekend was inducing in her. Like her only memorable school chemistry lesson, when things went badly wrong during an experiment involving magnesium and hydrochloric acid and the wild-eyed teacher was left laughing maniacally as she tried to keep the lid on the explosive concoction for fear of accidentally wiping out Form 3A, Bella felt the emotions fulminating inside her. Part of it was the impotent exasperation of the older sister for her impertinent sibling; part of it was sheer blind terror.

She felt a sudden urge to scream.

'I suppose so,' she said meekly. 'But you'd better not snore.'

II

After nearly thirty years in what he loosely called 'the theatre industry', Harrison Fforde was finally grateful for the breathing lessons he'd had at drama school. For almost that entire time, he'd regarded the techniques of his voice coaches in rather the same way as he'd viewed Pythagoras's theorem, or quadratic equations: purely academic and utterly incidental to his everyday life. Now, though, in the silence of his bedroom in the creepy old country house, he found a use for them.

Not the quadratic equations, obviously.

He could feel his heart pounding in his chest from the moment he entered the room. It had started even before he shifted the small wardrobe against the door, although that had certainly exacerbated the breathlessness, and he knew perfectly well what it was. You didn't stand in the wings of a minor regional theatre waiting for your grand entrance before a thin Wednesday matinee audience without knowing what nervous anticipation was.

Wednesday afternoons at Norcester Rep were one thing. At least he knew what he was letting himself in for, and had supposedly dedicated his working life to that kind of charged moment. Here, in the terrifying gloom of a candlelit room in the ancient, probably haunted confines of Abbots Chantry, he had no idea what to expect.

It was the main reason he'd drunk so much at dinner. He'd figured that the only way he was going to get through a night on his own, in a bedroom whose decor gave off massive Hammer horror vibes, was to get as close to paralytic as he could manage in the couple of hours between the sandwiches arriving and the assembly being packed off to bed.

He hadn't done too badly, given the window of opportunity available, although he was still far too sentient for his liking and now had the added pressure of Professor Stone's request to stay awake and listen for anything 'untoward'. Whatever that meant.

Fifteen minutes after he'd put his diaphragm through the few paces he could remember from voice class, during which he succeeded in reducing the pounding to a mere rhythmic thumping, he realised he was starting to fall asleep in the huge armchair near the window.

'Come on, Monkton, get a grip,' he said aloud, using his real name as he often did when chastising himself.

It felt more authentic.

'Try some tongue-twisters. Or limericks. That should keep you awake.'

He got up out of the chair and opened the window, letting in a blast of air that would have seemed depressingly cold on a normal night but, with the heating only minimally available in the generator-powered house, actually made a surprisingly small amount of difference.

'There was an old woman of Norcester
Who loved to recite E. M. Forster.
Her friends couldn't stand it:
They hired a bandit
Who took her to London and lorst 'er.'

The wind had died down considerably and a few flakes of snow were beginning to drift in from the north.

'A house that belonged to some abbots
Saw everyone at it like rabbits.'

Fforde wasn't entirely satisfied with the near-rhyme, which he'd only achieved by contorting the pronunciation of 'abbots', but he knew where he was going with it and needed the set-up.

'Some frisky young nuns
Turned up with some puns
And abandoned their Catholic habits.'

His brain was motoring now, and the alcoholic fug that had shrouded his thoughts was starting to lift.

'The Norcestershire old upper classes
Could only just wipe their own—'

A noise from the corridor outside his room stopped Fforde's latest masterpiece dead.

He waited, trying to hear it again, but nothing came.

He hadn't imagined it. There had definitely been a creak in the floorboards. Right outside his room.

The pounding was back.

'It's all right, Harry. You've got this.'

Even in his hazy recollection from earlier, he knew that

A Game of Murder

Professor Stone hadn't actually forbidden them to investigate anything 'untoward'. He'd merely suggested that he didn't want to be held responsible for their safety. In fact, now that Fforde thought about it with a slightly clearer head, the Professor's request for them to stay awake must have been a clear hint that he actually *did* want them to investigate anything 'untoward'. Why else would he have asked them to be alert?

If only his innate bravery matched his clarity of thinking.

It didn't. He knew it didn't. He understood quite well that all his bravado was nine-tenths bluster. He suspected the other members of the reading group knew it as well, but they'd been kind enough not to mention it in open conversation thus far. And yet, if that long-forgotten arithmetic hadn't deserted him completely, that still allowed for one-tenth genuine pluck, didn't it?

One-tenth would have to suffice.

Fforde shoved the wardrobe to one side, appreciative that it was empty, and leaned his ear against the door.

The nervous anticipation from the wings lifted Fforde's resolve and, after a moment's careful listening for a repeat of the creaking, he opened the door.

Just a crack.

Just enough to hear another floorboard creak.

It was further away this time, and Fforde assumed the foot that had caused it had moved, along with the rest of its connected body, down the corridor towards the main staircase. He opened the door a little further and peered out, ready to pull back and barricade himself in again if a crazed killer happened to be lurking outside.

The corridor was empty. He checked both ways.

Then he tiptoed out.

Doing the little dance he'd acquired at drama school, when he'd mastered the technique of avoiding the giveaway floorboards on nocturnal trips through the mixed dorms of the students' quarters for a variety of short-lived romantic entanglements, he made his way slowly and noiselessly down the corridor. Unlike those nights so long ago, he had no idea what he was expecting to find, but the thrill of identifying and solving clues in the murder of Felicity Penman was still fresh in his memory and he was determined to feel it again in this new investigation. If anyone was going to come up with something useful from this long, cold night, then it would be Harrison Fforde.

It was only when he reached a junction in the corridor, where an adjoining landing headed off to his right, that he realised he was hopelessly exposed, and it wasn't because of the open fly in his pyjamas.

Urgent whispering was coming towards him, and he had nowhere to hide.

Retreat back along the corridor to his bedroom was out of the question: there was no way he would reach it undetected. He could make a dash for the stairs and try to run down them, but there was a strong chance he would run into the owners of the whispers, and he had no desire to do that. They could, of course, belong to Professor Stone and someone else, out and about on a security recce. They could just as easily be the voices of a killer and his accomplice – or even his next victim.

The thought horrified Fforde and he knew he could not

simply abandon the poor person to their fate. Equally, he didn't fancy his chances against a potentially armed murderer.

As he pressed back against the wall, fear gripping his insides and the whispers getting closer, the house offered up the perfect solution. A panel in the wall behind his fingertips shifted and gave way, and Fforde knew he had found his escape route.

He slipped inside the priest hole and slid the panelling back into place.

Above the sound of his heart beating, Fforde could make out two voices, one male and one female. With the kind of fortuitousness that seemed to happen in detective novels all the time, but only rarely in real life, in Fforde's experience, the voices stopped precisely beside the panel where he was hiding. For a few moments, he heard their conversation clearly.

'You know it's not safe to be out here,' the man was saying, and the Scottish lilt told Fforde immediately that it was Monty Butler.

'You're here, aren't you?' said the woman. Her voice was not so instantly recognisable and Fforde couldn't place it.

'That's different – you know it is.'

'I don't see how.'

'Because as the estate manager, I've got an excuse if someone catches me around the house in the middle of the night.'

'And I haven't?'

'It's not the same. Now do as you're told.'

The pair began to move on, out of earshot, but a final phrase from the woman triggered something in Fforde's memory and he knew who it was.

'Don't start,' said Siobhan through gritted teeth.

Fforde left it a solid five minutes before daring to venture back into the corridor. There was one thing on his mind, and that was to find the Professor and report back to him. How could the academic be anything other than impressed both at his resourcefulness and at his information? He had taken it upon himself to go out into the house in the middle of the night – well, it had to be half past ten at least – and had come up trumps with what could prove to be vital clues to the murders of Keren Lowe and Hemingford Grey.

He marched down the corridor, not caring about the creaks he was making, before stopping suddenly in the middle of the landing.

He didn't know which room was Stone's.

And, more to the point, he had sudden and severe doubts about the value of the information he had to impart to the Professor.

So Monty and Siobhan had been out around the house at night when they were meant to be safely locked up in their own room. So what? Monty, as he had so astutely reminded his wife, was the estate manager and perfectly entitled to wander about the place wherever and whenever he saw fit, subject only to any restrictions that might be placed on him by Lord and Lady Verity. Fforde didn't imagine there'd be many of those. It was entirely up to him whether he was willing to run the risk of happening upon a killer with a weapon, and even if he did, Fforde rated Monty's chances pretty highly in a one-to-one confrontation. As for Siobhan, she too held a position in the house that allowed her to roam freely. Monty might have expressed his doubts about her authority to venture abroad in these circumstances, but Fforde couldn't see anyone else making any objections if she were to be discovered.

The only thing he couldn't work out was why the two of them were having their whispered discussion in the corridor at all, rather than in the comfort and privacy of their own bedroom. Perhaps Monty had set off first, and Siobhan had followed him out, only to be told off by him when they were already partway through their expedition. Fforde had no idea where they might be going – the staff quarters were in another part of the house altogether – but that wasn't too odd, and anyway it was none of his business.

He summed up the entirety of the information he would be able to impart to Professor Stone. It came to not very much, certainly less than he'd originally hoped, and he abandoned the idea of disturbing Stone now with so little to tell him of any worth.

Heading back to his own room, he eased the door open and slipped inside, clicking it gently shut behind him.

He was about to turn round when a movement caught his eye in the mirror that stood on top of the dressing table to his left. In the gloom, he couldn't make out what the shape was, but he could see that it was large, draped in white like an apparition, and rushing across the room towards him wielding a spade in its hands.

Harrison Fforde screamed like a little girl and spun round to meet his doom.

Two paces away from making violent contact with him, Olive terminated her charge and dropped the spade in surprise.

'Mr Fforde – what on earth are you doing in my room?'

III

The scream from down the corridor was the first thing that had made Lauren nervous since she'd gone to bed. She was used to creaky houses, thanks to the pre-war semi she'd grown up in, and nighttime prowlings by her younger brother Simon had meant she was also extremely familiar with odd noises at strange times, not to mention curious odours rising up from the kitchen.

But she froze at the scream.

At first, she couldn't be sure if it was a man's scream or a woman's, then decided only a man of singularly resonant vocal capabilities could reach that high a pitch involuntarily, and there was only one person in the house who fitted that description.

Harrison Fforde.

Lauren shivered and wondered what she was supposed to do. Did the scream mean that Harrison was in mortal danger? Or was it already too late to save him from whatever fate had befallen him in this sinister house? Perhaps the rest of the house had been roused by the sound and even now hordes of rescuers were rushing to his aid. But then she'd have heard their footfall in the corridor, wouldn't she? And if they were running to help, how would it look if she were the only person not to come to his assistance?

On the other hand, there would be little advantage to be gained from dashing out of her room if she were to come face to face with whoever had caused him to scream in the first place. There was no point in sacrificing herself needlessly.

All these thoughts and more passed through Lauren's mind before she could even get out of the chair where she was sitting, laptop on her knee, scraping the last vestiges of battery power from it to make some frantic notes for her new idea about the strange goings-on in a remote, snowbound country house where a killer seemed to be playing a game of murder.

Before she'd crossed to the door, her next move had been decided for her.

'It's all right. I'm OK.'

Fforde's voice echoed down the corridor, a slight tremble audible in his booming tones.

'No need to leave your rooms. Sleep well.'

Lauren let out a sigh. Fforde could be a bit of an idiot sometimes, and now was not the moment to be toying with everyone's emotions. She would have words with him over breakfast: if he thought that was a funny practical joke, then he'd need his sense of humour recalibrating, and right now she felt like just the person to do it.

She returned to the laptop and sat down again.

A scream rings out from down the corridor, she tapped out, and then leaped up in fright as a sharp knock came at her door.

'Harrison, if that's you—' she began, hurrying over and turning the key in the lock. She hadn't bothered with the Professor's extra layer of security, given that the lock was supplemented by two large iron bolts, top and bottom, which would, she was sure, defeat anyone hoping to make a discreet entrance.

After sliding them both back and whipping open the door, Lauren realised what a silly mistake she'd made. Not because she might just have let in a killer, taking advantage of Fforde's disruption to try their hand at gaining access to another victim. No, not that.

The silly mistake was opening the door to Colorado Hughes.

Of course, if Colorado Hughes was himself the killer, they would turn out to have been one and the same silly mistake.

Only time would tell.

The American grinned a wide, toothy grin, showing off his fine dentistry and creepy demeanour, but it was not the smile that Lauren noticed first. It was the fact that he was wearing an electric blue silk kimono, hanging open to reveal the smallest pair of briefs Lauren had seen since the time she babysat for her neighbour and the neighbour's five-year-old son had come running to meet her dressed only in his little-boy underpants.

On that occasion, the child's mother had been embarrassed enough to apologise. Colorado Hughes was showing no signs of following suit.

Instead, he brought one hand from behind his back and proffered Lauren a rose. Her immediate reaction was to wonder where on earth he'd found a rose at this time of year in the middle of a snowbound country house, but she had no chance to quiz him on his floral expertise.

'My leading lady,' he said, sidling across the threshold with a smooth ease and prompting Lauren to take two steps backwards. He glanced over his shoulder down the corridor then pushed the door closed behind him.

'I'd like to talk to you about your role as the face of my new documentary,' he went on, edging further forwards. 'As a director, I always feel it's important to get to know my cast ... intimately. Wouldn't you agree?'

Lauren appraised the vision of consummate Californian confidence who stood before her. Colorado Hughes was perhaps an inch taller than she was, with a mop of dark brown hair on top of a boyish, yet not unpleasantly so, face. In the dingy light from her laptop, if she squinted, she could almost persuade herself he had a hint of a young Tom Cruise about him – cheeky *Risky Business* Tom, not the cocky *Top Gun* variety – and she suddenly understood how people could find themselves trapped in the casting couch system that was supposed to have disappeared in the wake of the #MeToo movement but was still, if this example was anything to go by, all too prevalent.

He might be a sexual predator, abusing his power and influence to get his way, but it was a big step from that to murder, and somehow she couldn't picture his youthful arrogance behind either of the deaths at Abbots Chantry. Not only did he not seem the type (whatever 'the type' was), what possible motive could he have for killing two of the house's staff?

No. She didn't need to worry about being murdered by Colorado Hughes, she was sure of it.

Fighting off his romantic advances might be a different matter.

'I'm sorry, Mr Hughes,' she said, sounding a lot more resolute than she felt. 'I'm afraid I don't go in for that sort of thing.'

'Whaddya mean?' He sounded bemused more than insulted. 'Sex? Or sex with guys? Cos it sure as hell ain't this that's putting you off.'

He indicated the physique beneath the kimono which, Lauren was quite prepared to admit, looked toned and tanned.

'Don't tell me you're one of those dykes?'

She smiled sweetly at him and decided to play him at his own game. 'No, Mr Hughes. I just don't "put out", as you Americans phrase it, on one day's acquaintance, no matter how appealing the goods on offer.'

She wafted what she hoped was a sassy hand in front of his torso.

'So you can put this away.'

Hughes looked like he might want to argue with her about her English propriety, then changed his mind and pulled the kimono round him.

'I'm not used to being turned down,' he said indignantly.

'I can imagine,' said Lauren, still smiling.

'There's people out there would kill for the opportunity I'm offering you.'

'If you mean fronting the film, I'm sure there are.'

'No, I don't mean—'

'But I'm afraid my decision stands, and if you wouldn't

mind sticking to Professor Stone's request to stay in your room for the rest of the night, I'd suggest now might be a good time to leave.'

Hughes clearly wasn't used to be spoken to like that. He started to go a little bit red in the face, rather like the Fat Controller in those train books Lauren had read to Simon as a small boy, but he seemed to be struggling to verbalise his feelings.

Lauren didn't give him the chance. She strolled over to the door, opened it and ushered him out.

As he shuffled angrily past her into the corridor, Hughes looked at her with menace in his eyes.

'You're gonna regret turning me down, babe,' he said.

Lauren clung on to her smile as he left.

'You know, I really don't think I am,' she said, and closed the door.

IV

More than an hour had passed since Professor Stone heard Fforde screaming. It had been enormously tempting, after the actor's subsequent announcement to the house that all was well, to go directly to his room and give him a dressing down. Stone couldn't fathom what Fforde was playing at, but whatever it was wouldn't be helping the general mood of the guests.

That mood had been playing on his mind ever since he'd packed everyone else off to bed and interviewed the Veritys in vain on the staircase.

Their hosts should, by rights, be devastated at the loss of not one but two of their staff. But instead of high emotions, they'd responded with subdued melancholy at best, and Stone couldn't simply write it off as the stiff upper lip for which the aristocratic classes were, even in the second quarter of the twenty-first century, still renowned. Buttoned-up was one thing: completely repressed was another. Maybe his Lordship's childhood, generations removed from the wayward hedonism of his forebears, had been one of isolation and subjugation in an attempt by his parents to prevent him repeating history. That wouldn't automatically account for his wife's pinched despondence but it would hardly be surprising if she mirrored the behaviours and demeanour of her husband in matters of the heart. Maybe they were, even now, weeping with abandon on each other's shoulders in the privacy of their own room.

Maybe, but he doubted it.

There was more to their reaction at their staff members' deaths than met the eye.

Among the rest of their number, Stone had observed tension and fear – only to be expected with a double-murderer on the loose. Monty and Siobhan had been more anxious than the rest, but the fact that it had been Siobhan's sister who had been selected as the first victim would naturally have placed her on higher alert than the others, and Monty would doubtless be vigilant on his wife's behalf. Ronnie had been visibly terrified by the whole experience, and Stone expected Bella would have her hands full keeping her sister calm and together the next day. As for the Americans, their focus seemed to be on capturing as much of the action as they could, and he pictured them locked away in some little edit suite in Soho or Studio City a few weeks hence, foraging through the weekend's footage for the most vivid and sensational shots to stitch together in their putative documentary.

Olive, of course, was a law unto herself. Inscrutable, stolid, unimpeachable.

The thought of Olive put the Professor in mind of the day's work she had been required to endure. Besides duties such as retrieving Hemingford Grey's body from the clump of trees near the drive where she'd found him, she had faced the unpleasant task of constructing two makeshift coffins for erstwhile colleagues on the household roster of employees. He was pretty sure that undertaker assignments were not going to form part of her contract of employment at Abbots Chantry – nobody was likely to include coffin manufacture among a gardener's responsibilities on the off-chance – and regardless of her handiness with the tools she appeared to be able to lay her hand on at a moment's notice, it was a big ask to get her to fashion rudimentary resting places for Grey and Keren Lowe. From what he'd seen of the long-closed chapel, too, it didn't exactly measure up to a luxurious working environment in which to carry out the task.

The fact that she'd only put up minimal resistance to the request was greatly to her credit, even if she was a prime suspect in the activities that had led to the distressing job, and she'd completed it diligently – and fast.

Of course, the Professor's review of the guests and staff currently residing at Abbots Chantry would not be complete without a checklist of each of them as potential suspects for the murder of Keren Lowe – for Stone had now concluded beyond doubt that it *was* murder – and Hemingford Grey. The unhappy gift shop manager had seemed, for a while, to be in the frame for Keren's death, but had successfully ruled himself out by dint of becoming the killer's second victim. Leaving aside the reading group from his contemplations, Stone considered the two remaining Americans in the house. They had been alarmingly quick to divert their filmic intentions from *Murder on the Polar Express* (in whatever contorted aberration they were expecting to come up with) to the real-life events unfolding before them. It crossed his mind, perhaps a little unfairly, that this – or something like it – might have been their plan from the start, and it was possible that the two deaths that had occurred were a springboard they intended to use to launch their true-crime documentary on the world. If so, it was a wild scheme with terminally high stakes for Keren and Hemingford. Could Colorado Hughes and Marin Cypher really be that callous and premeditative? In his experience, Americans could be both aggressively ambitious and outrageously self-interested, but even he had to admit that such a plan, if it existed, would be a hell of a reach.

Among the staff, Monty and Siobhan could probably be discounted by virtue of their close familial bonds with Keren – although that didn't guarantee them a free pass; there were plenty of families in which one sibling was willing to murder another – while the Veritys themselves seemed unlikely candidates. What would they have to gain, and why would they kill their own employees? Ronnie remained a person of interest to the Professor, his affection for Bella notwithstanding: Ronnie seemed detached from the rest of the company and her lack of warmth towards her own sister could be indicative of something deeper and darker. As for Olive, if she were to prove the perpetrator of these appalling deeds, then there would be a twisted irony to the fact that she had been required to build coffins for her own victims.

And now, in the dead of night and with a houseful of probably unsleeping people all around, there was something niggling Stone about those coffins.

Or, to be more accurate, about their contents.

He could, of course, wait until morning and share his

concerns with the rest of the reading group. That would have the advantage of safety in numbers against any potential attack by the killer, as well as the benefit of daylight – such as was able to leak into the dingy compass of the chapel. On the other hand, there would be plenty more people about, and any attempt to return to the temporary mortuary might be fraught with awkward explanations or hindering hangers-on. Granted, Hemingford Grey had fulfilled that role for much of the previous twenty-four hours and he was no longer in a position to do so, but Stone did not want to risk someone else stepping into his shoes and obfuscating his investigation.

On balance, and notwithstanding his decree to the rest of the house, now was the time to go prowling.

He picked up the only light in his room – another replica of the original medieval candlestick from the lounge – and let himself out into the corridor.

He wouldn't have had the candle lit at all if the night outside hadn't been quite so thickly dark. Without it, though, he was in danger of tripping on a rug or even falling down the staircase in the inky blackness, and he decided a little flickering light offered less risk of attracting unwanted attention than a large, late-middle-aged man clattering headlong down the stairs.

It took him more than ten minutes to make his way from his landing in one wing of the building to the hall where Lord Verity's note had purportedly been left on a table for Keren Lowe. Every footstep held the threat of a creaky floorboard, especially on the stairs themselves, and with the corridors and hallways all adorned with furniture, suits of armour and assorted bric-a-brac of the antique variety, he trod extremely cautiously for fear of upsetting something noisy.

There was, of course, the additional concern that the perpetrator might be on the lookout for their third victim, and with no clue as to their motive – never mind their identity – everyone had to be viewed as a target.

Just as everyone had to be viewed as a suspect.

At the foot of the stairs, he almost abandoned his quest when he thought he saw something move in the shadows over towards the front door. In the candlelight he could make out nothing clearly, and he had no desire to venture closer for a better look. From what he could tell, there seemed to be a small puddle of water glinting just inside the door and he frightened himself by peering hard into the darkness and convincing himself there could have been a figure hiding in one of the alcoves either side of the entrance. If someone had gone outside at this time of night, bringing melting snow back in with them and concealing themselves from him when they heard him descending the stairs, it would take a braver man than him to accost them right there.

It was probably his mind playing tricks on him anyway. Those suits of armour were very lifelike.

He reached the door of the chapel and let out a long, slow breath of relief. He'd heard no sounds anywhere along the way, and while he was sure there wouldn't be much sleep going on, at least it suggested people were obeying the instructions to barricade themselves in their rooms and not emerge until morning.

With the possible exception of that terrifying shadow in the hall behind him.

The heavy iron latch that opened the door made more of a clanking than he'd hoped, and he glanced around involuntarily before letting himself inside. Closing it was easier as he could soften the falling latch with his fingers to deaden the noise.

Then he leaned back against the door and sighed again.

The chapel seemed to eat the candlelight and the temperature felt at least half a dozen degrees lower than the corridor outside. Stone shivered and pulled his jacket tighter round him. If he'd been a religious man he'd have offered up a prayer for protection to whatever deity he'd believed in; as it was, he muttered an expletive against the ghosts who dwelt in these shadows, then ordered himself to pull himself together.

A youthful diet of Peter Cushing and Christopher Lee in late-night television horror fests had instilled in him a healthy level of scepticism about all things supernatural: as a mathematician and amateur philosopher, he put no store in the fantasies of paranormal or psychic realms. On the other hand, it would do no harm to be wary.

Stone circumnavigated the entire chapel, checking every corner and crevice of the place with his ineffectual light source, before deciding that he definitely was alone. During the whole circuit, he hadn't dared to look into the middle of the space, where the two coffins were laid out side by side across the tops of the pews, which served as a kind of catafalque. Now, convinced of the absence of any lurking spectral being – or actual killer, come to that – Stone turned to the centre of the chapel and stared down at the bodies of Keren Lowe and Hemingford Grey.

Olive had a career in funeral directing if she wanted it. That much was apparent.

The corpses had been arranged formally in their caskets – which appeared to have been put together using old tea chests and beer crates – with their hands clasped across their abdomens in a respectful posture of repose. Next to each other in the same ritualistic pose, they could have been the tragic bodies of an engaged couple who met their end just moments before tying the knot and were now destined to spend eternity in a gruesome parody of wedlock. All it needed for the full Guillermo del Toro treatment was for Grey to slowly raise a hand and reach across to grasp that of his fellow victim.

Stone shuddered at the prospect and shook his head to free himself of the grotesque imagery.

Olive really should have put a lid on those caskets.

Gripping the candlestick a little tighter, he advanced towards the boxes and lowered his face to inspect the features of the two unfortunates before him.

Grey's clothes shone damp in the golden light and Stone realised the lower temperature in the chapel had meant the snow that had seeped into his coat among the laurels hadn't had a chance to dry out. At least the place was doing its required job of refrigeration, keeping the bodies from decomposition until they could be handed over to the authorities.

The only evidence of hideous violence was the patch of red leaking across the white shirt he wore beneath the coat, and Stone understood why people often described the dead as looking like they were sleeping.

If only that were true.

Stone went over in his mind all the things he knew about Hemingford Grey. He'd been the gift shop manager at Abbots Chantry for years, predating both Siobhan and Keren, and that meant he probably knew more about the house than anyone bar the family themselves. He'd certainly hinted at dark goings-on, although he hadn't given any clue as to what they might be, or whom they might involve. Before his demise, he might have made a decent suspect in the murder of Keren Lowe, what with his luring her away from the lounge with the mysterious note from Lord Verity, his obvious familiarity with oddities such as the medieval candlestick, even his prickliness with his Lordship over dinner on Friday night. The reading group had speculated about pretty much everyone, from Lord and Lady Verity to the visiting Americans, and if it hadn't been for the hulking mass of his corpse, with its chest open in graphic confirmation of his lifelessness, he might have been high on their list.

His presence in the chapel, grim and terminally immobile, did rather rule him out.

While there had been no possible dispute about the method of Grey's dispatch, Keren Lowe, by contrast, was a conundrum. As Stone turned his attention to her visage – paler and more waxy than Grey's, something Stone put down to more time elapsing since her demise – he leaned in closer still before catching a faintly malodorous whiff and backing away again.

He fished a handkerchief from his coat pocket and covered his nose with it before peering down at Keren once more.

Would it be disrespectful to touch her skin?

Yes, of course it would. But he did it anyway.

Putting the candlestick down inside the casket, wedging it underneath her right shoulder to keep it upright, he reached forward and eased Keren's collar away from her neck. His fingertips brushed against the folds of her skin and he recoiled slightly – mostly because it was much colder than he'd expected, and the image of a frozen leg of lamb leaped unbidden into his mind's eye. Trying again, he pulled the material far enough away from her throat to be able to inspect the rope burn that was clearly visible round her neck.

And suddenly Stone's mind was in overdrive.

Even allowing for the fact that the collar would have reduced the friction burn from the rope, there was no way this mark was severe enough, or cut deeply enough into her skin, for it to have been the means of her death. The rope had snapped, of course, and the fall from the height of the tower might have been enough to finish the job, but Stone smelled a rat.

Or a gerbil, at the very least.

And then there was the medieval candlestick that Bella had discovered later on, the original on which Stone's replica in the coffin was modelled. Could that have been the murder weapon, somehow concealed and then reinstated in the billiard room for reasons beyond his present comprehension? Or maybe the killer had used something else entirely and the plummet from the tower had merely been a piece of dramatic stagecraft designed to mislead observers into believing it to be a straightforward case of suicide. If suicide was ever straightforward.

Stone tried to make the chronology work in his brain. They had all heard the scream, although the reading group had been sequestered underground at the time, and Lauren had raised the anomalous question of whether someone throwing themselves from the tower would have screamed anyway. But if the scream had prefigured a physical attack by the killer, that person must have moved awfully quickly to have then tied the rope round his victim, manhandled her to the window and pushed her out.

Hemingford Grey had discovered the body at the foot of the tower, and there was now no way to ascertain exactly how long had passed between the scream and the discovery – another possible reason for the killer wanting Grey out of the way as well – but it seemed like a tall order, and Stone searched for other possibilities in his mind.

What was certain was that if the cause of death had indeed been the candlestick or some other blunt instrument, then there would be obvious signs on the corpse of Keren Lowe. And yet her face looked almost serene in the dim light, with no indication of violence or trauma. Gingerly, and attempting to preserve as much of Keren's dignity as he could, he lifted her head from the bottom of the casket and ran his fingers round the back of her skull, feeling for any injury through her thick black hair.

He found none.

But as he laid her gently back down, something at the corner of her lips caught the flickering candlelight and he leaned in for a closer look.

It was impossible to tell for sure but Professor Stone was convinced that Keren Lowe was frothing at the mouth.

The Kitchen

I

It was Monty who broke the bad news to Lauren over breakfast.

'I'm sorry to have to tell you this,' he began as she hovered around the buffet Siobhan had prepared. 'There's been even more snow overnight. I don't think we can expect help to arrive any time soon, and there's certainly no way off the estate.'

Lauren's heart, which had endured something of a rollercoaster overnight as she'd fought off amorous Americans, heard surplus-to-requirement screams and struggled for the past four hours to keep her eyes open, sank to a new low. She'd tried to stay awake by fleshing out some scenarios for the new book she was brewing but she realised she'd been slipping in and out of slumber when she looked back at her laptop notes to discover a stream of consciousness babble about a half-naked Californian roaming the landings in the small hours. She was sure the idea had been prompted by Colorado Hughes knocking on her door – he had, hadn't he? – but the rest of the rambling narrative seemed too far-fetched, even for one of her novels. When the laptop's battery finally died somewhere around four a.m. (she hadn't dared plug it in for fear of using up what little power remained from the generator), she'd resorted to getting up and pacing around the room to avoid dropping off, but the semi-aware visions kept coming and she was afraid she was losing touch with reality. She'd been grateful to hear the first sounds of movement in the corridor outside her room at about six, and hoped it was the Professor starting the day. If he was up and about, that meant it would be safe for the rest of them, provided they stayed in groups as they had done yesterday.

When she'd left her room a few minutes later, there was no sign of Professor Stone and she'd made her way directly to the dining room, following an unmistakable scent of cooked breakfast.

Monty was already halfway through a huge plateful of sausages, bacon and baked beans. Lauren fancied she might also have spied white pudding half-concealed under a fried egg, which certainly didn't seem to be on offer to the regular guests in the heated dishes at the buffet. Maybe that was one of the perks of sleeping with the chef. She finished loading her own plate and sat opposite him, smiling a thin smile to break the ice but not really feeling it.

'Are you sure it's OK to be on your own in here?' she asked, the thought popping into her mind that she'd found him alone.

He looked up from the sausage he was ripping apart and grinned.

'I'm fine,' he said. 'A true Scotsman never goes anywhere without his *sgian dubh*. I don't suppose you know what that is?'

'Actually, I do. It's one of the vital clues in a Lord Quaint novel we read not so long ago – *Delivery of Death*. But I thought they were supposed to be ceremonial daggers these days?'

'Oh, they are. But if the worst came to the worst, they'd do a half-decent job of repelling boarders. Let's put it this way: I'd fancy my chances with mine if anyone wanted to try and attack me.'

Lauren was curious. She'd thought the little weapons that were traditionally tucked into the top of a sock when a kilt was worn were only meant as a nod to the proud history of marauding Scotsmen. She never suspected they were carried as a matter of course, regardless of the occasion or outfit, and she certainly didn't imagine they were ever used in anger. Even now she wondered if Monty was pulling her leg: given his stocky frame and the rugby-playing past he'd alluded to at dinner on Friday night, he was unlikely to need a knife to protect himself in the event of a scrap.

The next thought that struck her made her feel instantly nauseous.

She was alone in the dining room with this stocky, rugby-playing Scot, and Professor Stone would have told her she had only herself to blame if she were to be sliced and diced right there.

She put down the forkful of scrambled egg she'd been about to put in her mouth and stared at Monty across the table as he ate. Even if he was the killer, and even if he'd wanted to make her his next victim, there was no way he could reach her from over there, and if he got up and came to get her, she could simply run round the table to escape. It might look a bit like a Tom and Jerry cartoon but she thought she might be able to evade him if necessary. It would be a different matter if he climbed up on the table, but she'd have to cross that bridge when she came to it.

Meanwhile, she'd gone right off her breakfast.

And then reason kicked in and she began to relax. Of course Monty wasn't going to try and attack her. With the aroma of frying animals wafting through the house, the dining room would be full of people at any moment. He'd have chosen a much more propitious place and time to do it. And besides, if he was the perpetrator of two murders already, wouldn't Siobhan have at least suspected something and sought help, rather than calmly going off to the kitchen and cooking up a feast? Lauren didn't want to start considering possible motives but he obviously knew both victims and had access to the various parts of the abbey where they'd been killed. And hadn't Bella said something about that candlestick mysteriously appearing in the billiard room *after* she'd been up there with Monty? What was that all about? If it was a clue, then it was both extremely puzzling and highly circumstantial, and it was quite likely that it had nothing whatsoever to do with Monty.

No, she decided, she was safe in the dining room. At least for now. Apart from anything else, Siobhan had self-evidently survived the night, so either Monty wasn't the killer or his own wife wasn't on the hit list, and if Siobhan wasn't a potential victim, then why on earth would Lauren be one?

She was about to try the scrambled egg when a loud voice behind her made her jump.

'Everyone still alive, then?' boomed Harrison Fforde, his tone far too jocular for the hour and the situation.

Lauren was on the point of conjuring up a barbed response but before she got the chance to deliver it, Fforde was followed into the room by Lord and Lady Verity. Monty started to get up but his Lordship waved him back into his seat, and instead Monty looked at him expectantly. After the lunchtime arrival of their hosts yesterday, Lauren was more than a little surprised to see them up and about so early, but then if they'd had as sleepless a night as she'd endured, then they would be hungry. She just hoped they weren't as irritable as she felt too.

'Ah, good – you've managed to find something to eat,' said Lady Verity. Lauren thought she saw her left eye twitch but a wink would have been wholly out of place under the circumstances. Probably the lack of sleep.

'Siobhan, your Ladyship,' said Monty.

'Ah, yes. Of course.'

'We've been up a couple of hours so she thought she might do something useful.'

'How did you sleep, Miss Sherwood?'

It was the most Lauren had heard Lady Verity speak since they'd arrived thirty-six hours earlier and she wasn't ready with a response.

'Um... Well, I didn't really.'

'Me neither,' interrupted Fforde, who was busy slopping copious quantities of tinned tomatoes onto his plate. 'Had a bit of a run-in with your gardener, actually, which kept me awake much of the night.'

'Run-in?' asked Lord Verity.

'Well, not so much a run-in as a barge-in. I got a bit lost and found myself wandering into her room by accident. The sight of her bearing down on me in her nightgown rather put the willies up me, I'm afraid. You might have heard me…'

So that explained the scream.

'I did wonder what had happened,' said Lord Verity. 'Olive can cut quite an imposing figure if you're not expecting her – although I must admit I've never seen her in her nightgown.'

Fforde waved a dripping spoon at his host, sending droplets of red soaring across the carpet.

'I'd suggest you keep it that way. Couldn't sleep a wink after that.'

'Yes, well, despite all your tall tales in the world of fiction, we don't spend all our time running around half-naked having affairs,' said his Lordship, with a note of what might easily have been regret in his voice.

Lauren put the mental image of Fforde accosting the nightie-clad gardener to the back of her mind and concentrated on eating while the others chatted aimlessly around her. It was only when the two Americans arrived that she felt an urge to move.

'Thought we'd grab a bite before we get out there for some more footage,' said Marin Cypher by way of explanation when Fforde asked pointedly if they had plans for the morning. The actor's transparency seemed so obvious to Lauren that she thought the filmmakers must see right through him, but they seemed to be tolerating him.

Which was more than could be said for her. Colorado Hughes, in particular, was positively pedantic in his shunning, but he must have had a word with Cypher too, because even the cinematographer was ignoring her.

They could be so petty.

Well, so could she.

On the pretext of not wanting to leave Siobhan alone in the kitchen – it had only just occurred to her that the tour guide was theoretically in danger, and she wondered why Monty hadn't stayed with her – Lauren excused herself and left the dining room. Strictly speaking, she wasn't too comfortable walking down the hall on her own, but compared to a chilly half-hour in the company of the Americans, it was the lesser of two evils.

When she reached the kitchen, she discovered that Siobhan wasn't alone at all: Bella and her sister Ronnie were there on monitoring duties. Ronnie was busy at the sink, washing the pans that Siobhan had used to rustle up breakfast. Bella had a tea towel in her hand and was mopping things up as quickly as Ronnie could get them clean. Siobhan herself was sitting at the large oak table, directing Bella where to put the utensils once she'd finished drying them.

'Morning, Lauren,' Bella chirped as she walked into the room. 'How was your night?'

'Long,' said Lauren, feeling the full depths of her tiredness now that she'd acquired a full belly and the disdain of the Americans. 'How about you?'

'Oh, full of excitement,' said Bella, who then shot a look of concern in Siobhan's direction. Lauren knew what she must be thinking: having lost her sister and a colleague yesterday, it was unlikely that Siobhan would consider the weekend's activities as anything approaching exciting. Devastating, yes; heartbreaking, quite possibly; harrowing, almost certainly. But exciting? Lauren knew there were people in the world who found life-threatening endangerment to be the ultimate thrill.

The sort of people who jumped off tall bridges with their feet strapped to a springy rope. Or who threw themselves out of aeroplanes at mind-boggling heights in the name of charity fundraising. Or, frankly, who stood up in front of a class full of six-year-olds and attempted to teach them something.

No, Siobhan would not be regarding this country-house event as exciting.

Bella was trying to make up for her *faux pas*.

'What I mean is that between my nocturnal visitor and the mysterious goings-on in the gardens, I had a pretty eventful night, all told.'

Lauren was concerned to hear that someone had been prowling the corridors.

'Nocturnal visitor?'

Bella laughed and indicated her sister. 'Only Ronnie. She didn't fancy spending the night locked up on her own, so she decided to come and join me in my room.'

'Oh, I see. Nothing too alarming then.'

'Depends on your view of Ronnie, I suppose.'

The subject of the conversation grabbed Bella's tea towel from her hand and flicked her with it.

'There's no need to be rude.'

Lauren was curious. 'And what exactly was going on in the garden?'

Bella took the tea towel back from her sister and picked up another pan to dry.

'You tell me. All I can say is that I saw a dark, hooded figure crossing the lawn in the middle of the night. Somebody was disobeying Professor Stone's instructions.'

'Who?'

'If I knew that, young lady, it wouldn't be a mystery, would it?'

Lauren felt a surge of adrenaline that reminded her of the tragic events at The Quaint Bookshop. Appalling and horrifying as the murder of Felicity Penman had been, she couldn't deny that there was a twisted thrill to be derived from investigating such a bloody deed. Now, in the snowbound confines of this creepy old monastery, she was feeling the same intoxicating chill.

She stared meaningfully at her partner from that investigation.

'We should check out the garden, Bella. They're bound to have left footprints.'

Bella paused for a moment. 'You do know it's been snowing again?'

'Not that much. There'll still be a trace of something visible under the new fall, I'm sure of it. What do you say?'

She could see a gleam in Bella's eye, as if she, too, felt the familiar churning in the pit of her stomach.

Ronnie stepped between them, a pair of wellingtons in her hand.

'Well, if you two are going out there, so am I.'

Lauren was uncertain about adding a supernumerary to the reading group pairing, and searched for an excuse to put her off. 'We shouldn't leave Siobhan on her own in here.'

At the mention of her name, Siobhan seemed to jump into life and she stood up quickly from her seat at the table.

'Don't worry on my account,' she said briskly. 'I'm going to the dining room to clear up the breakfast things. Monty can give me a hand. We'll be fine.'

Before any of them had the chance to object, Siobhan scuttled from the room, leaving the three of them eyeing each other up.

'Well, you can't leave me on my own now,' said Ronnie. 'You'll have to take me with you.'

Five minutes later, they were all togged out in overcoats and wellies and trudging through the drifting snow in the direction of the place where Bella had seen last night's figure in black. As she'd suspected, the footsteps were not exactly obvious until Lauren actually spotted them, at which point they became glaringly plain and they all reprimanded themselves for failing to see them before.

Lauren allowed Bella to lead the pursuit of the prints – she had been the one to see the figure, after all – but Ronnie, with only a tenuous familial link to their amateur sleuthing, was relegated to backstop, with Lauren keeping half an eye on her: she was, after all, an unknown quantity, and Professor Stone had been adamant that nobody except the reading group could be ruled out from suspicion. The trio followed the clues in single file, away from the house and in the direction of a long stone wall up ahead. At the wall, the disturbed snow took off to the right, then turned a corner before leading them to a little wooden door surrounded by an evergreen bush of some kind. As they passed through one by one, Lauren realised they were entering a sectioned-off part of the garden and she wondered what it might be for – vegetables for the kitchen seemed the obvious answer.

'The old monastery knot garden,' said Ronnie by way of explanation.

When they were all inside the walls, they stopped in a line and stared ahead of them.

There, in the middle of the neat square that was separated from the grounds, was an area that looked completely unlike the rest of the kitchen garden. All around, the snow lay pristine and flat. In the centre, where low bushes carved out a circle at the heart of the space, there was nothing short of devastation.

Someone had attacked the plants violently with an implement of some kind, ripping up the vegetation and trashing what had evidently been a neat array of greenery. Shrubs, herbs, undergrowth and winter flowers had been torn from their bedding, the soil distributed recklessly across the surrounding snow, and any semblance of order and neatness ruptured irrevocably by a forceful hand.

'Somebody's been at that with a rake,' said Ronnie redundantly.

That much had seemed obvious to Lauren, but the unanswered questions were plentiful as she surveyed the wreckage. Who would have done such a thing, and why? What possessed them to do it in the middle of the night, when everyone had been expressly forbidden to leave their rooms? And what possible connection could it have to the deaths of Keren Lowe and Hemingford Grey?

She was still mulling those impenetrable puzzles when Bella spoke with fierce determination.

'I'm going to find that rake if it's the last thing I do.'

11

There was an apocryphal story that Harrison Fforde had heard from several acting sources, each of them claiming to have heard it from someone who was there when it happened, about Peter O'Toole. According to the legend, O'Toole went on a lunchtime drinking bender with a friend before deciding to see a matinee. As they watched the opening scene unfold, O'Toole allegedly leaned across to his friend and nudged him with the words: 'You'll like this bit. This is where I come on.'

Fforde had never really believed the tale, although anecdotes about the great star's drinking habits were legion. It didn't stop it being a good story, though, and, as an old journalist drinking buddy had once drummed into him as they propped up a bar of their own at Norcester Theatre Royal and Opera House, one should never let the facts stand in the way of a good story.

Fforde recalled the urban myth now as he watched Professor Stone make his entrance. He'd been conspicuous by his absence all morning – Fforde had looked out for him at breakfast, wanting to apologise for his outburst during the night – and Fforde was beginning to form the notion that Stone might have one set of rules for himself and another for everyone else. With that kind of exceptionalism, he'd probably make a good politician.

'Ah, Professor, there you are,' he said, hurrying over to greet him. Having spent several hours in the company of the two Americans – partly to comply with the safety instructions but also in a continuing bid to ingratiate himself with them – he was ready for a change of personnel. His mission to win over the filmmakers had ground to an embarrassing halt after he'd given them a detailed rundown of his curriculum vitae, only for Colorado Hughes to express surprise that he'd never appeared in *The Bill*.

'I thought every British actor had been in *The Bill*,' the Californian had opined. 'If you can't even get a guest spot on that show, why would we wanna give you a job?'

It was particularly painful because it was true, Fforde realised, and he'd drifted away from the pair as they circumnavigated the house looking for the ideal shot, Marin Cypher taking innumerable pictures on his phone and tablet, and Hughes directing him towards the best angles in the snow. He'd never let them get out of his sight, conscious of a self-appointed reading group responsibility to stay reasonably close by, for his own safety as much as for keeping an eye on them, but they had continued their conversation without reference to him and he had even wondered if they knew he was there half the time. When they finally went back indoors, Fforde was grateful to be able to warm himself in front of a fire that Siobhan had got going in the lounge while Hughes and Cypher leaned tight over the tablet, studying the images they'd only just captured.

When the door opened imperiously, Fforde was fully expecting to see Lord and Lady Verity sail into the room, possibly attended by one or more of their staff (whom they would undoubtedly have called servants) and with a retinue that implied their lives held more value than those of anyone else at Abbots Chantry that weekend.

Instead, Professor Stone had swept in.

He was quite alone.

The Americans ignored Fforde as he went to greet the Professor. He felt unusually solicitous towards him and wondered momentarily if that meant Stone was looking a little older, more careworn: was he taking his arm and guiding him to a chair because he was pleased to see him, or because he seemed frail and needed looking after? Fforde hadn't seen much of his parents in their declining years – they rarely left their seaside cottage on the south coast and he seldom had the funds to go and visit them – but he had a clear recollection of noticing the exact occasion when they had looked old. It was soon after his fortieth birthday, when he had made a special effort to call on them, only to discover they had become practically housebound in the six months or so since he'd last seen them, and all his plans for paddling on the beach had been swiftly dropped in favour of an ice lolly from the van that toured their village once a week. In the subsequent eighteen months before their eventual departure, within two weeks of each other, he had attempted to visit as often as he could, but he still felt guilty that he hadn't been with either of them at the end, leaving that onerous task to the properly trained experts of the help-at-home service that had still operated in those days. Maybe that's why he now felt duty-bound to pay particular care to Professor Stone: he wasn't a father figure, exactly – they were too close in age for that – but perhaps he was the closest thing to one that Fforde had.

'Where have you been?' he asked the older man when he was finally settled in an armchair near the fire. 'I thought we were not supposed to wander off on our own?'

Stone shooed him away, as if he was giving off a rather unpleasant aroma.

'I haven't been on my own.'

'Then where—?'

'I've been out in the grounds with Olive.'

'The gardener?'

'Yes, the gardener. Do you know of any other Olives here this weekend?'

There was no need to be sarcastic, thought Fforde, though he didn't say anything.

'Was that sensible? I mean, isn't she just as much a suspect as everyone else?'

'Oh, Olive's all right,' said Stone, waving his hand dismissively. 'And besides, I wanted another look at where Hemingford Grey's body was found.'

Fforde waited.

Nothing happened.

'Did that help you at all?'

'Help me?'

'I mean, did seeing the location again give you any insight into his murder?'

Stone gave him a look as if to question whether Fforde was doubting his rationale.

'I'm no nearer to working out who did it, if that's what you're asking.'

Fforde wasn't sure if that was what he was asking, but refrained from pursuing the line of questioning.

'There was the small matter of the broadband to be examined as well,' said Stone.

'The broadband? What about it?'

'I wanted to see if there was any chance we could get it up and running without having to wait for an engineer from the phone company.'

'Oh, I see. And can we?'

'Well, I doubt *we* could in any circumstances. But Olive is a different story.'

'She is?'

'Oh, yes. She's not just a pretty face.'

Fforde pictured the gardener's swarthy features in his mind's eye. The truth was that she wasn't a pretty face at all, but he allowed the Professor his aphorism without challenge, especially as he carried on talking without stopping.

'What she can't do with that spanner doesn't bear thinking about. And I dare say she's just as handy with any other tool you'd care to put in her hand.'

Fforde considered this and found himself speaking aloud the thought that followed hard behind.

'What about a candlestick?'

Stone shot him a look, then glanced over his shoulder at the table where the Americans were still huddled.

'You might do well to keep your suspicions private,

Harrison,' he said quietly. 'It wouldn't do for any of our suspects to go blabbing to any of the others about what we're saying about them.'

'So you do think she's a suspect?'

Stone shook his head. 'In the absence of any evidence pointing us unequivocally towards the killer, we've got to keep our minds open, haven't we?'

'Minds open, traps shut,' said Fforde, miming a zipper across his mouth. 'Got it.'

'Good.'

They sat in silence for a few moments until something occurred to Fforde.

'So did she?'

Stone looked across at him with a curious expression on his face.

'Did who what?'

Fforde thought his question had been clear but he repeated it nonetheless. Perhaps the old man was starting to lose his marbles.

'Did Olive manage to fix the broadband?'

'Oh, that. No.'

III

It felt to Bella as if they had only just finished clearing up the breakfast dishes. Now she was in the kitchen again helping prepare lunch.

If she'd wanted a life of domestic drudgery, she could have stayed with Trevor. At least he went out to work every now and then.

It didn't help that Ronnie was hovering at her elbow, like an abandoned puppy desperate for a loving new owner. She'd spent most of the night whimpering on the other side of the huge four-poster, and Bella had wondered what she'd been dreaming about. She'd forgone the opportunity of asking her when she woke up in the grey morning, not really wanting to have to empathise with whatever her sister had had to endure in her sleep, but the faint cries Ronnie had let out at semi-regular intervals suggested she might not be enjoying the best rest of her life.

Throughout the morning, Bella had tried to find moments when she could whisper privately to Lauren about her mission to track down the rake, but Ronnie had stymied her at every opportunity, lurking on the pretext of making up a trio for safety's sake. She'd have loved to explore the stable yard, the sheds and the outhouses, but Ronnie had put the kibosh on that too: there was no way Bella was going to invite her along on this particular detective ride. Now the situation was impossible. The three of them had been nominated to come up with lunch, Siobhan's exhaustion at her grief having finally overcome her, causing her to collapse on a *chaise longue* in the lounge under the care of her husband. Lady Verity had been terribly apologetic – although maybe not as sincerely as Bella might have hoped, as one of her house guests – and requested that Ronnie take over kitchen duties for the next meal. Siobhan might be feeling a little better by evening, she suggested, which only served to make the prospect of rustling up a hot dinner for eleven loom large in Bella's mind, accompanied by a side-serving of resentment and a gravy boat of panic.

Ronnie had immediately grabbed her sister and Lauren to share the task and here they were again, slaving over the kitchen table to cut loaves, butter them economically (for who knew when more supplies might be able to reach them?) and find something edible to put between them.

'We need to talk,' Bella hissed from the opposite side of her mouth to where Ronnie was slicing.

Lauren didn't reply but gave Bella a panicked grimace, as if to say, *What am I supposed to do about it?*

Bella hadn't a clue what either of them was supposed to do about it, but she needed Ronnie out of the way. She'd come up with a variety of theories about the rake and desperately wanted to test them out on someone. She didn't imagine for a moment that any of them would stand more than a cursory inspection before falling apart at the seams, but until she tried them out on at least one other member of the reading group, she couldn't be sure.

One thing she did know for certain was that she wasn't going to co-opt her sister to the investigations.

She was racking her brains for a solution to the conundrum when one walked in through the door.

Or two, to be more precise.

Siobhan and Monty strode into the kitchen with a purposefulness that had been lacking over breakfast.

'Ah, thank you for getting started on lunch,' said Siobhan, giving the volunteered trio a warm smile. Bella thought she could detect a hint of puffiness around her eyes and some redness in the whites, but tears were only to be expected under the circumstances. What was a little stranger was that Monty seemed to be trying to control himself, his teeth gritted, his hands tense and his skin displaying a livid, mustardy pallor. Losing a sister-in-law might provoke one to sadness, despondency, misery even, but this looked much more like stifled fury and Bella got the distinct impression that he and Siobhan had recently been arguing.

'Where are we up to?' Siobhan went on, taking an apron from a drawer and tying it round her waist. Subliminally she was making it clear that the kitchen was under her command again, and if Ronnie had any ideas about taking control of the periscope then she would need to rethink them pretty fast.

'Lots of buttered bread, not much filling,' said Bella, feeling no inclination to protect her sister from the usurper. If she knew Ronnie, she wouldn't be bothered about handing over the reins in any case. Then the thought of a periscope with reins made her smile involuntarily, and she hoped Siobhan would read it as a 'pleased-to-see-you' smile rather than the 'where-the-hell-have-you-been-while-we've-been-slaving-over-a-hot-butter-knife' kind.

'We'll be needing the dried ham,' said Siobhan, clearly intending her remark for her husband but declining to look at him as she delivered it.

'Righto,' he replied, also not making eye contact. He headed for a door that Bella hadn't noticed before, and when he opened it she was amazed to see racks of food stacked on shelves, in piles and across the floor of what appeared to be a pantry designed to survive the end of the world. Never mind a lunch for eleven, this storehouse of wonders could keep a cavalry squadron well fed for months and still have supplies left over for the horses.

As Monty disappeared inside the treasury of provisions, the kitchen door opened again and Lady Verity made what Bella considered to be a grand entrance: she flung the door back on its hinges and stood there, one hand against her forehead in the traditional pose of a despairing maiden in a silent movie awaiting her knight in shining armour to rescue her from the clutches of the moustachioed villain. The full tweeds, deerstalker and Burberry wellingtons detracted from the Clara Bow look somewhat but Bella was taken aback nonetheless, not least by the similarity of expression to that which Siobhan had worn on her own entrance minutes earlier.

'Ah, here you all are,' she sighed dramatically, and stepped over the threshold.

'Where else would we be?' asked Siobhan, a distinct edge

in her voice. Bella suspected Monty hadn't heard the last of whatever their argument had been about.

'I'm sorry, Siobhan, have I done something to upset you?'

So she'd detected the tone in Siobhan's response too.

Bella decided to step in to avert any further ructions within the household.

'We were just preparing some sandwiches for lunch.'

'Oh, how lovely. I don't know how you all do it in such circumstances.'

Siobhan, now hovering over the sink, muttered something under her breath.

'I beg your pardon?' asked Lady Verity sweetly.

'Nothing.'

'No, I distinctly heard you mumble something. Would you mind sharing it with the rest of us? Please?'

Siobhan turned quickly – more quickly than Lady Verity seemed to be expecting – and was about to open her mouth when Monty appeared at the pantry door again, a jar of pickled something-or-other in one hand and a large pink joint in the other.

'Ah, Lady Verity. I thought I heard your dulcet tones.'

'Monty,' she said, 'I was just discussing the luncheon menu with Siobhan but I missed what she said, so I simply asked her to repeat it.'

'Ham,' said Siobhan forcibly.

Bella was surprised to hear the house's tour guide refer to its mistress's appearance in such a derogatory way, then realised Siobhan was pointing at the hunk of meat in Monty's left hand.

Monty must have had the same worry because he swiftly

put the meat and the pickle jar down on the table and diverted Lady Verity back the way she had come, taking her by the elbow and steering her out of the door. Bella was completely mystified by the look he threw back over his shoulder as he departed: was it intended for Siobhan, and if so, did it signify an attempt to protect her from the lady of the house by removing her from Siobhan's domain, or was it something else entirely? Perhaps it hadn't even been for Siobhan. But then who was it for, and what did it mean?

Bella was still searching for answers to these impossible questions when Siobhan let out an earthy expletive.

'Well, I don't think there's any need for that,' Bella said, looking in shock at Siobhan.

'I'm sorry. It's just that she winds me up.'

'Her Ladyship?'

'*Ladyship* – really! She's nothing more than a jumped-up bitch.'

Bella stared at Siobhan, then at the door, which was still standing ajar. She moved across to it quickly and pushed it to, checking first outside in the corridor that her Ladyship wasn't still within earshot and Siobhan hadn't just signed a rather fruity resignation letter.

'I'm sure you shouldn't be talking about your employer in these terms,' she said, shooting a glance of desperation towards Lauren, who had spent the last five minutes immobile beside the dresser. Bella didn't know if her young friend was enjoying the entertainment or in a state of shock herself.

'Do you want to pop the kettle on, Lauren?' she said as she ushered Siobhan away from the sink and towards a chair. 'I think Siobhan could do with a cup of tea.'

'I'll crack on with the sandwiches,' said Ronnie in an uncharacteristically helpful intervention.

'Here – have a little sit down,' said Bella, nodding at Lauren and Ronnie to approve their activities.

'I don't want a little sit down,' said Siobhan. 'I want to kill her.'

Bella decided she needed to remove Siobhan from the kitchen altogether and executed a swift change of manoeuvre. Vetoing the door into the hallway for fear of running into Lady Verity again, she aimed instead for another door that she hadn't noticed before, tucked away in a corner beyond the end of the dresser.

'Let's get a change of scene, shall we? What's in here?'

Without waiting for an answer, she pulled the door open and guided Siobhan through it.

On the other side, they found themselves at the top of a flight of stairs. Bella spotted a light switch on the wall – one of those old brown bakelite contraptions that snapped with a satisfying certainty – and instinctively flicked it, forgetting Monty's orders to use as little power as possible. Immediately, the space was illuminated by a cold, bare bulb and she could see the stone stairs leading down into darkness below. Judging by the bare brick of the walls and a faint mustiness in the air, Bella realised she must have inadvertently chosen the door that led to the cellar, and she turned back to take Siobhan into the kitchen once more.

'Are you sure it's wise to split up?' asked Lauren as they reappeared into the comparative warmth.

'Oh, yes. You weren't planning to attack Ronnie, were you?

And however much I joke about her, I'm sure she's not a killer, so you'll be quite safe with her.'

Lauren gave a pointed look at Siobhan, whose face was still screwed up into a ruddy grimace of fury.

'I meant you.'

'Don't worry about us. We'll be fine,' said Bella, and led Siobhan to the hallway door.

She peered out to make sure the coast was clear, then took Siobhan's hand and went out into the corridor.

'Is there somewhere nice and cosy we can sit for a bit?'

Siobhan seemed to snap out of whatever funk she'd fallen into.

'The study. We could have gone there.'

'Well, we still can.'

'No, down the stairs.'

Bella sensed that things were starting to get a bit too much for Siobhan.

'Let's go in here, shall we?'

She pushed at the first door they came to and discovered that it was another sitting room, evidently less favoured than the lounge they'd been entertained in so far. The furniture was all in dark, heavy wood, the wallpaper thickly flocked in lurid deep green, and there was a stale aroma of disuse and dust in the air. But Bella sighed with relief: it wouldn't have done for Siobhan to have launched into a diatribe that could have been heard throughout the ground floor and maybe beyond.

Once inside, though, with the door securely shut, the diatribe was unleashed.

'Now, what's Lady Verity done, exactly?' Bella asked.

'Don't get me started on that stuck-up cow. She only

married him for the money, you know. Before that she was just like the rest of us, but now she's got ideas above her station she's Miss High-and-Mighty.'

Bella had had an aged aunt who used that expression – 'ideas above her station' – and had, as a small child, asked her what it meant. The aunt had concocted some fabulous lie about the architect of St Pancras who, she claimed, had originally designed the hotel frontage without its famous clock tower but, when the building was completed, had decided it needed something extra and forked out for the finishing touch from his own pocket, only to be snubbed for an honour by Queen Victoria for thinking himself too grand, with ideas literally 'above his station'. For years, Bella had relayed the story to countless acquaintances and friends, only to be met with uncomprehending and disbelieving looks from people who apparently knew her aunt had made the whole thing up. It was, typically, Trevor who had set her right on the subject, ridiculing her in front of a garden full of guests one summer evening round a barbecue, and it had taken all her inner strength not to grab one of the red-hot skewers from the grill and plant it firmly in a place where kebabs didn't normally go.

Not in that direction of travel, at least.

Now she came to think of it, she wondered why Ronnie hadn't quietly told her the truth at some point in their youth. She really could be an annoying little sister. But then again, perhaps she believed the story too, and was clinging on to Auntie Norma's mythical fable with the same avid innocence as she had that family folklore about being related to Shakespeare's granddaughter, and therefore to Shakespeare himself. Just because their father had told them it as indisputable fact, it didn't make it true, as she'd learned from a visitor experience assistant at one of the houses in Stratford-upon-Avon, who'd declared categorically on a school trip that Bella's father was wrong. He had to be because Shakespeare's granddaughter, despite being married twice, had had no children.

And thus had ended Bella's childhood dream of becoming a writer as famous as her supposed forebear.

They were buggers, those visitor experience assistants.

Anyway, Siobhan was still ranting about Lady Verity.

'Bloody gold-digger. God knows what he saw in her.'

Bella wanted to know how Lord Verity had met his wife but she couldn't get a word in – edgeways, straight on or in any other format she could think of.

'And now she runs this place as if she were born to it, bossing us around, taking things that aren't hers and acting as if she owns it. Well, she doesn't. She only married into it, and she's bloody lucky that we've all been willing to go along with it. Did you see how she reacted to the news that Keren had been killed?'

Bella would happily have offered an opinion on this but it seemed that Siobhan's question was, in fact, rhetorical.

'She didn't bat an eyelid. Didn't stop to grieve for a moment. She might as well have killed the poor cow herself.'

Siobhan finally took a breath, but only to inhale ahead of a gigantic sobbing spree, the emotion of the past forty-eight hours catching up with her once more. Bella toyed with the idea of going off in search of Monty, but too many negatives militated against that course of action. Not only did she have no desire to go walking the corridors alone with an unidentified killer still on the loose, she was far from certain that Monty's presence would do anything to alleviate Siobhan's misery. He might even make things worse, especially since he'd last been seen with his arm round the object of Siobhan's ire.

'That's it, dear. You let it all out,' she said at last as the sobs subsided into snivelling.

Bella couldn't really imagine what it would be like if Ronnie had been the victim of a double-murderer and she had no desire to find out now. But she was sure she'd be just as upset as Siobhan, possibly even marshalling her emotions to lash out, as Siobhan was doing, at anyone who happened to be in the vicinity. For Siobhan right now, that was Lady Verity, but half an hour earlier it had evidently been Monty. If Bella stayed in this sitting room with her much longer, she figured, she might be next.

'Right,' she said decisively, not relishing that prospect at all. 'Time for some lunch.'

IV

Friday night's dinner had been an awkward affair, there was no denying it. But, for different reasons, Professor Stone was finding Sunday's buffet lunch an equally tricky occasion.

He looked round the table at the *dramatis personae* who peopled this chilling mystery.

At one end of the table, Ronnie was having a quiet conversation with Olive, who, for safety reasons, had been invited to join the repast. Monty and Siobhan were studiously avoiding each other, while Lauren and Harrison were vying for the attention of Colorado Hughes and Marin Cypher. Lord and Lady Verity were picking at the sandwiches on their plates, as if they didn't really know what to do with the half-slices Siobhan had cut: perhaps they were more used to fingers of cucumber sandwiches, or quartered segments with salmon or beef paste.

Ten. Eleven including himself.

Someone was missing.

It was only when he realised the misplaced guest was Bella Bourton that Professor Stone began to feel really concerned. Thinking back over his morning, he registered that he hadn't seen her since last night – although nobody else had remarked on her absence, so he assumed someone must have seen her this morning.

He decided to check.

'Has anyone seen Bella today?'

The table fell silent as everyone turned to the Professor.

'Yes. Why?'

He looked at Siobhan, whose countenance suggested she was as anxious about Bella's welfare as he was himself.

'It's just that I haven't seen her at all this morning and I was starting to get worried.'

'Oh, you don't need to worry,' Siobhan said, waving a dismissive hand in the Professor's direction. 'I was with her in the green sitting room a few minutes ago.'

Her exhortation not to be concerned did nothing to calm Stone's anxiety.

'How long ago – exactly?'

Siobhan seemed taken aback and looked at the watch on her wrist. 'Ten minutes, maybe? Fifteen at the most.'

The Professor was out of his chair and heading for the door before Siobhan had finished her sentence. As he went, he collected Olive, who was also quick to get up.

Two opposing theories had formed in Stone's mind about Olive. One was the most obvious, the conclusion that the group had reached when she'd first appeared with Hemingford Grey's body in a wheelbarrow: she remained high on the list of suspects. She had the means, certainly, but any sense of motive was still obscure and dim in his thinking. The other theory was that she might be their best ally in tracking down the actual killer, with her insider knowledge of the house and its occupants, as well as being handy with a toolbox in all kinds of circumstances.

Either way, he figured the wisest thing to do with her was to keep her close by his side. If she wanted to kill him, he'd be ready, and at least he was removing the potential threat from the others; if it wasn't her at all, she could turn out to be incredibly useful.

'Which way's the green sitting room?' he asked in an urgent tone as they emerged into the hall.

Olive led the way down the corridor, past a particularly gruesome stuffed deer that was mounted in a niche in front of a painted backdrop of a Scottish glen, then turned right down a side passage. Two doors down, she stopped and waited for Stone to catch up.

She wasn't too many years younger than him, he estimated, but her speed had left him breathless.

'This one.' She pointed at the door, which was firmly closed.

Stone could feel his heart pounding and knew it wasn't just because of his lack of fitness.

'What are we waiting for?' he asked, and pushed it open.

The green sitting room was empty.

They returned to the dining room almost as quickly as they'd left it, and Stone was in a masterful frame of mind.

'Right. Nobody is to move from this room. Understood?'

Lady Verity seemed especially unsettled by his commanding tone.

'May I ask why?'

The Professor felt a twinge of irritation. Why couldn't people just do what they were told in an emergency? It had been the same at the university: rules and regulations were there for a reason but young people seemed to make it a doctrinal principle to challenge them at every opportunity. He'd once had a discussion with the dean in which the academic chief had expressed his delight that youngsters under their care were finding their own voices and pushing back against the forces of officialdom. Stone had responded that they were all wilful little toerags who should be sent back to sixth form to learn some manners and the conversation had ended with a cordial agreement to disagree. He was younger then and had mellowed in his opinion somewhat in the intervening years, but Stone had never really come to terms with the theory that raw individualism was a virtue to be applauded.

He swaddled his irritation in layers of *politesse* and replied with all the pleasantry he could muster.

'Because Bella has gone missing and Olive and I are going to find her and I don't want to come back to discover that other members of our party have gone wandering off in the meantime necessitating a further search that will endanger not only their lives but ours as well. Will that suffice, m'lady?'

Lady Verity clearly had no idea whether Stone was being sarcastic or genuine; in the absence of any riposte, he nudged Olive's arm and made for the door once more.

'Can't we help?'

Lauren's voice reached the Professor just as his hand rested on the door knob.

He turned back to see her looking eagerly towards Harrison, as if inviting him to join her as she offered her services in the search for their reading group colleague.

Her expectant face and obvious dedication to Bella's safety melted something deep inside the Professor and he modified his stern demeanour for her benefit.

'I'm not sure that's a good idea, Lauren.'

'Why not? Two pairs will cover the ground twice as quickly as one, and you know you can rely on me and Harrison.'

Lauren's broad, innocent grin took him back to the early days of the reading group, when Felicity Penman was still alive and had brought the intrepid foursome together at The Quaint Bookshop for a purpose they could not have guessed at when they first met, but which had forged a bond between them that would, he had no doubt, last the rest of their lives. No one goes through an experience like the one they had together without it affecting them permanently.

'All right, then,' he said. 'But you must do exactly as I say.'

Fforde in particular seemed less than enthusiastic about that last edict, but they were in no position to argue: if they wanted to participate in the hunt for Bella Bourton, they would have to agree to Professor Stone's terms.

'Can we come too?'

Stone was surprised to hear Colorado Hughes volunteering for the search party. But then he realised: Hughes wasn't offering to help. He wanted his cinematographer on the job, capturing every moment on video for their documentary feature.

'No, you can't,' he said.

On his way out of the dining room behind Olive, Lauren

and Harrison, he picked up the candlestick that was standing on a sideboard near the door, left there by whoever had handled it last. If they were going roaming around the deserted house, it might just come in handy.

Lord Verity's warble wafted after him into the hall.

'Excuse me – that's a valuable antique.'

Stone pulled the door closed behind him and lowered his voice.

'I wasn't sure about asking you to join us, Lauren, because we have now left nobody from the group among the remainder of the household, and that troubles me.'

A frown passed across Lauren's face.

'Why should you want one of us to stay with them?'

Stone sighed. 'How many detective novels would you say we've read at the bookshop, Lauren?'

'I don't know – a couple of dozen, perhaps. Maybe more.'

'Definitely more,' interjected Fforde. 'I keep a careful record of them.'

Stone raised a surprised eyebrow, which Fforde noticed.

'I know you all think I'm a slob in my bachelor pad but there are some things I take extremely seriously,' the actor protested. 'LPs in alphabetical order of band or musician, catalogued cuttings from my theatre performances … and a register of the reading group's books, together with our communal verdict on them. Call me peculiar—'

'Oh, I do,' interrupted Stone.

'—but some things have to be just so,' Fforde concluded.

'Out of interest,' said Lauren, looking oddly at Fforde, 'when you say alphabetical order, do you count first name or surname? I mean, does Ed Sheeran come under E or S?'

Fforde lifted his head from the close huddle they had formed and pulled his shoulders back.

'I am delighted to say that Ed Sheeran comes neither under E nor under S as he has no place in any self-respecting music fan's record collection.'

'Oh, that's a bit harsh,' said Olive unexpectedly. 'He's got some rather good tunes if you ask me.'

Professor Stone was regretting inviting Lauren and Harrison to join the search.

'I think we're getting off the point. Now, if you want to join this little expedition – against my better judgement, I have to say – then you'll need to follow my orders. OK?'

'OK,' said Lauren, her face expectant once more.

'Oh, all right. If you insist,' said Fforde, leaning in again.

'Right. You two start on the ground floor of the main house. Check the doors leading off the hall on both sides, but don't go any further than the kitchen. When you've done that, come back to the main stairs and do the same thing on the first floor.'

'Where will you be?' asked Lauren.

'Olive and I will spread a bit further afield. With her knowledge of the house and estate, we can try some of the more out-of-the-way spots without risking getting lost. But we're only looking for Bella, remember? Don't go off on some secondary jaunt trying to find clues to the murderer or anything like that. Understood?'

Lauren and Fforde both nodded decisively and were about to head off down the corridor when Lauren hesitated.

'Yes, Lauren?'

'Why *did* you want one of us to stay in there with them?' She jerked a thumb at the dining room door.

'Because, my sweet little innocent, one of them has to be a double-murderer, and sitting cooped up in a room with the employers and colleagues of your victims is bound to make him – or her – uncomfortable, especially if they're left for a decent amount of time. If one of us were still in there, we would be able to watch out for hints in the conversation or anything suspicious in anyone's actions. As it is, it feels like we're wasting an opportunity.'

'Oh, no! Why didn't you say so? I feel like I want to be back in there now.'

'No, I'm sorry, Lauren. You can't do that now – it would look too dodgy after you were so keen to come and look for Bella with us. But if you make a quick search of this floor and upstairs, you could probably be back in there within ten minutes or so on the lookout for any strange behaviour. How does that sound?'

'Like a plan,' said Lauren, and grabbed Fforde's arm to lead him down the hall.

'Unless...' said Fforde, resisting Lauren's guidance.

'Unless what?'

'Unless we find Bella.'

'That's the point of searching, isn't it?' said Stone, not understanding where Fforde was going with his train of thought. Train might be a bit generous, of course: Fforde's thought might be merely a handcar on the rails of conjecture heading relentlessly for the buffers of futility.

'No, I mean *find* her. Not *find* her.'

The riddles were sorely testing Stone's patience now.

'Yes, that's what we're hoping to do. Find her.'

'No, we're hoping to find her, as in see where she's got to.

But what if we ... find her ... you know...' Fforde seemed unable to finish the sentence. 'Find ... her ... body?'

He whispered the last word, as if saying it could somehow make it happen.

Stone was shocked. In his head, the search for Bella was a practical exercise in reuniting everyone in the same place of safety. He had not allowed himself to consider any alternative. In his heart, he knew Fforde had put a harsh spotlight on another terrifying possibility: a different, but equally plausible reason for her absence.

It was possible that Bella Bourton had already become the killer's third victim.

The Study

I

Self-preservation featured highly on Harrison Fforde's list of priorities for life. It might not have been at the very summit of the list but it certainly made the top ten, and under the right circumstances – such as being stranded in a remote, snowbound country house while a game-playing killer picked his way through the names of the guests and staff – it might easily have risen to the top three. As a result, he hadn't really wanted to join Lauren in the search for Bella. He had derived a sense of security from the herd and was perfectly willing to endure whatever time there was going to be until rescue arrived in the same room as everyone else, even if that included the killer. By his reckoning, no further murders could practically be committed while they remained together. In contrast, prowling the gloomy rooms of Abbots Chantry with a young woman of indeterminate physical ability seemed like the worst possible outcome.

'Keep up, Harrison,' said Lauren, several yards ahead of him in the hallway. The absence of electric lighting hadn't been so bad in the large reception rooms of the house, where fires in the grate and strategically placed candles had offered a vestige of beneficence – a glimmer of hope, one might say – but out here in the cold, dark corridor, the walls seemed to lean in oppressively, danger lurking unquestionably round every corner.

'Stop going so fast,' he replied, the sound of his voice echoing off the panelling and swirling round his ears in a whine of mockery. 'I'm not as young as I used to be.'

'Then stop behaving like a child,' came the reply, pertinent and provocative in equal measure.

It stung because it was true. Harrison knew by now that not only had he never grown up properly, he also never would. The things of adulthood – maturity, serious relationships, a credit card – had escaped him thus far and there were no signs that he would get any nearer to enjoying any of them in this lifetime. Such was the sacrifice he had been forced to make for his art.

Oh, come on. Who was he kidding? Art? A few creaky old repertory productions of plays that should have been retired long ago did not constitute a life of cultural creativity. He had found a place in the landscape of British theatre and settled for it. It wasn't so bad. The odd job that came up, when he managed to persuade some casting director to give him another shot, had been perfectly acceptable in the grand scheme of things. He had long ago abandoned any hope of stardom or fame – whatever they meant in these social media-driven times that had left him far in their wake when it came to public profile – but he'd had his diminutive share of acclaim in front of the footlights, even once acquiring a fan who turned up at the stage door a few times, collecting his autograph on her programme and a selfie on her mobile before vanishing as randomly as she'd arrived. He'd later found out that Margaret – that was the name below her mugshot on the court report in the *Norcester Echo* – had not been quite honest with him when she'd told him how big a fan she was and begged him to show her his dressing room. At least it had explained where his wallet had disappeared to. The police had been very sympathetic about his being scammed but held out little hope of recovering either the wallet or its contents, and their lack of optimism had, indeed, proved correct. He didn't mind losing the twenty quid and loose change so much as the dog-eared black-and-white photo of Selina that he'd kept for sentimental reasons: there was no way his ex-wife would be willing to replace it, so her image was lost to him for ever, except in those semi-regular dreams he experienced which woke him up drenched in sweat and gasping for breath. He'd never been able to remember the exact contents of the dreams, only their physical effect on his body, so he couldn't tell whether his unconscious mind still felt fondly towards her or was terrified of her.

Funnily enough, it was his immaturity that Selina had ultimately blamed for the collapse of their marriage.

Women could be such temperamental creatures.

'Have we checked this one?' he asked as they passed yet another dark wooden door. They all looked the same to him, and he could only get his bearings from the variation in the stuffed animals that lined the hall. He was sure he'd seen that squirrel eating an acorn minutes before.

'Yes – that's one of the sitting rooms.'

'How many have they got?'

'Don't know. They're all named by colour and so far we've seen a red one, a yellow one and a green one.'

'Only brown, scarlet, black, ochre, peach, ruby, olive, violet, fawn, lilac, gold, chocolate, mauve, cream, crimson, silver, rose, azure, lemon, russet, grey, purple, white, pink, orange and blue to go then.'

He'd barely reached violet before Lauren had stopped and turned back. Now she stared at him, bewildered.

'What on earth are you talking about, Harrison?'

'Have you never seen *Joseph and the Amazing Technicolor Dreamcoat*?'

'No, I haven't.'

'I was in a production in Weston-super-Mare once. Those are the colours of his coat. It's a bugger to learn, you know, but once you've got it, it never leaves you.'

'Clearly. Now can we get on with looking for Bella, please?'

'Sorry. Yes, of course.'

When they reached the main staircase, halfway along the hall, Lauren stopped again.

'Should we finish down here or do upstairs next?'

Fforde weighed it up: the corridor ahead of them looked uninviting, while the plushly carpeted stairway was lit with a couple of warm, candle-powered lanterns and looked much more appealing.

'Upstairs, I think.'

'There's only a few more doors down here, so we'll check those when we come down again.'

Fforde felt a little wary about wandering into the rooms along the landing as several of them had been temporarily transformed into a home away from home by the guests at the house. But there was no other way to check that they were empty, and he didn't suppose there'd be anything incriminating left lying around in any case, so he steeled himself against potential impropriety and opened doors willy-nilly. Handily, Lauren was equally forthright and between them they cleared the landing in a few minutes.

Back at the bottom of the stairs, they assessed their situation. With just a handful of doors to go, there was no sign of Bella. There was also no sign of the Professor and Olive, but that didn't seem too surprising to Fforde, given that they had the whole of the rest of the estate to cover.

'Do you think it's a good or a bad sign that we haven't found her yet?' he asked Lauren as they pushed open the first of the remaining doors to find a walk-in closet stuffed full with trenchcoats, boots, hats and umbrellas.

'It's got to be good, hasn't it?' said Lauren, moving on to the next door.

'How do you figure that out?'

'If she'd been murdered, she'd stay in one place. If she's mobile, she's got to be alive.'

Fforde had serious doubts about Lauren's reasoning. For one thing, her body could have been stashed somewhere they were unlikely to find it on a cursory search of the house and grounds. For another, anyone with the agility to do what they had done with Keren Lowe's body – staging her death to look like suicide by leaping from the tower window – would have no problem shifting Bella's slight frame wherever they wanted. No, deadness was no guarantee of a stationary corpse.

Yet he still found himself slightly grateful not to have found

Bella when he reached the last door, nearest the grand entrance.

With a perfunctory shove, he swung the door open.

Bella Bourton was sitting in a large office chair behind a huge mahogany desk in what was clearly Lord Verity's study.

She glanced up from the book she was reading and smiled at him.

'Hello, Harrison.'

Fforde felt something peculiar rising inside him. He couldn't tell at this early stage whether it was a gush of sudden relief or a wave of angry incredulity but the result was much the same.

'Bella!' he boomed, making her jump in her seat. 'What the hell are you doing in here?'

She regained her composure rather more quickly than Fforde did, and waggled her book at him.

'Reading about knot gardens. What are you doing?'

'You're supposed to be in the dining room with everyone else. We've been turning the house upside down looking for you because the Professor has got it into his head that you've become the next victim of our resident murderer.'

'Where on earth did he get that idea?'

'I don't know. Maybe it was something to do with the fact that we're all under express instructions not to go wandering off alone, and when you didn't turn up for lunch, he put two and two together. Not unreasonably, I might add.'

'Oh, I couldn't put up with all those miserable faces from the staff over the dinner table. I thought I'd eat something a bit later so I took Siobhan as far as the door then went back to the kitchen.'

'And now you're here in the study. Alone.'

Bella was about to reply when Lauren appeared at Fforde's shoulder, peering into the study and sharing his look of amazement at seeing their reading group colleague comfortably ensconced at the desk.

'Thank goodness you're OK,' she said enthusiastically.

'Why wouldn't I be?'

As Lauren stepped inside the study and moved towards Bella, Fforde glanced out of the window to the gravel forecourt at the front of the house.

Walking calmly up the drive came Professor Stone and Olive, the gardener.

'We need to let them know you're safe,' he said, and darted to the front door.

'Professor! We've found Bella. She's been here in the study all along.'

Stone quickened his step and Olive kept pace with him as they crossed the gravel and entered the house. The relief was etched on his face as he hurried into the study and gave Bella a warm hug.

'Well,' he said at last, after releasing her from his embrace and looking around the other four faces in the room. 'It looks like we've got the band back together. Shall we do some sleuthing?'

11

She had nothing against the gardener personally, but Bella found it very odd that Professor Stone seemed to have welcomed her into their group without even running it past the other members. Olive might be completely innocent – although Bella had her doubts about that, given what she'd discovered and the background reading she'd been up to – but it was hardly the place of any one individual to invite rogue guests into their deliberations.

She looked at Lauren and Harrison to see if they were showing any signs of feeling the same way, and was quietly pleased to see that they were. Lauren had her brows furrowed in a slight frown. Fforde looked positively steaming, but that could have been the remnants of his railing at her a few minutes earlier for not being with the crowd in the dining room.

Then again, he often seemed as if he was seething away to himself; it was so hard to tell what was really going on under the surface.

'Professor,' she ventured, trying to come up with a choice of words that wouldn't sound too harsh.

'Bella.'

'Perhaps Olive would be more useful keeping an eye on the others?'

Bella had barely exchanged a handful of words with Olive – that was one of the reasons she could make no firm judgement about her culpability or otherwise – but she had to hand it to her. She could clearly read subtext.

'If you're going to talk about me, I'll just pop into the dining room,' she said.

Before the Professor could intervene to change her mind, Olive had left the room, closing the door behind her.

The Professor looked stern.

'That was a bit uncalled-for, don't you think?'

'Actually, no,' said Bella, feeling braver than she had any right to feel under the circumstances. 'We don't really know anything about Olive, do we? And if we're going to share our theories about who killed Keren and Hemingford, it's best we do it in the privacy of our own little group.'

'Mmm,' said Fforde enigmatically. 'Our Professor here has his own theory about Olive. Thinks that because she's handy with a spanner, she can't possibly be the killer.'

Bella turned that over in her mind for a moment before replying.

'Surely being handy with a spanner would be more likely to put her in the frame?'

'Aha!' shouted Fforde. 'That's exactly what I said.'

'Well, not exactly,' said the Professor. 'But my point is that I don't believe Olive to be a danger, particularly when she's physically with us. And she could have given us some helpful inside knowledge if you hadn't just sent her packing, Bella.'

Bella felt her confidence ebbing away and was grateful when Fforde changed the subject.

'Look, if you want to do some sleuthing, shouldn't we start thinking about possible motives for the murders?'

'Agreed,' said Stone. 'Do we still think it most likely that someone killed Grey because he knew their secret?'

'I never thought it was likely,' said Fforde. 'I know sex is one of the biggest reasons for killing someone, but I can't see him resorting to blackmail.'

'You didn't speak to him in the gift shop. He sounded pretty sinister to me. And before that, he'd been really pushy trying to find out about our investigation into Felicity's murder. I think he was just nosey, but I didn't like it.'

'If he was nosey, that's all the more reason to think he might have known a secret,' said Lauren. 'But who was he blackmailing?'

'Lord and Lady Verity are the ones with all the money,' said Stone thoughtfully. 'There's no point in blackmailing someone who hasn't got any, is there?'

Here was a subject Bella felt she could speak about with some authority. She might not be best pals with her sister but she'd gleaned enough over her time at Abbots Chantry to be able to put the Professor straight on this one.

'But they don't,' she said.

The Professor looked at her. 'Who doesn't what?'

'Lord and Lady Verity – they don't have any money. That's why they rely on volunteers like Ronnie.'

Bella was quietly pleased with the effect her intelligence had on the others.

'Why do you think they're sucking up to the film people the way they are? They need the location fees from *Murder on the Polar Express*.'

It took a moment for Professor Stone to gather himself. When he spoke, it was less complimentary than Bella had hoped for.

'Well, that might have been useful information to have shared with us all a little sooner. Is there any other morsel of pertinent detail that you'd like to share with us, Bella?'

Bella felt Lauren take a step nearer to her. 'Don't pick on Bella. I've got a feeling she *has* got a helpful thing or two to tell us. Am I right?'

She pointed at the book Bella had deposited on the desk and made an encouraging gesture.

'Oh. Yes. That.'

Bella's bravery drained from her once more as she realised everyone was looking at her expectantly. All she really had to go on was a nocturnal vision and a book on flora. And she didn't mean the margarine. That, at least, she might have known something about.

'Right…'

'Go on, Bella. You've found something, haven't you?'

She could hardly bear to see Lauren's wide eyes. The poor girl was so trusting, so sure she'd come up with something groundbreaking. It was going to be hard letting her down gently.

'I don't know. It's probably nothing.'

'Come on, Bella – don't put yourself down,' said Fforde

encouragingly. 'Wasn't it you who put the crucial pieces together in the Felicity Penman investigation?'

'Er, no. I don't think it was.'

'What have you found?' The Professor sounded more than a little impatient.

'All right, I'll tell you. I saw something last night, about an hour after we all went to bed and barricaded ourselves in.'

'What?' Professor Stone had stepped up from impatient to irritable.

'I'm not sure. But there was someone wandering about in the grounds.'

'Who?'

'If I knew that, my information would be a lot more useful.'

'Is that it?'

Bella could tell she'd disappointed the Professor, but in fairness, she'd never made any grand claims for her news.

'Well, I do have something else—'

Fforde threw his hands up in exasperation.

'I thought you'd found the smoking gun. I thought you were going to tell us who the killer was and how they'd done it. Instead, all you've got is a mystery figure traipsing about in the snow.'

Lauren took another step closer to Bella.

'Hold on. She hasn't finished.' She turned to Bella and gave her a warm smile. 'You said you had something else. Is it to do with the knot garden?'

Bella nodded.

Professor Stone suddenly looked keen.

'The knot garden? What about it?'

The fact that the Professor knew about the knot garden

came as a surprise to Bella. She thought the expedition that she, Lauren and Ronnie had undertaken earlier that morning would be shedding fresh light on a part of the estate that had so far remained obscured to the rest of the group.

She was wrong.

'You know about the knot garden?'

'I've been there.'

Shock number two.

'Hemingford Grey told me about it and I went out to see it yesterday morning.'

Bella was really curious now.

'How did it look?'

'What do you mean, how did it look? It looked like a knot garden covered in snow.'

'It was intact, then?'

'Intact? Yes, I suppose so. The only disturbance was a set of footprints that led there from the kitchen door. Other than that, it was just a walled garden. Quite picturesque, actually.'

Lauren rested a hand on Bella's arm. 'What does it mean, Bella?'

The testy edge returned to Professor Stone's voice. 'What does what mean?'

Bella breathed out slowly. 'Lauren and I went out there with Ronnie this morning after breakfast. It was in ruins.'

It seemed nobody quite knew what to say to that.

'Someone attacked the knot garden with a rake. I've been trying to get my hands on it ever since.'

The Professor looked perplexed. 'Why?'

'Why what?'

'Why have you been trying to get your hands on it?'

Bella knew her answer was insubstantial, and she feared the group might think her inexperience in matters detectional was coming to the fore again.

'Just a feeling. I think it might be significant.'

Fforde was nodding slowly. 'And if it has something to do with the footprints the Professor found yesterday, then it very well might be.'

'But how? All I found was a set of prints that went from the kitchen to the knot garden, then on to the estate manager's office. Nothing particularly odd about that.'

There was something about the Professor's tone that suggested he was softening in his resistance to Bella's anecdote.

Fforde pursued the line of thought. 'Except that nobody would make a casual trip to the knot garden in the middle of a blizzard like the one we've been having.'

Lauren's eyes were bright with excitement. 'Unless it was part of their job.'

'Job?' Bella wasn't sure what she was driving at. 'What do you mean?'

'She means Olive.' The Professor looked ominous. 'You warned me to look out for her, Harrison. Said she could be dangerous with that spanner. And if she is the one who's been making nocturnal trips to the knot garden, that doesn't look good for her.'

Bella was getting thoroughly lost.

'Why not? Why shouldn't she go to the knot garden?'

'In the middle of the night?' said Lauren. 'In the middle of a snowstorm? And not just one night. She went twice, on successive nights – first to visit it, then to destroy it. No, that's decidedly dodgy.'

Bella could feel the rumblings of a runaway train about to set off from panic station.

'We don't even know for sure it was her.'

'You just said you saw her, didn't you?'

Bella was on surer ground here. 'No, I didn't. I said I saw *someone*. A tall figure in a dark hood. It could have been Harrison for all I know.'

'It couldn't,' said Fforde emphatically. 'I was in one of the bedrooms an hour after we all went to bed.'

He stopped and eyed up his audience.

'But it couldn't have been Olive, either. Because the bedroom I was in was hers.'

Bella didn't imagine that any performance Harrison Fforde had given on the stage had ever had such a dramatic effect.

Unfortunately, his confession – swiftly explained away by his account of wandering the landing in defiance of Professor Stone's orders – helped not one iota with their investigation. His reporting of the whispered conversation he'd overheard between Siobhan and Monty was a little more pertinent, but still didn't add much to their musings. A married couple arguing about being discovered roaming a house that they lived in was hardly a revelation: even Sherlock Holmes would have struggled to identify the guilty party from that useless titbit.

Lauren and Harrison were getting into yet another squabble – they'd gone back to their topic *du jour*, with Lauren accusing him of glory-seeking to ingratiate himself with the Americans and Harrison fighting back with claims of her stabbing the group in the back – when Bella noticed Professor Stone had gone very quiet.

'Shut up!' she ordered the niggling pair, somewhat to their surprise. 'What's the matter, Professor?'

Lauren and Harrison immediately stopped their argument and looked at the older man, who had definitely turned a shade paler.

'Just a thought I had last night.'

'What thought?' Bella pressed. She didn't know where Stone was going with this, but she had a feeling she might be pointing in the same direction.

'I'm not sure. I dismissed it and went to bed, and this morning I've been rather preoccupied with Olive and the scene of the Hemingford Grey murder, so I haven't really considered it again.'

'But...?'

Stone looked a little sheepish. 'I did a little prowling of my own last night.'

So that was why he hadn't torn Harrison off a strip for his nocturnal perambulations: he'd been up to the same thing.

'After everything you said to us?' Fforde seemed about to start an argument.

'Never mind that,' said Bella. 'Where did you go, Professor?'

'I went to the chapel.'

Lauren let out a tiny gasp. Bella couldn't be sure if it was admiration or horror.

'And...?'

'And apart from a sense that I was being watched in the hall, I found something rather odd. While the cause of death for Hemingford Grey was clear, it wasn't quite the same with Keren Lowe. There seemed to be no obvious signs of mortal injury on her body.'

Fforde grunted dismissively. 'She fell from the top of the tower with a rope round her neck. Which of those lethal means of dispatch are you doubting?'

'Shut up, Harrison,' said Bella again, and he instantly fell into line. She'd have to remember that particular tone of voice.

'She didn't die from strangulation and she didn't die from the fall,' the Professor went on. 'I believe she may have been dead before her body even left the billiard room.'

'The candlestick?' asked Lauren.

He shook his head. 'Remember I said there were no obvious signs of trauma?'

'What, then?'

A chill descended on the back of Bella's neck. She glanced at the book she'd been reading then stared at the Professor.

'You're going to tell us Keren was poisoned, aren't you?'

III

Lauren had no idea how Bella knew. All she was interested in now was seeing the evidence for herself.

'We have to be sure,' she urged the others as they assimilated the shocking development that Professor Stone had readily substantiated. He told them it had been a forgotten hypothesis until this moment: Bella's potential corroboration of his tenuous theory turned it into a full-blown suspicion.

'But I don't know if I want to go to the chapel right now,' said Bella, a look of considerable distaste on her face. 'We don't know what we'll find.'

'Two dead bodies and a lot of spiders, I'd have thought,' said Fforde, who looked as queasy as Bella.

Lauren turned to Professor Stone for support. He shrugged.

'You're welcome to see for yourselves,' he said, and stood aside from the doorway he'd been blocking.

'Come on,' said Lauren. 'We might find something useful.'

Bella didn't seem to want to move. Fforde stood beside her and put an arm round her shoulders.

'It's all right, Bella,' he said. 'I'll give you a quick lesson in controlling your nerves. We do it all the time in the trade. Any actor who tells you they're not shit-scared standing in the wings waiting to go on is either lying to you or on ketamine. What you have to do is close your eyes, take a big gulp of air, hold your breath for a count of fifteen, then let it out slowly through your mouth. It helps to make a farting sound with your lips while you're blowing out.'

Bella had already got her eyes closed and was building up to taking a deep breath.

'And this is supposed to calm me down, is it?'

'No idea, but it'll give the rest of us a jolly good laugh.'

Bella opened her eyes, saw she was being teased and thumped him playfully on the upper arm as she laughed herself.

'There, you see,' said Fforde. 'It's working already.'

Although she'd been the one to encourage the others into viewing the bodies, when it came to crossing the threshold of the murky chapel, Lauren was as reluctant as Harrison and Bella. Probably more so, given her fear of spiders. Harrison's jibe about the place being full of the hideous arachnids had been intended to wind up Bella but it had worked its creepy-crawly hooks into Lauren's subconscious, and she conjured up images of Saturday night parties with schoolfriends when some idiot or other had found old movies on YouTube and proceeded to terrify the more delicately natured girls with clips of web-laden crypts and graveyards shrouded in gossamer blankets.

The Professor went ahead to where Olive's two makeshift coffins stood, resting across the tops of the few pews that filled the nave of the chapel. Lauren and the others held back. If they felt anything like she did, they would be extremely wary of peering inside the boxes. She'd seen enough of those movie clips to know that there should be scratchy violin music playing at this point, together with close-ups of their eyes displaying apprehension as it grew into fear, then complete horror at the moment that the corpses sat up in their coffins and reached out to grab them.

Pull yourself together, she thought, and took a bold step forwards.

As she neared the first box she caught sight of the blood that drenched Hemingford Grey's chest. The torso was a mess, with one big hole torn into it at the centre of the ribs, and several smaller ones dotted around it. What kind of maniac had plunged the wooden stake into Hemingford Grey, then repeatedly stabbed him with follow-up jabs, knowing they would do no more damage than the fatal first wound? She found it hard to believe that anyone in the house could be capable of such a frenzied attack.

She was surprised not to see the murder weapon lying beside him, and for a moment she wondered where it had gone. For some reason, she'd imagined that Professor Stone would have instructed Olive to leave it with its victim as she built the coffins, offering as much evidence as possible for the police, whenever the law were finally able to make it through the snow to rescue them. Of course, that might well depend on the uncertain abilities of the Californian location manager who'd trudged off into the snow more than a day earlier in search of assistance and who might well be buried under a snowdrift having lost his way in the remote English countryside. They should never have let him go alone. But they couldn't change any of that now, and they could only deal with the nightmare that was in front of them.

Right now, that nightmare was Hemingford Grey's gruesome body.

By rights, she thought, they should probably have left him where Olive had found him, but she'd already transported his body to the conservatory in the wheelbarrow so that ship had sailed long before the rest of them even knew he was dead. It was only a marginal step from there to laying him out in a wooden box – some might even say it suggested a degree of ethical maturity – and on reflection it made some sense to remove the stick. Leaving it lying beside him would have been unseemly.

If the forensics team had an issue with that decision, it would pale into insignificance beside the fact that everyone's fingerprints were already all over the corpse from manhandling it into the chapel. It was something the detectives would just have to work round as they investigated the double murders.

Unless the reading group managed to solve them first.

That, of course, would involve answering a number of questions that they hadn't so far been able to answer. Why, for instance, had Keren Lowe and Hemingford Grey become the victims of the country-house killer? And why this weekend? Among themselves, the group had speculated about extramarital affairs and blackmail, based on a few odd comments and strange looks between members of the household for the most part, but they were no nearer to identifying a culprit with any degree of certainty.

Lauren's father had once told her that the longest non-technical word in the English language was floccinaucinihilipilification, which he'd translated as the estimation of something to be worthless. At twenty-nine letters, it outranked antidisestablishmentarianism by a mere one, but that was all it took. She'd never seen either word in print in the wild, and had serious concerns that if she ever did, putting floccinaucinihilipilification and antidisestablishmentarianism next to each other on the pages of a book would cause no end of problems for the typesetters, especially if they were determined to avoid superfluous hyphenation. While she'd never bothered to verify either the record-holding claim or the meaning of floccinaucinihilipilification, she'd always loved the word and had searched relentlessly to find a context in which to use it authentically.

In her musings about the two murders, she thought she might have found it: she estimated them to be worthless.

With a twinge of heartlessness about bypassing Hemingford Grey's corpse, she edged round to the second coffin. Behind her, Bella crept over tentatively to examine Grey.

Keren Lowe looked serene.

It seemed odd to Lauren that the victim of a killer could appear so peaceful, and yet there she was. The dignified pose Olive had given her – hands clasped together across her midriff, eyes closed as if she were merely sleeping – made Lauren wonder if their theory that she had been murdered could actually be correct. Surely there should be more traces of the violence that had caused her demise, besides some inevitable bruising from the fall? But then, she remembered, that was why they were here: the Professor didn't believe she had met a violent end at all.

Stone was standing on the opposite side of the coffin from Lauren and lowered his head to inspect Keren's lips more closely.

When he found what he was searching for, he pointed it out to her.

'There – do you see?'

In spite of her misgivings, Lauren couldn't resist leaning in closer herself.

'What am I looking at?'

'In the corner of her mouth. A fleck of spittle. It's easy to miss but it's definitely there.'

Lauren found it hard to believe that such a tiny piece of evidence could actually be real. If it was indeed spittle, then how had it survived this long since Keren's death? Lauren could only put that down to the prevailing conditions in the chapel, which must have preserved it in the same way that they were delaying any deterioration of the bodies. But even if it was real, it could simply have appeared on Keren's lips as she gave her final desperate cry: it proved nothing, not even that she'd been murdered.

And then Lauren smelled it.

It was barely there, almost a whiff of nothing on the chilly air, and if her senses hadn't been finely attuned and her nerves on edge, Lauren might easily have missed it.

The faint smell of mouse wee.

Lauren had no idea how she knew what mouse wee smelled like, but as a child she had become annoyingly familiar with both gerbil and hamster wee, and this wasn't them. It could conceivably have come from a rat, but Lauren's educated guess was that rats' wee would have given off a more pungent odour, and this was weak, as well as faint.

'Can you smell that?' she asked the Professor.

'What?'

'That,' she repeated, putting a finger close to Keren's lips to indicate the source of the aroma.

Professor Stone resumed his leaning and sniffed heavily. The speed with which he jerked his head away suggested that he could indeed smell that.

'I noticed it last night too,' he said.

'What is it?'

Bella's voice came from the back of the chapel, where she had retreated from Grey's coffin to join Fforde, who was still loitering near the door. She'd evidently decided to allow Lauren and Stone to do this particular piece of research on their own.

'Do you think all dead people smell musty?' asked the Professor, addressing his morbid query to Lauren.

Apart from Felicity Penman's body, glimpsed across the aisles at the bookshop, Lauren's experience of dead people was non-existent. She shrugged.

'Musty?' Fforde's curiosity must have been aroused since he gave up pretending to peer at the inscriptions on the walls and turned his attention to the corpses for the first time.

'There's a definite suggestion of must,' said the Professor. 'What was the last thing she ate?'

Lauren tried to recall if she'd seen Keren at breakfast the previous morning. From the timings, that would have been her last meal, but she couldn't remember if the woman responsible for serving up the breakfast had actually partaken of any herself.

'Shredded Wheat? Yoghurt? Black pudding?'

Stone shook his head. 'It's none of those.'

'No, it's mouse wee.'

The Professor could look decidedly condescending when he wanted to.

'You're not suggesting that Keren ingested mouse wee as her final meal, I hope?'

'No—'

Bella chirped up. 'Maybe she liked those herbal drink thingies that taste like grass?'

'Spirulina?' said Fforde, leaning back against one of the pews. 'I tried that once on the advice of another member of the company in an Ayckbourn farce I was doing in Great Yarmouth. She said it would help with my digestion.'

'And did it?' asked Lauren.

'Gave me the runs, if that's what you mean. But I can safely assure you that nobody *likes* drinking those.'

'Must be the hemlock then,' said Bella in a matter-of-fact tone of voice.

Three faces turned to the harmless middle-aged woman standing in the doorway of the chapel.

'I beg your pardon?' said Professor Stone eventually.

'She said, it must be the hemlock,' offered Lauren helpfully.

'I heard what she said,' the Professor continued. 'I just didn't understand what she meant by it.'

Bella jerked a thumb back towards the hall. 'I was looking at it in that book in Lord Verity's study when Harrison came in and shouted at me. Hemlock smells of mouse wee.'

'What was the book?' asked Lauren cautiously.

'*The Toxicologist's Almanac*,' said Bella. 'I found it on a shelf in there.'

Lauren's mind was working overtime, only without the additional pay she'd normally have expected from extracurricular activities at school. The very existence of a toxicological textbook on the shelves of Lord Verity's study was odd. Why wasn't it in the library with all the other non-fiction books? His Lordship's study was a place of learning, there'd been no doubt about that, but she'd noticed, even in the short time she was in it, that its sleek mahogany bookcases were lined with fiction for the most part. By contrast, Lauren could recall from her visit to the library the previous day, while the Americans were scouting locations with her, that there was an entire section there given over to manuals, atlases, dictionaries and other assorted textbooks. Surely the place for *The Toxicologist's Almanac* was nestled up alongside *Pharmacy for Beginners* or *Chemistry Debunked*? It was a suspicious anomaly which, despite her normal propensity for deference towards aristocracy, raised doubts once again in Lauren's mind about their hosts for the weekend.

Could Lord Verity be hiding something sinister behind that jocular, jowly face of his?

'Bella,' she said slowly, the pace of her delivery markedly at odds with the speed of her thoughts. 'I'd like to take a look at that book.'

IV

There was a big difference between seeing something and noticing it, Professor Stone was realising.

Really noticing it.

He'd seen the tiny bubble at the corner of Keren Lowe's mouth the first time he'd checked out the bodies. It had glistened in the candlelight as he'd stared at her face in the small hours of the morning. But after registering a passing thought about its oddness, he had relegated it to a subterranean burrow deep in the mines of his memory. It might have enjoyed the rest of his life tucked away in its little mental filing cabinet, never to be recalled by his conscious mind and doomed to spend eternity roaming the echoing halls of amnesia with only the goddess Mnemosyne for company.

But then Bella had mentioned hemlock, and Greek tragedies had stepped into his brain.

He was pretty sure he could dispense with Socrates and his hemlock-based demise as incidental to this particular investigation. Keren, on the other hand, seemed to embody a modern-day Greek tragedy, with its very own flawed central character and an intervention from the gods – in this case, taking the form of a human to mete out her fatal peripeteia.

It seemed so obvious now Bella had mentioned the lethal herb: whoever had made the footprints from the kitchen to the knot garden had endured the elements with the express purpose of securing a cache of the stuff with which to dispatch poor, unfortunate Keren.

But who? And why?

He paused in his march back towards the study, thinking he'd ask Bella if her line of thinking was similar to his. When he looked back for the others, who had been following him dutifully from the chapel only several steps behind, only Fforde and Lauren were there.

Bella had disappeared. For a second time.

'Where's Bella?' demanded Stone, his voice betraying his inner anxiety. He didn't care about that: Bella's safety in this house of death was more important than looking weak to the rest of the reading group.

Lauren looked surprised at the question.

'She said she was just going to pop back to the dining room to make sure that everyone was OK. I think she was mostly worried about her sister, though.'

That made sense. In the absence of any children of her own, Bella's innate motherly instincts easily transferred to other people. Stone had seen it happen in front of his eyes with Lauren, and he imagined she would feel the same kind of empathy towards her younger sister. No matter how annoying she claimed Ronnie could be, nothing would eradicate the sororal bond between them.

Bella was just being Bella.

'Right, the rest of us have to stick together. Understood?'

Fforde looked like he might be about to object – probably the same old complaint about Stone assuming he was the authority figure among them – but Stone wasn't going to give him the chance. Apart from anything else, he *was* the authority figure among them, both in terms of seniority of years and with regard to his standing thanks to his former post in academia. For all Fforde's posturing (and he really was good at posturing), all he had to show in comparison was Third Murderer in a long-forgotten production of *Macbeth* that had starred a soap opera has-been trying to extend his career, and a brief stint on a children's television series as an oversized penguin with kleptomaniac tendencies. Even that had come to an ignominious end, Stone had discovered from Google, when life imitated art and Fforde was suspected – though never directly accused – of purloining his black-and-white beaked onesie to entertain at some off-the-books parties. He might have got away with the kiddies' ones, but when Emperor Guin-Guin had been papped by the tabloids with a scantily clad supermodel snorting something highly suspicious off his long yellow bill, Fforde had found himself swiftly unemployed, despite his protestations that a member of the production crew must have raided his wardrobe without his knowledge.

Yes, in a straight fight between them, it was only natural that a mathematics professor might think himself the more natural leader of the two.

'Right, where's that book of Bella's?' he asked

superfluously as they entered the study. The book was lying exactly where she'd left it on the desk.

It was open at a page headed 'Poisonous plants and their uses'.

Professor Stone struggled to come up with any uses for poisonous plants other than poisoning someone, but he supposed there were more things in heaven and earth, Horatio...

'Now, what does it say about hemlock?'

He found himself being crowded on either side at the desk by Lauren and Fforde, both peering over his shoulder to read the same text he was perusing. He decided to let that pass on the grounds that their interest in the volume was just as legitimate as his, but when he fell upon a paragraph relating to the aroma of toxic vegetation, he picked up the book and read aloud.

'This is interesting. "A musty smell can be indicative of natural toxins, especially the fumes emitted by plants of the conium variety, such as poison hemlock." Looks like we might have found our culprit.'

'For Keren, at least,' said Lauren, appearing thoughtful. 'But it still leaves a load of questions unanswered.'

'Such as?'

'Such as how she came to ingest it. And was it self-administered, or did someone force her to consume it?'

Stone realised she was right. They might have found what Fforde would probably have called 'the smoking gun' of the means of Keren's demise, but it brought them no closer to knowing how – or when – she had taken it. There was still a chance that she had taken her own life. Never mind that it made little sense for her to have poisoned herself, tied a rope round her neck and leaped from the billiard room window in the tower. Until it was ruled out by solid evidence, it remained a theoretical possibility, however unlikely – as per the Holmesian dictum.

Lauren was expanding on her theory. 'Do you remember, in *Murder on the Polar Express*, how Lord Quaint deduces that Lavinia Glitch is framing her new husband for a murder that hasn't actually been committed?'

'You're not suggesting Keren Lowe is trying to frame somebody, are you? Because we know she really is dead – we've just come from the chapel.'

'No, no,' said Lauren, slightly irritably. 'But surely the whole suicide scenario is a set-up to cover up a murder. Hemingford Grey worked it out somehow, or maybe stumbled across the killer in the garden, and became the second victim.'

'So is this what Bella was talking about when she mentioned the knot garden?' asked Fforde. 'You think the hemlock might have come from there?'

'I would think, given the fact that Bella told us it was ruined when she and Lauren went to look at it this morning, that's a distinct possibility. Someone was trying to cover their tracks.'

Lauren moved over to the window and stared out at the front drive of the house.

'Which makes it more likely that Keren didn't kill herself.'

'How so?' The Professor had his own ideas about it, but he wanted to hear Lauren's theory.

'We know it wasn't her that Bella saw in the middle of the night. She was already dead by then.'

'Agreed,' said Stone.

'So unless she had an accomplice who went out last night to hide her suicide by destroying the garden, somebody else was responsible for harvesting that hemlock. And if we can find out who that was, the chances are we've got our killer.'

Fforde grunted. 'There's only one person with that kind of intimate knowledge of the gardens, surely. Not to mention a rake.'

Olive. He meant Olive.

Stone thought about it and came up with a selection of doubts.

'There are quite a lot of leaps in that logic,' he said eventually. 'But at the moment it's the best we've got.'

'What's the best we've got?' asked Bella, making everyone jump in shock.

'What the—? Where on earth did you turn up from?' asked Stone.

'There,' said Bella, pointing behind her into the corner of the study.

The Professor looked at where she was indicating and realised that the bookcase nearest to the wall was sticking out slightly further than its neighbours, at an odd angle that made it seem like it hadn't been fitted properly.

'What do you mean, "there"?'

Bella retraced her steps into the corner and took hold of the ill-fitting bookcase. With a deft movement of one hand, she eased it forwards, pivoting on one axis like a door, to reveal an entrance behind it.

'There. It's one of the house's secret passageways. Weren't you paying attention when Siobhan told us all about them?'

Stone had to admit he wasn't. There had been quite enough on his mind, as they explored the passage that led away underneath the lounge, when they'd heard the blood-curdling scream of Keren Lowe meeting her doom.

'How many of these things are there?'

'Oh, just the two that I've found so far. There's one going from the lounge to the conservatory, which we were all in when Keren died, and there's another that crosses it, going from the kitchen to here. I thought you all knew about them.'

Now Stone came to inspect it, it was so similar to the one in the lounge that he chided himself for not having guessed it was there.

But Bella seemed to have something else on her mind besides secret passages.

'Look, we can't stand around here gossiping about the house and its quirky ways.'

'We can't?' asked the Professor. He had no idea why not, except for the room full of anxious people across the hall, two dead bodies in the chapel and the knowledge that a murderer could well be stalking their next victim from among the guests.

'No, we can't. We've got a rake to inspect.'

Lauren sounded excited. 'You've found it?'

'Certainly have.' Bella looked pleased with herself.

'Well, where is it?' This seemed like a real breakthrough – their first, if Stone was really honest about it, and he didn't want to pass up the opportunity of capitalising on Bella's discovery.

'I don't actually have it...'

Stone's heart sank.

'... but I know where it is.'

Stone's heart lifted again. Maybe not to quite the same elevation that it had been at when Bella first mentioned the rake, but noticeably higher than when he'd suspected it might be a dead end.

'Where, Bella? Can we look at it?'

'We can, but we might have to prise it out of Olive's hands.'

The woman was talking in riddles.

'What are you saying?'

Bella gave a dramatic sigh. She'd obviously picked that up from Fforde.

'If you'd let me speak, I'll tell you what I've just discovered.'

Stone slumped in the chair behind the desk, where hemlock was silently taunting him from the pages of *The Toxicologist's Almanac*. Lauren and Fforde closed in around Bella, wanting to hear her story, but they were younger than him and his feet were tired with all the running around.

'We're listening,' said Fforde.

'All right, then. After I checked on everyone in the dining room – they're all fine, by the way, thanks for asking – I thought I'd join you back here by taking the shortcut from the lounge.'

'The secret passage?' said Lauren.

'Exactly. The secret passage. Only I lost my bearings when I was down there and instead of turning right to get to the study, I turned left and ended up at the passage door that leads into the conservatory. But I didn't go in as I heard voices on the other side.'

'I thought everyone was in the dining room,' said the Professor, who was becoming rather irritated by the entire house full of people ignoring his express instructions to stay in one place. It was bad enough when the other members of the reading group did it, but for almost complete strangers to undermine his authority in this cavalier manner was something he was definitely going to take personally.

'It was Siobhan and Lady Verity,' said Bella, apparently tolerating the interruption because she'd left this vital information out of her narrative. 'I think Lady Verity is probably allowed to walk around her own property with one of her staff, don't you? Even if there is a killer around.'

Stone didn't actually think so, especially not after having given orders to the exact contrary, but he wanted to hear the rest of Bella's story so chose not to argue the point.

'What were they doing in the conservatory, Bella?' asked Fforde.

'Having a row, from the sound of it. It was all in whispers but I've had enough of those kinds of arguments with Ronnie to know that's what it was. I couldn't hear what they were saying but I could see them through a crack in the wall, where the passage door opens, and their body language was plain enough. Anyway, that's not the point.'

'It isn't?' Stone could feel his impatience stirring again: before long it would be fully awake and pacing about, ready to join its twin sibling irritation among the creases on his brow.

'No. The point is that while they were having a go at each other, Olive turned up at the outside door.'

'Olive?' This was getting ridiculous. Why had *she* left the safety of the dining room to go outside?

'Yes. Carrying a rake.'

Even Stone had to admit this was an exciting new

development. What had Lauren said? If they could find the rake's owner, they might well have found the murderer. And who, on an estate like this, would be the likeliest owner of a rake?

The logic was still full of holes, but better to have a rake than not to have a rake.

Fforde was looking dark. 'So we're back to Olive again as the chief suspect?'

'That doesn't make much sense,' said Stone, trying to work it out in his head as he spoke. Things were not looking good for Olive, but at the same time, he had questions. 'If she'd used the rake to cover her tracks by destroying the knot garden, why would she then go galumphing about the house with the very device she'd employed to conceal her duplicity?'

Fforde nodded charitably. 'True. Good point.'

'And you didn't fancy asking her why she was carrying a rake?' said Lauren, her attention still on Bella.

'Certainly not. For one thing, if the rake does point to Olive as the killer, I have no desire to confront her on my own. And for another thing, if I'd stepped into the conservatory at that moment, I'd have given away the fact that I'd been eavesdropping on Lady Verity, and I don't think that would have gone down too well with our hostess, whether she's a murder suspect or not.'

Stone stood decisively and picked up the book from the table.

'You did the right thing coming back here to find us, Bella. Safety in numbers and all that. But now we're at full complement, I think it's time to get our hands on that rake.'

The Conservatory

1

It came as something of a surprise to Bella that nobody else wanted to return to the conservatory via the secret passageways. Not only were they the most direct routes to the various parts of the house that they served, they offered the bonus of being able to navigate Abbots Chantry undetected. Any slight advantage they might be able to get over the hidden killer among them had to be exploited to the full; surely Professor Stone, at least, could see that?

Apparently not. Professor Stone seemed as reluctant as the others to head down into the subterranean world of the passages.

He argued that if the killer did indeed belong among the ranks of the household, it was extremely likely they would know about the tunnels, and possibly even be using them to sneak about the place. That made them highly dangerous places to be. Consequently, he vetoed the idea of Bella using the tunnels again alone, as she had been doing all afternoon, even though that would have allowed the other three to approach the conservatory innocuously while simultaneously giving Bella the opportunity to creep up unannounced on whoever was still occupying the room.

Bella argued that would give them a further edge in the event of a confrontation, or a means of escape to fetch help from elsewhere in the house. But the Professor was having none of it: they would all stick together, like the three musketeers in the novel by that French chap.

Bella didn't know anything about a novel by any Frenchman. She'd tried some Asterix books as a youngster but found the little moustachioed Gaul and his oversized friend rather too boyish for her liking so had moved rapidly on to Tintin, who was famously Belgian. One of only two famous Belgians she could think of, in fact, the other being Hercule Poirot. It must say something about Belgium that the only examples she could think of as representatives of the nation were fictional characters. As for musketeers, her only contact with anything like that was a children's television series she dimly recalled, repeated during summer holidays in her childhood and possibly starring Brian Blessed as the permanently hungry one. There was Disney's theft of the name for his Mouseketeers, she supposed, but they didn't really count.

There were four of them in any case, so the Professor's analogy fell down before it even got started.

Any plundering of her memory for further enlightenment was academic. When they reached the conservatory, there was no sign of Lady Verity, Siobhan Butler or Olive the gardener.

Or the rake.

Instead, huddled side by side on a wicker settee in the

shade of a large potted palm tree, Colorado Hughes and Marin Cypher were poring over a tablet with eager looks in their eyes.

The Americans barely looked up when the quartet entered the conservatory, so engrossed were they in what they were watching on the screen. Bella scanned the room for the rake but could see no trace and she was starting to feel as if all their efforts were once more in vain when Lauren let out a little squeak of surprise, or shock, or possibly alarm.

The girl was standing behind the wicker settee peering between Colorado and Marin's shoulders at the tablet. Bella guessed she might have been trying to see how much video they had that included her.

But now Lauren had one hand over her mouth and the other pointing at the screen.

'What is it, Lauren?' Bella asked, hurrying over to where she was standing.

'There.' Lauren pointed. 'By the back door.'

Bella leaned in closer, ignoring the indignant noises she seemed to be prompting from the filmmakers as she invaded the space between their heads.

'Can you rewind about thirty seconds?' Lauren asked Marin, who was holding the tablet.

'I guess,' he replied fussily, and manipulated the screen.

At first Bella couldn't make out what she was looking at. Then she realised the pair were reviewing footage they had previously shot – part of their collection of mood imagery that they had talked about filming for the benefit of interested producers or investors back home. Colorado had seemed more excited at the prospect than his colleagues: Bella recalled from dinner on Friday night the now absent location manager downplaying the dramatic possibilities of snow, largely on the basis of cost. But they had gone ahead with the atmospheric material anyway, it seemed.

Now, instead of seeing Lauren or the snowbound gardens in their video, Bella could see the very room they were standing in, and she realised the footage had been shot just minutes earlier, when Lady Verity and Siobhan had still been in the conservatory. In fact, she could just see them leaving through the door into the hall, Lady Verity calling something back over her shoulder. Bella could only guess at what had transpired: the Americans had happened upon them in the conservatory and either the women had been embarrassed about being caught in the middle of an argument, or the filmmakers had started shooting their background material and the ladies had taken exception. Either way, the conservatory was now the domain of the Hollywood duo and they were enjoying their seclusion to go over everything they'd got 'in the can', as Bella thought they phrased it.

Yet as she looked, she realised she could make out someone else in the frame. Outside the back door that was frosted with the cold, and unmistakable in her frame and stature, stood the impassive figure of Olive.

And she was carrying the rake.

Bella, from her vantage point behind the passageway door, had witnessed Olive's arrival in the conservatory with the rake but she'd crept away immediately afterwards and so saw nothing of what followed. She must have missed the entrance of the Americans by moments. But she could see it now, and she realised that Olive had left just after Lady Verity and

Siobhan. For some reason, she'd hovered outside the back door – maybe trying to decide what to do next, or where to stash the incriminating rake – and been caught on camera.

As Bella watched, the figure moved away from the conservatory and across the small courtyard to the kitchen door. There, she could be clearly seen kicking her boots against the wall to knock off the worst of the snow.

After that, she propped the rake against the wall, opened the kitchen door and disappeared into the house.

Bella blinked. She looked up from the screen and out of the conservatory, towards the kitchen door opposite, seeing in real life the same view she'd just observed on the tablet in Marin's hand.

There, leaning against the wall by the kitchen, stood the rake.

The top of its handle had been broken off.

'Oh my God,' said Bella, pointing blankly at the implement outside. 'It's the rake.'

Fforde was nearest to the door and he was outside in the cold air before anyone else had even moved. In four short steps he was by the kitchen door and had grabbed the handle of the rake, swinging its head up towards his face to get a better look at the tines.

'Stop,' yelled Bella, dashing out in his wake and holding out a hand in a clear sign of warning. 'Don't touch that rake!'

Fforde froze, and it wasn't because he had no overcoat.

Gingerly, as Bella took two careful paces towards him, he lowered the rake and replaced it exactly where he had found it.

'What's the matter, Bella? I was only holding it by the handle.'

'Doesn't matter,' she said, an urgent edge in her voice. 'That might look like strands of cow parsley caught on the other end of it but it's not. If we're right about Keren being poisoned, that's hemlock. Same family, very different outcome.'

'I wasn't going to touch the plant,' Fforde protested.

'You don't need to touch it. Even inhaling its toxins can be seriously damaging to your health.'

'Oh, come on. It can't be that lethal.'

'She's right,' said Professor Stone, emerging from the conservatory with *The Toxicologist's Almanac* in his hands. 'Listen to this: "Poison hemlock's primary toxin is coniine, which interferes with the body's nervous system causing suffocation, respiratory paralysis, seizures and death. Coniine can be consumed through ingestion or absorbed through the skin or by inhalation." I think it might be worth paying attention to Bella, you know, Harrison.'

Fforde took two immediate steps away.

Bella crouched where she stood, a full three yards from the rake, and focused her eyes on it. The handle had snapped a few inches from the top, and Bella knew exactly what had happened to the missing part: it had ended up buried in the ribcage of Hemingford Grey. But now she was more interested in the other end of the rake, where bits of plant material were caught between its teeth. The strands certainly looked like the cow parsley she had enjoyed on walks across fields on the outskirts of Norcester, in the days when she'd have to come up with an excuse to leave the house for an hour or so every now and then to get a moment's peace from Trevor. It had never occurred to her that what she'd assumed was cow parsley might, in fact, have been poison hemlock.

From her cursory reading of the book in the study, she'd gathered that there were a great many similarities between the two related plants, and in some cases it might take an expert to spot the differences. She definitely didn't class herself as that, and would be taking no chances with these fronds of vegetation, but the almanac's description of dark green, fern-like leaves and purple spots on the stem might give her a clue.

In the end, it wasn't the appearance that persuaded her she was staring at genuine hemlock: it was the smell. Even at this distance, the aroma was pungent.

She stood up quickly and moved backwards, stretching her arms out to indicate to the others that they, too, should stay away.

'That's our culprit,' she said simply. 'Mouse wee. And I'll bet the bit of the handle that's broken off is what was used to kill Hemingford.'

'Very impressive,' came an American voice from behind her. She turned to see Colorado Hughes, his phone held high in front of his face, watching her as she identified the noxious weed. At his shoulder stood Marin Cypher, his tablet capturing their every move.

It seemed they could always be relied upon to find a way to antagonise someone.

'I hope you're not filming this,' said Lauren, moving over to put her hand across Hughes's lens. He tried dodging it but there was no way she was going to let him capture their investigations on camera. As he whipped his hand away and tried to get another angle, she was just as quick and put her whole body between him and the rake.

What a dick, thought Bella, and took no further notice of him.

'Do you think Olive knows?' asked Fforde, staring warily at the rake.

'About the hemlock?'

'Well, yes. And the knot garden.'

'I don't know. But it'll be interesting to see the look on her face when we bring the subject up with her.'

Professor Stone slammed the book shut and moved to the middle of the little courtyard where they were standing.

'I think we should pause our deliberations there,' he said decisively, nodding in the direction of Hughes and Cypher, who had stepped back inside the conservatory and were now conducting their filming from the other side of the window, where Lauren was finding it harder to block the view.

'Maybe we could go back to the study for a chat?' asked Bella. She'd never really warmed to the Americans and now the feeling had waned to barely tepid.

'Good idea. I want to check something out anyway.'

'What's that?'

'A book we read when the group first started.'

'Which one, Professor?' asked Lauren. 'Maybe Harrison and I can help?'

'That's the thing,' he replied. 'I can't actually remember. All I can recall is that it was a Poirot story about a philandering artist who gets poisoned with coniine, and there are two sisters who are suspects. Unlike our current situation, where one is a victim.'

'That's ringing a vague bell,' said Lauren, and Bella watched as she and Harrison sifted through the files of their memories. It would have been long before she joined the group at Felicity Penman's invitation, and even longer before the poor bookshop manager met her tragic death. Bella's own acquaintance with the stories of Christie was limited to the ones she'd seen as movie adaptations, plus the couple of more obscure ones they'd read in the time since Felicity's murder. She hoped Lauren or Harrison could come up with the goods on the one Professor Stone was trying to remember.

'Aha!' said Fforde suddenly, making Bella jump.

'You remember it?' asked the Professor, an eager tone in his voice.

'No, but I've got a way of finding out.' He lowered his voice so he would be inaudible to the men beyond the pane of glass.

'We just need to lose our American friends. Then I suggest we skip the study and head straight for the library.'

The Library

I

It didn't take much for the foursome to escape the beady eyes of the would-be film moguls. Fforde blustered a diversion outside so the pair were drawn away from the others, who then darted into the now empty conservatory and disappeared through the secret passageway. When Hughes and Marin realised they'd vanished, they clearly assumed they'd gone back out into the hall, and followed them at a hurrying pace.

Fforde simply waited a few moments before following his reading group colleagues, and closed the passageway door behind him.

'I'd love to see the look on their faces when they realise we're not in the hall,' he said, catching up with the others. Somehow, Stone still had some power left in his phone battery and was using its torch to light the way ahead.

'Oh, I think we can probably picture it, can't we?' said the Professor with a little chuckle.

'My only concern is that rake,' said Bella. 'Those two idiots know it's dangerous, but what if someone else comes along and picks it up?'

Lauren concurred. 'It's evidence in a murder case too, so we don't want it to go walkabout.'

'I'll get Monty to handle it,' said the Professor. 'He'll be able to stash it somewhere safe for the police.'

Fforde had a nasty feeling that giving the prime piece of evidence to someone who could, arguably, still be a suspect was not necessarily the brightest idea, but he couldn't think of an alternative that didn't involve putting himself or one of his friends in considerable danger so he let it pass. The thought didn't seem to have occurred to Bella or Lauren.

They turned right where the two tunnels met and were back in the study before anyone could say *Toxicologist's Almanac*. Nobody did, because the book was in Professor Stone's hands and they'd already retrieved the information they wanted from it. But, of the four rooms connected by the subterranean passages, the study was nearest to the library and therefore the quickest way to reach their destination unseen by anyone else.

Stone waited by the door, holding it slightly ajar as he peered out into the hall.

'Don't want to run into those Americans again,' he'd explained as the others waited patiently behind him.

When they were sure the coast was clear, they tiptoed along the corridor to the next door, slipping inside and closing it quietly.

Fforde looked around at the floor-to-ceiling shelves and marvelled at the dedication of proper book collectors.

The room was gargantuan, double-height with a gallery running its full circumference and at least four sets of steps leading from the ground floor to the mezzanine. Along every wall, filling every possible space, were ranked tier upon tier of dark wooden bookcases, each crammed to overflowing with hardbacks, paperbacks, numbered volumes and assorted picturesque spines. Some of the books looked impossibly old, with jackets that were falling apart or only held together with Sellotape. Their covers seemed more uniform, with faded gold lettering imprinted on leather in various shades of brown or blue. Others seemed newer – relatively, at least – featuring modern typefaces and dustjackets with photographs or illustrations marking them out as more recent additions to the library. At first glance, Fforde could see no particular method of cataloguing the volumes: they certainly weren't aligned by anything so logical as an alphabetical sequence of author surnames. But as they roamed the shelves, each murmuring their own version of amazement at the extraordinary literary collection before them, he realised that the books were arranged in sections, with non-fiction separate from fiction and countless subsections ranging from Arcana to Zoology.

At least that was something. Beyond that, though, how on earth anyone was meant to find a specific work in this giant mausoleum was anyone's guess.

Fforde's heart, momentarily lifted by the sight of the library, sank again.

'Look for the crime section,' suggested Bella. 'There's bound to be a huge selection of Agatha Christies in here, especially if she stayed here.'

'What do you mean, *especially if she stayed here*?' asked Lauren.

Bella went oddly silent, as if she'd let something significant slip.

But there was no time to pick her up on it. Fforde had miraculously stumbled on precisely the book he was looking for.

'It's something I picked up from your brother,' he bluffed to Lauren as the four of them gathered around one of the reading tables in the centre of the room.

'Simon? What did he tell you?'

Now that Fforde's throwaway brag had started him on a journey down White Lie Highway, under further questioning from Lauren, he realised he had no idea how to get off it. 'Oh, nothing in particular. I just studied the way he did his research when he was tracing Felicity's background, and adapted his techniques for my own purposes.'

'But he does everything on the computer.'

'I know. But the same principles apply in the real world too. If you run into a brick wall, instead of trying to go over it, go sideways until you reach the end, then go round it. There's always an end.'

The Professor grunted. 'Sounds like me with the knot garden wall.'

'Exactly,' said Fforde, not really understanding the reference but grateful that Stone had moved the topic away from Lauren's forensic dissection of his blustering. 'And in this instance, we could have spent hours scouring these shelves for a Christie section which might not even be here. If she did indeed stay at Abbots Chantry, as you seem to be suggesting,

Bella, then she's more than likely to have her own special library somewhere in his Lordship's private quarters. Maybe it's back in the study – who knows?'

'Should we go back there and look, then?' asked Lauren.

'No need. That's what I'm trying to tell you.'

Fforde produced the volume he'd been carrying behind his back and dumped it on the table.

'*Who's Who in Detective Fiction*,' read Professor Stone. 'I didn't even know such a book existed.'

'Nor did I. But I bet it's got what we're looking for.'

Immediately he started rummaging through the hefty volume, stopping when the name 'Christie' appeared in bold type across the top corner of the leaves.

'Dame Agatha Mary Clarissa Christie, Lady Mallowan, DBE,' he read.

'Never mind all that,' said Stone impatiently. 'Does it list her novels?'

'Of course it does,' said Fforde, and laid the book flat. After a short biography of the novelist herself, there was an entire section given over to the alphabetical listing of every book and short story collection penned by the maestro herself, with a paragraph about it that included its publication date, alternative American title where appropriate, and a brief synopsis. Given the Queen of Crime's prodigious output, the section ran to numerous pages.

He took a step backwards to allow Stone to inspect the pages for himself.

Bella interposed herself between the two men and reached for the book.

'You start at the front and I'll go from the back,' she said, turning over a few leaves and holding them open so the Professor could still read the earlier titles.

From his position beside her, Fforde watched as Bella went from *Witness for the Prosecution* and *Why Didn't They Ask Evans?* to *Three Blind Mice* and *Three Act Tragedy*. When her finger reached *The Thirteen Problems*, she stopped.

'Have you found it, Bella?'

'No,' she said slowly. 'But I've just realised I don't know what I'm looking for.'

Fforde laughed.

'Good point. Maybe Lauren or I should take over.'

He was about to reposition himself on the book side of Bella when she paused again.

'Oh, look at this.'

'What?'

'*The Thirteen Problems* was known in America as *The Tuesday Club Murders*. That's a bit of a coincidence, isn't it?'

Professor Stone sounded amused. 'I think Richard Osman would describe it as an *hommage*. No plagiarism intended.'

'No, I didn't mean that,' said Bella. 'It's just that we meet on a Tuesday. And now we're a bit of a murder club, aren't we?'

It was Fforde's turn to pause. A chill ran down his spine, did a U-turn somewhere about his lumbar vertebrae, and re-emerged between his shoulder blades as a shiver. He was much happier when they'd been a simple book club.

'Reading group,' he said sombrely. 'Isn't that right, Professor?'

'Oh, yes. Always a reading group. Never a book club. Or anything else.'

'Yes – why is that, Professor?' asked Lauren. 'I've always wondered.'

'Pure snobbery,' he said proudly, and let the matter drop.

Less than thirty seconds later, Professor Stone had the answer.

'*Endless Night, Evil Under the Sun*... Ah, here it is. *Five Little Pigs*.'

'Oh, yes!' exclaimed Lauren. 'I remember that one. Poirot solves a cold case at the request of the guilty party's daughter.'

'No spoilers, now,' warned Stone distractedly.

'Oh, come on, Professor,' said Fforde. 'We've all read it.'

'I haven't,' Bella added, a little timidly.

'Well, I'm sorry, Bella, but if we're going to crack this case, I think you might just have to sacrifice the ending of *Five Little Pigs*.'

'Not necessarily,' said the Professor. 'We might be able to extract what we need from this synopsis without giving the game away for Bella. As I recall, it was rather a neat solution to the problem.'

'Wouldn't expect anything less from Poirot,' Fforde nodded, settling himself against the bookshelves.

'I can recall it really clearly,' said Lauren, warming to her theme.

'Shame you couldn't remember its title,' grumbled Stone.

Lauren ignored him. 'Two sisters, an artist, his model and a murder. Everyone thinks it's one person but it's been another all along. I remember thinking I might borrow a version of the plot for one of my novels.'

'Now that would be plagiarism,' pointed out Fforde. 'Unless you can disguise it really well.'

'It was the sisters who made it interesting. And there was a really good red herring.'

'Sounds right up my street,' said Bella. 'Especially with sisters. You might have noticed that Ronnie and I have a rather up-and-down relationship.'

'Was it just the two of you growing up?' asked Lauren.

'Yes. And I was the older sister, so I was the one who had to deal with all the problems.'

'And now we've got a murder mystery of our own, complete with a pair of sisters,' said the Professor.

'Why did your mother leave you to deal with Ronnie?' asked Lauren.

'She was just always rather unkind to us that way. Some mothers are like that with their children, aren't they?'

And that was when it hit Harrison Fforde.

'Maybe not,' he said suddenly.

Everyone stared at him.

'Maybe not what?' asked Bella.

'Maybe not a mystery. And maybe not a *pair* of sisters.'

Professor Stone was looking particularly eagerly at him. 'What are you thinking, Harrison?'

Fforde couldn't quite believe he might have happened upon the key to the entire puzzle. He, Harrison Fforde, the one with the ridiculous name and equally pitiable acting career. The one who always felt out of place among the smart brains of The Quaint Bookshop reading group. The one who never guessed the perpetrator in the detective novels they read.

He just might have come up with the solution.

A grin broadened on his face as he returned the others' gaze.

'I'm thinking there were three members of Bananarama.'

11

From where Professor Stone stood at the front of the gathering, it looked like one of those *dénouements* from the Lord Quaint books: everyone assembled in the library of a remote country house, cut off by the weather and with no hope of escape or rescue while a murderer roamed among them. The very act of survival came down to whether the amateur sleuth could solve the case before the killer struck again.

In this instance, of course, there were four amateur sleuths standing at the front of the gathering, but that didn't prevent Stone from putting himself in the rather pinchy patent leather shoes of Lord Quaint himself, metaphorically tapping out his pipe in the grate and standing imperiously before the fireplace. The fact that a huge fire was blazing put the dampeners on the scenario a little – how could he tap out his pipe among roaring flames? – but he realised he was letting his mind wander and pulled himself back to the reality in front of him.

'My lords, ladies and gentlemen,' he began in the time-honoured fashion that would have worked perfectly well in the university refectory at the end-of-semester dinner but which fell a little flat with only one lord and an assorted bunch of bemused-looking civilians.

He tried again.

'We are gathered here today…'

No, that wouldn't do at all.

'Look, we know there's a murderer in the room. We've followed the clues and now we're going to tell you who it is.'

Hardly classic Quaint but at least it was short and to the point.

A bit too much to the point, if Lady Verity's reaction was anything to go by. She immediately let out a small cry and swooned onto her husband's shoulder.

Guilt could do strange things to people, Stone mused. At least, it could if it was responsible.

'You mean you know?' asked Lord Verity, easing his wife's face from his tweeds and encouraging her with a little gesture to support her own head.

'We'll come to that.'

'Oh, so you don't know,' said Ronnie, giving her sister a hard look as if to ask why she'd been left out of all the fun. Or was it a twinkle that said, *Looks like I've got away with this*?

This was going to be harder than he thought.

When the fourteen of them had first sat round the dining table on Friday night (Olive having been excluded as a mere outside labourer, he presumed), Professor Stone could not have imagined the turns the weekend was about to take. He'd assured Bella, for instance, that the tragedy that befell Keren Lowe was not the same as that which had befallen Felicity Penman: lightning doesn't strike twice, he'd foolishly declared.

Well, not only had lightning struck twice, it had decided it liked striking so much that it had taken out a season ticket and struck a third time, less than twenty-four hours after its second excursion. It was quite probably rubbing the thunderclouds together even now, charging up its natural electrodes for a fourth outing, and it was only the fortitude, competence and 1980s girl-band expertise of the reading group that had prevented that quaternary turn around the croquet lawn.

Of that original fourteen, plus Olive, there numbered now only seven before him. The film crew's location manager had plunged out into the snow in the hope of reaching civilisation and fetching help for the besieged house. Keren Lowe and Hemingford Grey had met their untimely ends at the hands of the killer who remained, so far, unidentified. The other three members of the reading group were arrayed beside him at the front of the library, like some posse from the Wild West who had rounded up the Verity Gang and were lining up beside the sheriff – Stone, naturally – to administer justice. And Olive was nowhere to be found.

Which left seven of them.

The secret seven.

Seven deadly sinners.

Seven swans a-swimming.

His imagination was running away with him again.

Lord and Lady Verity were at the front in a pair of high-backed chairs that resembled little thrones. Behind them, their staff members Monty, Siobhan and Ronnie were perched on more basic wooden chairs, but all five shared one thing: they were staring at the Professor in a mixture of mild disbelief and appalled anticipation.

On either side of this central group sat Colorado Hughes and Marin Cypher – the first time Stone had seen them apart from each other, he noted. Marin continued to record everything on his camcorder, while Colorado had found some juice for his mobile somewhere and was filming with his arm stretched out in front of him.

Ten minutes earlier, when the reading group had formulated their plan for this revelation, Professor Stone had been relishing the opportunity to flush out a killer. With Fforde's natural dramatic abilities, Lauren's flair for storytelling and Bella's uncanny instinct for human nature, he'd been convinced they could panic the culprit into a confession, without which they would have only suspicions and circumstantial evidence.

Now, with the task ahead of them, he wasn't anywhere near so sure.

'Let us begin with the murder of Hemingford Grey,' he announced sombrely.

'Why?'

Stone hadn't expected an interruption quite so soon, and hunted down the source of the question with a frown. Siobhan looked up at him with a genuinely quizzical look on her face.

'What do you mean, why?'

'I mean, why not start with Keren's murder? Surely it would be more logical to take them chronologically?'

Stone suspected Siobhan's vested interest in her sister's killer might be behind her line of questioning, but they'd decided on a course of action and he was not going to allow the personal priorities of one of the assembled company to throw him off now.

'If you wouldn't mind just going with it on this occasion?' he said, hearing it come out rather lamely.

Siobhan shrugged and sagged back down on her chair.

'Thank you. Now, as I was about to say, it seemed perfectly obvious from the outset that the killing of Hemingford Grey didn't fit the same pattern as that of Keren Lowe. She had been deliberately set up for murder, with props, red herrings and several possible means of dispatch arranged carefully in advance. I'll come back to that in a moment.'

He turned to Lauren, who picked up the baton without flinching.

'Poor Hemingford's death was quite different, we realised,' she said, looking as though she was enjoying her moment in the limelight. 'He had a hole in his chest when Olive found him in the grounds. It seemed highly likely that his murder was opportunistic, and quite probably unplanned.'

Next along the line was Bella.

'Just as Olive stumbled across his body, we think Hemingford Grey stumbled across something the killer didn't want him to find, and had to be removed in order to save their own skin.'

When the narrative reached Fforde, he drew himself up as if he were playing a character, took a deep breath in, and declaimed his line like he was giving his King Lear at last.

'Hemingford Grey was unlucky enough to have discovered a secret. It might have been a Verity family secret from generations past. Or it might have been … the identity of Keren Lowe's killer.'

Stone turned back quickly to study the reaction on the seven faces sitting in front of him.

There was a stunned silence.

The blood was thumping in his temple, and he counted at least a dozen pulses before anyone spoke.

'Piffle,' said Lord Verity at last. 'There *are* no Verity family secrets.'

'Are you certain about that, Lord Verity?' asked Stone, watching his prey fastidiously.

'None worth killing for, that's for sure.'

The expression on his wife's face suggested something rather different, but now was not the moment to pull on that particular thread. There were other priorities to be addressed.

'Well, let's park that one for now,' said Stone, and looked at Siobhan. 'And so we come to the death of poor Keren Lowe, Siobhan's sister and the much-missed catering manager of this establishment.'

'You can say that again,' mumbled Lord Verity.

'Sorry?'

'Oh, nothing. I was just remarking on the quality of the meals since we lost Keren.'

Lady Verity unaccountably burst into tears, perplexing the Professor. Siobhan's food hadn't been all that bad.

'Anyway,' he continued after Lord Verity had put a comforting arm round his wife's shoulder. 'Keren's death has proved something of a mystery.'

'Not so mysterious,' said Monty.

Stone was getting more than a little frustrated at the constant interruptions. Lord Quaint never had to put up with this kind of insubordination.

'Really?' he said. 'And why's that?'

'The rope round her neck. The jump from the tower. I don't

think it would take Miss Marple to work that one out. I'm just sorry that none of us recognised she was so unhappy.'

Lady Verity began sobbing again.

'Ah, well, that's where the mystery comes in,' said the Professor, trying to wrest back control of the meeting. 'I don't think she was unhappy. Hemingford Grey told us as much before he died. And that was the first clue to our suspicion that perhaps Keren Lowe hadn't killed herself at all. Perhaps Keren had been murdered.'

He was hoping to leave a dramatic pause but his aspiration was cut short by the opening of the library door.

Olive's timing could hardly have been worse, he mused.

But it turned out Olive's timing had had nothing to do with the opening of the library door. From outside in the hall stepped a weary figure, its leathery features drawn with exhaustion and its shoulders slumped as if weighed down by dismal failure.

Everyone turned to look at the location manager.

'What?' he asked in his Californian drawl. 'What did I miss?'

Even Colorado Hughes and Marin Cypher looked surprised to see him.

'When did you get back?' demanded the director, allowing his mobile to fall for the first time since the meeting had begun.

'Middle of the night last night,' replied the location manager, whose name Stone couldn't recall having heard. 'I got as far as I could but the snow stopped me and I had to turn back. It was late and I didn't want to wake anyone so I just slunk off to my room. I've been asleep ever since. So what did I miss?'

Stone shivered as he recalled the feeling of being watched in the hallway the night before, when he'd made his way to the chapel. He remembered the puddle of water in the darkness near the front door and realised he'd probably been staring right at the location manager as he crept ignominiously back inside the country house, melting snow the only betrayal of his return.

Then he had another chilling thought. Volunteering for a rescue mission provided the perfect alibi for someone wanting to kill two victims without ever being suspected.

But if that changed his thinking about who might have perpetrated the murders, he had no opportunity to air his new theory. Bella took a half-step forward for her next part in the delivery they'd already prepared.

'Welcome back,' she said to the location manager. 'We've had two murders since you left.'

She left him gaping at the news as she continued to the rest of the gathering: 'I was just about to explain that when I went up to the billiard room I found the candlestick from the lounge lying on the floor. Monty assured me it hadn't been there when he and Olive went into the room earlier.'

Another interruption from the audience made Stone sigh heavily. Clearly nobody else had cottoned on to the same hypothesis about the location manager. Maybe he should let things run their course, just in case the man turned out to be another red herring. He could always turn the tables at the last minute, if their original plan to flush out the killer proved erroneous.

'It must have been,' said Lord Verity. 'Candlesticks don't

just appear out of nowhere. Monty and Olive must have missed it when they first went up there.'

Monty began to remonstrate with his boss, arguing vociferously that there was no way they could have missed the candlestick on their initial visit to the billiard room, and certainly not in the position where Bella had found it, in the middle of the floor near the window.

Stone raised his voice and put his best pissed-off lecturer tone into it. 'If you wouldn't mind listening to us for a few minutes, then all will become clear.'

The frisson in the room settled once more and six faces turned back to the front. Hughes and Cypher were glued to their devices, but for once Stone was willing to let it pass.

'Leaving the candlestick to one side for the moment, we need to consider how Keren actually died. It wasn't the candlestick – despite her subsequent fall there was no sign of blunt force trauma to her head – and it wasn't the rope. Although her body showed signs of friction burns around the neck, it was neither strangulation nor a break that killed her.'

'Then what did?' asked Ronnie, switching her attention between Stone and Bella, who she presumably thought might be able to give her all the answers.

'Now that's where the story gets really interesting,' said Stone. 'Over to you, Bella.'

'Thank you, Professor. Now, after Hemingford was murdered yesterday and we went into our self-imposed lockdown overnight, I discovered one or two interesting things. I'll not trouble you with the secret history of Agatha Christie right now'—she skewered Lord and Lady Verity with a piercing look—'although I do think you owe it to her fans to reveal the truth about that. No, the most troubling thing I saw in the middle of the night was a figure crossing the lawn towards the knot garden. On subsequent investigation this morning, we discovered that the garden had been destroyed by a rake. Someone was clearly trying to cover up evidence. But what evidence could be found in a knot garden?'

She turned to Lauren, who was holding the book that Bella had been reading in the study.

'This, ladies and gentlemen, is *The Toxicologist's Almanac*. It contains lots of useful information about poisonous plants. And we found it in Lord Verity's study.'

'Now hang on a minute—' spluttered Lord Verity, bounding to his feet.

Fforde cut him short with a resonant bark.

'Sit down, please, your Lordship. Nobody's accusing you of anything.'

Lauren carried on. 'I was merely indicating the source of our research. Thanks to Bella's curiosity and Professor Stone's careful inspection of Keren's body in the chapel, we have been able to verify the real cause of her death.'

She stopped, allowing Fforde to savour the big moment.

'Keren Lowe was killed with poison hemlock. Cultivated in Abbots Chantry's very own knot garden. That was why it was destroyed in the night. To conceal the murder weapon.'

Stone allowed a few seconds for this to sink in before picking up the theory again. It was only a theory, he was acutely aware, and the arrival of the location manager might have thrown it into utter confusion – he could have been the curious figure Bella saw crossing the lawn, after all – but by watching their suspects closely, he still hoped to spot some twinge of guilt that would betray them. Even if the reading group hadn't got the facts completely correct, he was trusting that there was enough evidence to approximate the actual events. It might not convince a jury but it might be enough to flush out the murderer in the room.

'Keren Lowe was poisoned, then taken to the billiard room, tied to the rope and thrown out of the window in an attempt to disguise her murder.'

Lord Verity stirred again. 'But you'd need someone with superhuman strength to carry her dead weight up the tower.'

As if responding perfectly to a cue, a handle rattled and the door from the hall was flung open a second time, this time in a movement more suited to a barn than a library.

Appropriately enough, Olive came in.

In her hand, she hefted her huge, gleaming spanner.

'*Her*,' yelled Monty, pointing a finger at the new arrival. 'That's how the candlestick got there. It was planted as a red herring to confuse any investigation, and only Olive had the key.'

By now, four of the suspects were on their feet, either through fear or with the apparent intent of apprehending the culprit. Monty and Siobhan were both pointing at Olive, Ronnie clutched both hands to her face in terror, and Lord Verity looked very cross indeed.

Only Lady Verity and the film crew remained seated, although Marin Cypher was making as if to get up to follow any ensuing action sequences.

'Stop!' roared Professor Stone, and the room fell silent.

'If you would kindly resume your seats; we haven't actually finished yet.'

Monty made no indication of sitting down, although the other three sank down meekly. Olive took up a position in an upright chair near the door.

'I'm not just going to sit here and wait for her to plough through us with that spanner of hers,' said Monty, sounding more indignant than Stone had heard him the whole weekend, in spite of losing his sister-in-law to a calculating killer.

'There'll be no ploughing from Olive, I can assure you of that,' said Stone. 'You're forgetting a number of important features of this case.'

Lord Verity harrumphed irritably. 'Such as?'

'Such as the motive. What possible motive could Olive have had for murdering Keren and Hemingford?'

'That's easy,' retorted Monty. 'You've just said yourself that Grey was killed because he discovered something about the killer. And as for Keren, she was always annoying people. Who knows what she might have said or done to Olive that would prompt a murder?'

'Not good enough,' stated Stone. 'Any jury in the land would laugh that out of court as a feeble motivation. And besides, she's got an alibi for last night.'

Lord Verity seemed unconvinced. 'Alibi? What alibi?'

'Harrison here was with her in her room at the time Bella saw the figure out in the grounds.'

Seven pairs of eyes turned to Fforde, who took a moment to realise the implications of the Professor's words.

'Not like that, you twisted degenerates,' he shouted. 'I went into the wrong room by accident.'

It was time to push the nuclear button, Professor Stone

decided. All or nothing. If they were wrong, they would have to face the consequences and apologise.

But maybe they weren't wrong.

'No, it wasn't Olive who went out to the knot garden and destroyed all traces of hemlock among the herbs. Admittedly, we thought she might be trying to hide something when Lauren and the others saw her raking over footprints in the snow, but it turns out she was just making the place a bit more photogenic for our American friends here. No, if you're looking for a person with the means, motive and opportunity to kill both Keren and Hemingford, then you need to search for someone else, someone with the knowhow to disrupt Olive's attempts to repair the broadband and power, leaving us disconnected from the outside world and unable to preserve the victims' bodies, and thus making subsequent forensic examination so difficult as to be almost impossible. You need to find someone who, like Olive, had access to the billiard room in the period between Keren's body being found and the candlestick mysteriously appearing. And you need to find someone who shared a secret with Keren Lowe that was worth killing her to keep quiet. Someone who might have let slip in their behaviour towards her in the lounge yesterday morning that theirs was a relationship that extended beyond a work or family bond; a relationship that, if discovered, would put a grenade under everything they had built at Abbots Chantry. An extramarital relationship that threatened not only to ruin a marriage, but also to smash the cosy, comfortable life the killer had set up for themselves.'

Stone paused, letting his exposition sink in.

'The only thing I don't understand is why you started the affair with your wife's sister in the first place, Monty.'

For five dramatic seconds, the whole assembly was stunned into silence.

Then the room erupted into chaos.

Siobhan began screaming, Lord and Lady Verity jumped out of their seats, Ronnie stood up, sat down and stood up again, while the three Americans leaped about, frantically trying to capture the strongest reactions and best footage.

Only Olive remained implacable in her seat at the back of the library.

But the most disturbing reaction of all came from Monty Butler himself.

With a swift, fluid motion, he sprang from his seat, vaulted over the chairs formerly occupied by Lord and Lady Verity, and planted himself beside Professor Stone.

In his right hand he brandished a revolver.

Stone had no idea where the gun had come from, nor what Monty intended to do with it, faced with a room full of witnesses. He could hardly kill them all.

At the far end of the line, Stone heard the disgruntled mutter of his friend Harrison Fforde.

'Blimey. I thought I was supposed to be the dramatic one.'

'Shut up!' ordered Monty, waving the revolver along the line of four frightened readers. 'You think you're so clever, don't you? But you're not. All right, so maybe I did kill Keren and that stupid bore Grey, but you've got no concrete evidence. What did you just say, Professor? Any jury in the land would laugh it out of court. You can't prove anything.'

Stone glanced across the room at Colorado Hughes who, as

instructed by the Professor not half an hour earlier, had caught the entire debacle on his mobile phone.

Hughes gave him an eager thumbs-up.

'I think you'll find that an unprompted confession on camera will stand up nicely in court,' said Stone.

From behind him, a timid voice cut through the atmosphere like a chorister in a brothel.

'Except,' said Bella quietly, 'that you can't confess to something you haven't done.'

III

The gun trembled in Monty's hand; Bella's voice in her throat.

'It wasn't you, was it, Monty?'

She didn't know where she was getting the bravery to hold his stare – maybe something of Fforde's lessons about actors' breathing techniques had sunk in – but she wasn't going to back down now. She tried to gauge whether the look in his eye was defiance, fury or simply derangement. In any of those cases, she was standing at the wrong end of a gun barrel, although to her mind it looked quite old and Monty might easily be faking it with an antique from the house that wouldn't actually fire.

There was only one sure way of finding that out, and it wasn't one that Bella wanted to put to the test.

'What are you talking about, you sad old woman?' said Monty viciously.

'Now hold on,' said Fforde, stepping in front of Bella to put himself between her and the weapon. 'You don't get to talk to my friends like that. Besides, she's not old. She's probably not even fifty.'

'Harrison!' said Bella, affronted.

'What?'

'I'm quite capable of looking out for myself, thank you very much.'

She bypassed Fforde to confront Monty once more. 'It wasn't, though, was it? You're protecting someone.'

She felt a pang of envy, wishing she had someone who might protect her in the same kind of way. The closest Trevor had ever come to chivalry was leaving the room to break wind.

'It's all very gallant but it's not going to wash. My hunch is it's more than that.'

The Professor was staring at her, puzzled. She was going off script now and he obviously couldn't understand why. But from the moment their family connection had been revealed, Bella suspected there was more to Siobhan and Keren's relationship, and she'd seen and heard enough in the past day and a half, both in open rooms and from behind secret doors, to be able to guess the rest.

It was something only a sister could truly understand.

She turned away from the man with the gun and looked directly at Siobhan.

'Keren was your non-identical twin, wasn't she?'

There was no obvious reaction beyond a darkening of Siobhan's features, but the whole of the rest of the library let out a gasp. They probably hadn't even known they'd been holding their breath.

Bella had recently seen an online forum in which readers picked out examples of writers describing characters letting out a breath they didn't know they were holding. It was meant as an affectionate poke at a literary cliché, but now Bella had heard it with her own ears.

She'd never make fun of literary clichés again.

'I know what sisterly jealousy can feel like, but your twin having an affair with your husband – that must really hurt. Probably beyond endurance. I think it was you that poisoned Keren, maybe in her tea at breakfast. It was you that forged the note from Lord Verity to entice her up to the billiard room – we all saw her frown, so she clearly had no idea what it was about – and then you tied her to the rope and tipped her out of the window. You probably sliced the rope so that it would snap on the way down, just to add another touch of drama. After all, she'd look so much more striking splayed out in the snow than dangling from the window. It was you who let out the scream that we all heard, and nobody questioned that it hadn't come from her. The sound carried perfectly through the chimney breasts, down into the tunnels where you'd conveniently positioned us. You must have moved fast, though, to get up into the tower and throw her out.'

Bella had a head of steam up and nothing was going to interrupt her now.

'My guess is that Hemingford Grey was unlucky enough to stumble across you confronting Monty about his affair so he had to go as well. The rake handle was a stroke of genius. Disguise the real cause of death with a blunt instrument.'

She sensed the Professor edging forward further along the line. 'What are you talking about, Bella?'

'It wasn't the rake that killed Hemingford, Professor.'

'It wasn't?'

'No. When we looked at his body in the chapel I noticed there was a smaller puncture wound in his heart. He was already dead when the killer attacked him with the rake. And my money says we'll find the real murder weapon tucked into Monty's sock, won't we, Monty?'

Lauren gasped. 'Of course! The *sgian dubh*. So the rake injuries were only there to throw us off the scent.'

'Like the candlestick,' said Bella. 'And the note from Lord Verity. All obfuscation. And that's a word I learned entirely by myself.'

Professor Stone was staring at the man with the gun. 'How about it, Monty? Are you going to admit that it was really your wife who murdered Hemingford Grey and Keren Lowe?'

There was no opportunity for the estate manager to answer Stone's question.

Lady Verity let out a scream of her own and collapsed against her husband's shoulder, distraught. He looked thoroughly confused.

Lauren rushed over to her and took hold of her hand.

'It's all right, Lady Verity. You've got nothing to worry about. We know who did it.'

'That's the problem,' whimpered the feeble creature. 'My sister killed my sister.'

Bella felt a surge of satisfaction that their instincts had proved right.

'So it's true,' she said slowly. 'We guessed from the Bananarama reference that there was a third sibling in the house alongside Siobhan and Keren. We ruled out Olive because she was much older and Ronnie because she only had one sister, and that sister was me. Which leaves only Lady Verity. Or should I say … Sara?'

She looked at Fforde. It was only fair to allow him the big revelation. It was he who had come up with it, after all.

'Not twins, in fact, but triplets,' he announced, sounding very pleased with himself.

'And my husband was sleeping with us all,' muttered Siobhan.

'What?' Lady Verity sobbed again. 'You … you knew?'

Siobhan whirled on her sister, 'Of course I knew. Monty's never been able to hide anything from me. And don't think you'd have got away with it either, Sara. You were next on my list.'

Bella might have put the pieces of the murders together but there were still things she didn't understand.

'What I don't get,' she said, as much to Professor Stone as to Siobhan, 'is why Monty is willing to take the rap for two murders.'

The Professor shrugged. 'It might be something as romantic as misplaced loyalty but my money's on greed. As soon as Monty discovered his wife had killed her own sister – and maybe she even told him she was lining up Lady Verity next – there was nothing he could do but help her. If the truth were to come out, their happy little existence, creaming off a healthy pension from the profits of the estate, would all have come crashing down. It was Monty who cleared up the mess after Siobhan, planting the candlestick in the billiard room to confuse any investigation, and wrecking the knot garden in the middle of the night.'

Something else had apparently dawned on Fforde.

'So the woman I overheard him consorting with on the landing last night – that wasn't Siobhan at all. Her voice and mannerisms just led me to believe it was, when in fact it was Lady Verity.'

Lauren had a question.

'Why now? Why this weekend, when the house is full of people?'

'You've answered your own question there, Lauren,' said Stone. 'More people equals more suspects, more diversions from the real killer. I think Siobhan was hoping our reputation as detectives might have been hyped up by the press, and we would go off on some wild goose chase, misled by planted evidence such as the candlestick and getting the whole thing wrong. And I think she believed we'd make such a mess of the crime scene that we'd render any serious investigation by the police completely impossible.'

Bella looked from Monty to Siobhan, then to Lady Verity, then back to Monty again. They were all sharing glances between them but nobody seemed to want to speak.

'Well, Monty? We're right, aren't we?'

His lip curled into an unpleasant grin. Odd how handsome men could suddenly become rather ugly, given the right circumstances. While she could never have honestly called Trevor handsome, he could be downright hideous when Norcester United were losing.

'It doesn't matter whether you're right or wrong, you're still trapped here with a killer,' he said darkly.

Bella became aware of a horrible thought sidling up to her brain, and she tried to send it away unthought.

But it refused to go, and plagued her until she brought it to the front of her mind.

He's going to kill you all, the horrible thought whispered.

For one brief moment she believed it.

Then Harrison Fforde leaped into action.

In a dramatic move that would have made any stunt coordinator bristle with pride, he suddenly dodged out of the line-up that the reading group still formed.

Bella saw the whole manoeuvre in slow motion. He took two paces in the direction of the door, signalling frantically at Olive, who launched her spanner at him. Catching it in one hand, he checked his direction and lurched back towards Monty, bringing the spanner down heavily onto the estate manager's shoulder and sending the revolver flying across the library to land with impossible accuracy on a shelf marked 'Arms and Armoury'.

By the time Bella looked back, Fforde was sitting astride a prostrate Monty, and Lauren had Siobhan in a half-nelson. Both were moaning in pain.

Good. They deserved it.

The Quaint Bookshop reading group had been trying to work out how they would keep Monty and Siobhan subdued for as long as it took until help finally arrived, when help finally arrived.

From the windows of the library, overlooking the long, snowbound drive, Bella could see a strange effect in the sky above the dark trees. At first she couldn't make out what it was – she even wondered if it might be a very southerly manifestation of the northern lights – but then she remembered that they were usually green, and this luminous display was definitely blue.

When the realisation hit her, she blinked with relief.

What she was witnessing was the flashing lights of the emergency services.

'I think the police are here,' she said, turning back towards the room.

Monty and Siobhan had both been tied to their chairs, with gags round their mouths to prevent any attempt at sweet-talking. Professor Stone had given them all a lecture on the dangers of Stockholm Syndrome, in which hostages had been known to form bizarrely close relationships with their captors, and denied them the chance to put the psychological theory into practice. Instead, they had bound them and spent the past hour studiously ignoring them.

With Monty now out of her way, Olive had been able to restore the broadband with the last of the generator's power and the alarm had duly been raised. The Americans were in the middle of outlining a new feature film about a double murder at a snowbound English country house when the generator finally gave out.

Elsewhere, Lauren comforted Lady Verity as best she could after losing one sister at the hands of another. Lord Verity hovered nearby, fidgeting and looking completely confounded by the whole business. In the aftermath of the action, he'd explained that he'd always felt uncomfortable about employing his wife's siblings as staff, fearing it might all end unhappily; not as unhappily as this, he confessed, but then his own family was hardly a paragon of moral rectitude, so who was he to judge?

The Professor sat amiably with Olive, chatting away in a corner of the library as if nothing untoward had just happened. Fforde paced up and down as if rehearsing lines, glancing occasionally at the two malefactors and, Bella assumed, trying to formulate a narrative that he might be able to use as some kind of dramatic monologue when they finally made it back to the real world.

For her part, Bella stared out of the window at the scenery, watching the clouds loom and night gather over Abbots Chantry.

Eventually, Professor Stone had called the four of them together and they had agreed they would take it in shifts to stay awake for as long as it took to be rescued.

And now rescue had come, and their real-life country-house murder-mystery weekend was over.

As the four of them stood at the entrance to the old monastery, watching the rugged police vehicles make light work of the snowbound drive, Professor Stone began to laugh. It started as a low chuckle, building into a throaty chortle before finally erupting as a contagious, gusty guffaw.

In moments, they were all howling companionably.

'What are we laughing at?' asked Bella when she could finally catch her breath and the first Range Rover screamed to a halt in front of them.

'It's just funny, that's all,' said Professor Stone.

'What, two murders?' asked Lauren uncertainly.

'They certainly do seem to be following us around,' added Fforde.

'No, not the murders.' Professor Stone stood aside to point several burly officers into the house. 'The culprits.'

Bella waited for someone to ask. In the end, she did it herself.

'Monty and Siobhan? What about them?'

'We should have known from the start,' said the Professor. 'The Butlers did it.'

THANK YOU FOR READING
A GAME OF MURDER

IT WOULD MEAN SO MUCH IF YOU COULD LEAVE A REVIEW ON ALL YOUR PREFERRED PLATFORMS AND SOCIAL MEDIA TO HELP SPREAD THE WORD!

YOU CAN ALSO FOLLOW ME ON INSTAGRAM @MICHAELDAVIESAUTHOR, ON FACEBOOK @MICHAEL-DAVIES-AUTHOR, AND CHECK OUT MY WEBSITE WWW.MRGDAVIES.COM FOR UPDATES ON MY LATEST WORK.

DON'T MISS THE FIRST INSTALMENT IN THE COSY CRIME CLUB MYSTERY SERIES: *MURDER BY THE BOOK* PERFECT FOR FANS OF RICHARD OSMAN!

Nothing is deadlier than angry readers ... especially when you murder one of their own.

When the manager of The Quaint Bookshop is found slumped between the shelves, the four members of the shop's reading group decide to put into action all the skills they've picked up from their favourite fictional detectives.

If anyone knows how to solve a killer of a crime, it's a team of murder-mystery superfans. The police might be investigating but the reading group are on the case…

AVAILABLE NOW IN EBOOK, PAPERBACK AND AUDIO

Acknowledgments

When I first started writing about The Quaint Bookshop's reading group, I had no idea readers would take to the characters so strongly and so fast. Reaction to the intrepid foursome in their debut outing *Murder by the Book* was heartwarming: people really seemed to cherish the quirky quartet, some having their own preferences, others loving them for their ability to work together despite their differences.

As an author, you are blessed with permission to do what you want to your characters, but that is also a big responsibility. I hope no readers will feel I have been overly cruel with the dramas I have inflicted on Professor Stone, Bella Bourton, Lauren Sherwood and Harrison Fforde. Because it is to readers who have returned – or are meeting them for the first time – that I owe my greatest debt of gratitude. Without you, there would be no The Quaint Bookshop reading group, and I would be locked in my office, tapping away at my keyboard, for the sole purpose of amusing myself.

So thank you for saving me from that.

Part of the reason the reading group seems to have touched so many people is because of the hard work and support of a great many folk along the path from my keyboard to the finished book.

The first person to read it is always my beautiful, trusty other half Tricia, whose wisdom, guidance and love are terrific reasons to pay attention, let alone her actor's eye for story and ear for dialogue. Tricia, you are a marvel, and this book, like everything else, is for you and because of you.

Once the manuscript escapes the confines of the office, it passes into the hands of people who make it better, such as my good friend and confidant Richard Howarth, whose editor's skills are invaluable to the process.

And, of course, there's a veritable army of professionals at One More Chapter who suggest, prod, query, scratch their heads, invite, underscore, challenge and a whole lot of other useful activities to get me to look at it anew, shape it afresh and mould it into the best it can be. These include (but are not limited to) line and copy editors Victoria Oundjian and Tony Russell, proofreader Janet Marie Adkins and managing editorial assistant Kara Daniel. The gorgeous covers are the work of designer Lucy Bennett, while marketing is handled by consummate professional Katie Sadler and her team, including Chloe Cummings and Grace Edwards, without whom you probably wouldn't have heard of The Quaint Bookshop and its reading group.

At the helm of the publishing effort are my scrupulous and supportive editor Helen Williams and OMC's boundlessly energetic publisher Charlotte Ledger, who have nurtured the series from pitch to fruition with a gentle, encouraging steer and always a healthy dose of inspiration. Thank you both for your ongoing faith in me and the series.

So now the foursome has moved out of the bookshop into a

snowbound country house – and survived. Where on earth might they go next? And what might their author do to them this time…?

The author and One More Chapter would like to thank everyone who contributed to the publication of this story...

Analytics
Imogen Wolstencroft

Audio
Fionnuala Barrett
Ciara Briggs

Design
Lucy Bennett
Fiona Greenway
Liane Payne
Dean Russell

Digital Sales
Laura Daley
Lydia Grainge
Hannah Lismore

eCommerce
Laura Carpenter
Madeline ODonovan
Charlotte Stevens
Christina Storey
Rachel Ward

Editorial
Janet Marie Adkins
Rosie Best
Kara Daniel
Charlotte Ledger
Laura McCallen
Jennie Rothwell
Tony Russell
Sofia Salazar Studer
Helen Williams

Harper360
Emily Gerbner
Ariana Juarez
Jean Marie Kelly
emma sullivan
Sophia Wilhelm

International Sales
Ruth Burrow
Bethan Moore
Colleen Simpson

Inventory
Sarah Callaghan
Kirsty Norman

Marketing & Publicity
Chloe Cummings
Grace Edwards
Katie Sadler

Operations
Melissa Okusanya
Vanessa Coubrough

Production
Denis Manson
Simon Moore
Francesca Tuzzeo

Rights
Ashton Mucha
Alisah Saghir
Zoe Shine
Aisling Smyth

Trade Marketing
Ben Hurd
Eleanor Slater

The HarperCollins Contracts Team

The HarperCollins Distribution Team

The HarperCollins Finance & Royalties Team

The HarperCollins Legal Team

The HarperCollins Technology Team

UK Sales
Isabel Coburn
Jay Cochrane
Leah Woods

And every other essential link in the chain from delivery drivers to booksellers to librarians and beyond!

One More Chapter is an award-winning global division of HarperCollins.

Subscribe to our newsletter to get our latest eBook deals and stay up to date with all our new releases!

signup.harpercollins.co.uk/join/signup-omc

Meet the team at
www.onemorechapter.com

Follow us!

@onemorechapterhc

Do you write unputdownable fiction? We love to hear from new voices. Find out how to submit your novel at
www.onemorechapter.com/submissions